ENTHRALLMENT

ENTHRALLMENT

Meg Evans

Library of Congress Control Number: 2020909125

ISBN: 978-0-578-69611-9 (pbk.)

ISBN: 978-0-578-69612-6 (ebook)

Edited by Emma O'Connell

Cover design by Mila Milic

Printed in the United States of America

First edition: August 2020

www.megevansauthor.com

For my parents, with love

CHAPTER ONE

"DON'T GO IN THERE! He'll kill you!" My heart is pounding and my legs are jittering nervously. Filled with panic, I'm hidden behind my hands, peeking through my fingers. I can't watch her die; she's made it so far—she has to live. But the second I scream the warning, she goes inside and gets strangled. The movie is over. I drop onto the soft cushions with a heavy sigh.

"I told her not to go inside, damn it!" I shake my head in disbelief. "How can you be that stupid?"

Most of the horror movies I've seen ended in the exact same way—making me feel frustrated at their final scene. Yet I always choose this genre on Netflix anyway. In fact, I'm going to watch another one tonight.

Before I get consumed by another terrifying film, I need to stretch out a bit. My legs are stiff and my butt tingles; I've been nestled on the couch for too long. I stamp across the spacious living room to the open kitchen. The only noises now are the gurgling from the refrigerator and the swinging of the pendulum of my aunt's grandfather clock. The neighborhood where I live is so quiet that hearing a car passing by after eight p.m. is a miracle.

I come up to the pantry, which is my favorite place in the kitchen, and open the door wide. I stare at its contents for a good while, biting my lip, making up my mind.

Why is it always such a tough choice for me between Doritos, Oreos, and pretzels?

I'm unexpectedly jolted out of my food-searching trance by the wails of a siren. The violent sound assaults my ears, getting louder and louder. That's odd. I've only seen one ambulance here, two years ago, when our neighbor across the street had a sudden and severe asthma attack.

I turn around to face the living room again. Rapidly flashing blue and red lights invade the living room through the half-drawn curtains of its windows. A knot forms in my stomach when I realize that the ambulance has stopped outside *my* house.

Something must have happened to Maddie or Cynthia!

I drop an open bag of Doritos. The chips spill onto the floor and crunch under my feet. I don't care about the mess; I need to know what's going on.

I dash upstairs, my adrenaline pumping like it's trying to escape. Halfway up the stairs, I bump into my cousin, Maddie, rushing in the opposite direction. Her eyes are wide.

"There's an ambulance next door!" she shouts.

That would make sense. We live in a two-family house, and the other side of the wall is home to a nosy old lady whose favorite activity is gawking at people through her kitchen window.

A sudden relief washes over me. As much as I'm sorry for the neighbor, I'm glad it wasn't my family who called 911.

"My God. I thought for a moment that—"

Maddie isn't interested in what I have to say. She doesn't even pause, but scoots to the window closest to the front door. She opens the curtain and discreetly peeps outside.

"The paramedics have already gone inside. I can't see anyone; only the ambulance."

I slink back down the stairs and stand by her side, peering out of the window as well. A moment later my aunt, Cynthia, joins us. I don't have to see her to know

that she's shown up. I can smell the jasmine and rose notes of her fragrance.

"Poor Mrs. McConelly," Cynthia says, standing behind us. "I hope that everything's alright."

"She seemed just fine in the morning when she was scolding me for talking too loud on the phone," Maddie blurts out.

Cynthia throws her a meaningful look. "Maybe she was right."

"Mom, quiet hours end at six a.m.; I left the house at seven-thirty." Maddie tosses her head side to side.

"Are you sure you weren't shouting?" Cynthia insists.

"I'm sure." Maddie rolls her eyes.

"Zara, honey, have you seen anything?"

"No, I was by the pantry when I heard the ambulance. I ran upstairs to check on you guys first. When I came back down here it was too late, everyone was already inside her house."

"That's so nice of you to check on us, sweetie." My aunt grabs me by the shoulders and gives them a gentle squeeze.

We keep looking out the window. After lingering ten minutes, two men emerge from the house, pushing a gurney with a black bag on it. It must be poor Mrs. McConefry. A chill runs up my spine.

"Oh my God," Cynthia and Maddie say simultaneously. My aunt's eyes immediately well up with tears, whereas Maddie's jaw drops open.

I saw her just yesterday, and now she's dead. I won't meet her on the street ever again. I won't see her decrepit smile or her struggles to open the gate. I won't hear her complaints about me idling in the driveway for longer than the allowable two minutes. She's gone.

I'm suddenly aware of the mortality that we all possess and could lose at any moment. Staring at the black bag, I can feel deep in my gut that some changes are on the horizon.

CHAPTER TWO

MY CHEST HEAVES AS I DART through the woods, urged on by instincts of self-preservation.

There's no sign of life in the vicinity. The rustle of bushes and the howl of the wind are the only sounds that reach my ears. I'm alone and lost in this dark, hostile maze of thousands of trees. The woods are shrouded by the mist, making everything hazy. I must be very careful not to stumble over one of the ground-knotted roots. I can't fall. My heart is thumping. Even though I feel as if I've been here before, adrenaline courses through my veins. I can hear my own rapid breathing.

Out of nowhere, a scattered beam of light filters through the treetops and illuminates the path I'm bolting down. I gaze up, but the branches of the densely-packed trees are tightly interlocked like enormous arms and don't leave enough space for me to spot what's up there.

Is that my rescue? Am I safe now?

I stumble to a stop. My chest rapidly heaves up and down. I bend down and rest my hands on my knees, trying to collect my breath. The air is heavy and humid, which makes it difficult to breathe. The mist slowly dissipates and reveals the soggy ground I've sunk into. Oddly, the sound of the wind in the leaves has ceased, ushering in a deafening silence. Everything is unnaturally still. As I look around the quiet woods, I notice a mysterious silhouette about fifty yards away.

Someone is watching—or perhaps waiting.

I can tell that it's a man by the figure's stature. He's leaning against a thick trunk.

My nerves are on edge. Even from afar, I can sense his piercing look penetrating me. From the moment that I see him, a spark ignites in me, overwhelming me with a feeling of combustion. His gaze is both alluring and frightening. My heart tells me to approach, but my mind tells me to flee. The battle within me to determine my next move has me at a standstill. Suddenly, I hear my name.

ZARA...

Do I know him? I hear it again.

ZARA...

This time it's closer, as if he is speaking directly into my ear.

Who is he? What is he? The questions race through my mind.

ZARA!

Someone is yanking my arm. "Zara, wake up!"

I lurch up, shivering uncontrollably. Panic overwhelms me, and my heart is racing in my chest. The first things I notice are Maddie's heart-shaped face and her big amber eyes staring down at me.

"What happened?" I blink a couple of times as my eyes adjust to the light. I see my white desk in the corner of the room and my purple blanket across my legs. I'm tucked safely in my bed. It was just a nightmare.

"You weren't downstairs, so I came to your room to wake you up. When I got here, I heard you mumbling then saw you twitching, as if you were having a seizure." Maddie's face is pale, and her eyes are concerned. "Are you okay?"

"What was I mumbling?" I ask, pushing my dark hair away from my face.

"I don't know; I couldn't understand you at all."

I let out a sigh as the details of the dream come flooding back. It's the same one as always. It's haunted me for two months now, ever since Mrs. McConelly died. Whenever I wake up, I'm relieved that it was just a nightmare, but at the same time I want to go back to sleep, drawn to the mysterious man.

"Don't worry. It was just a bad dream," I assure her.

"If you say so." She stares at my sweaty face. She's so close that I can see the freckles dotting her naturally blushed cheeks. "You watch horror movies too often."

"No way will you make me watch your romantic comedies."

"Oh, no! You just hurt my feelings," she says, exaggeratedly upset.

"Shut up. I know you don't care."

"Nah, I don't." She pulls away. "Anyway, you scared the hell out of me, but since you're okay, I'll leave you alone. Also, I think you should get up if you don't want to be late for school."

My eyes immediately shift to the electronic clock on my nightstand. It's almost seven a.m.; I have about thirty minutes to get ready to leave.

"Shit!" I punch my fists into the bed. "Why didn't you wake me up earlier?" I shove the blanket aside and jump to my feet.

"Well, in my defense, I did come to wake you up," Maddie points out as I dart past her. "Plus, that's what they invented alarms for—so that you can wake up at the exact time that you want."

"Gee, thanks." I rummage through my closet to find the least wrinkled clothes.

"See you downstairs." She swiftly leaves my bedroom.

Forty-five minutes later, I run out of the house and slam the front door shut. I fiddle with the keys to my old red Volkswagen Golf, trying to unlock it, then raise my head for a fraction of a second and take a quick peep over the wooden fence which separates our section of the front yard from the part that belonged to our dead neighbor. Something is different there, but I'm unable to tell what it is right away. I squint to see better, and then it dawns on me that the 'FOR SALE' sign, which has been stuck in the ground for the last two months, is gone.

I guess we have new next-door neighbors, I think to myself while opening the car door.

I'm thrilled. I'm so done with all those potential buyers perpetually hanging around by my windows. Ever since Mrs. McConelly had the heart attack, a woman named Laura Pierson, a young and ambitious real-estate agent, has been dragging over throngs of people interested in purchasing the other half of the house every single day. Sometimes it seemed to me that Laura's promotion, or maybe even her life, depended on this sale.

I pull out of the driveway and screech away toward Willamette University. I have about ten minutes before my class starts, and six miles to travel. While driving along Rafael Avenue, just before the intersection with Shoreline Drive, a large truck almost rams into me as it takes a wide turn into the street. I slam on the brakes and send the driver a straight-up glare, but he doesn't even look in my direction.

What a douche! How can you be driving like there's no one else on the streets?!

I toss my head from side to side and let him drive past me. Now I have eight minutes left and over five miles to go. My car is not a rocket, so I'm not even hopeful I will make it on time now.

What a wonderful beginning to the day.

* * *

Several hours later, I'm in haste again, but this time I'm

heading back home. I can't catch a break today. My shift at Walgreens starts in exactly half an hour and I still need to stop by my house to pick up my uniform, which I forgot to pack while I was hurrying to collect my other things this morning. My manager will kill me if I'm late for the third time in a row.

The scene outside my place has changed significantly from this morning.

Hang on, isn't that the truck that nearly ran into me this morning? It is!

The vehicle is now parked in front of my house, almost unloaded. Among the white-clad uniformed men carrying heavy boxes into the house, I strive in vain to catch a glimpse of my new neighbors. I'm dying to know whether the folks who'll live on the other side are old or young; with or without children; friendly or abrasive. Or maybe it's just one person? If so, who is it: a woman or a man? In the ideal scenario, it'll be Chris Hemsworth's double. I'm not picky.

Nevertheless, even if our new neighbor turns out to be an unbearable, nasty grump whose hobby is to sunbathe in the backyard with a body way past its sell-by date spread out on a beach chair, I wouldn't be disappointed. I already have a dreamy object of desire who has all the traits I've ever wanted in my partner.

Daydreaming about him, I back out and leave the driveway, praying I'll make it on time to work. The moving truck is parked on the street along the curb and is blocking my way. I'm forced to use the other lane to get around it, but its size limits the visibility of oncoming traffic. Panicking that I might cause a head-on collision with another vehicle, I stop and crane my head out the window to ensure that the road is clear. It doesn't help at all.

That truck has been getting on my nerves since the crack of dawn!

Boiling mad, I quickly realize that the only way around this is to get one of the uniform-clad workers to move their truck. I fight with my seatbelt to unbuckle it, but it gets stuck. I'm frantically pressing the release on the top of the buckle, but the latch won't give. *What the hell is wrong with it? Damn you!*

My head drops back on the headrest. Great. Now I'm helpless *and* late.

As I stare hatefully at the truck, I notice a black, freshly-polished Bentley emerging from the other side of it, creeping toward me. The windows are tinted just enough for a hint of mystery while still allowing me to see that there is someone inside. As is my custom, I try to glance at the person behind the wheel, but my reaction is far from customary.

It's a man. Even though I can't see him too clearly, I get chills all over my body when our cars are side by side. My pulse skitters wildly, and a hot wave washes over me from head to toe. I immediately feel a gentle twinge right where my birthmark is, near my breastbone. I automatically reach up to touch it. I stop breathing, hearing, thinking. I have the impression that the rest of my senses have been turned off so that I can focus my entire attention on what I see before my eyes. When the car drives past me, I slide my eyes to the rear-view mirror. Only now do I notice a woman in the back seat.

I'm torn away from the weird hypnosis by the sound of someone knocking on the passenger side's window. I turn my head to the right and see Charlie, madly waving at me.

Oh geez, not now, I whimper in my mind.

Charlie is my age and lives a couple of houses up the street. We met in elementary school and became close friends. Over the years he developed a soft spot for me, and that was the beginning of the end. I wish I could say that the feeling is mutual, but I've always thought of him as a brother; there is no chance it's going to ever change.

Unwillingly, I press a button on the door. The window slowly rolls down. I force a smile.

"Hey, Zara! I haven't seen you for ages, girl!"

It's been only five days since I saw him last, but to him it obviously felt like forever.

"It's good to see you, buddy, but I'm late for work—could you please help me get out of here?" I fix my eyes on the truck in front of me. "I can't see anything ahead."

"Sure." He's not offended; at this point Charlie must be used to me brushing him off.

He jogs to the other side of the street. Even the way he moves turns me off; he seems so wobbly, as though he's about to fall flat on his face. Charlie motions from a few feet away to let me know that the road is clear, so I wave my thanks as I go around the truck. I'll have to break every traffic law in order to get to work on time. I'm trying to focus and make it there as quickly as possible, but it's tough to control my thoughts; they are occupied with the black Bentley and its driver.

* * *

Shortly before eleven o'clock, I pull into my illuminated driveway. I'm completely drained; my manager didn't fire me for being late again, but I had to stay until closing time. My brain is on ten percent battery and I'm about to crash. Walking along the fence that separates my yard from my neighbor's, I casually look over it, then abruptly stop; my heart suddenly races.

Either my mind is messing with me, or it's that black Bentley parked in the driveway on the other side.

I strain to see if it's exactly the same car I saw before, not just one that looks similar. I even lean over the fence. As I'm stretching to get a better look, the front door opens and two silhouettes step outside. I rapidly straighten up so as not to raise any suspicion. I wouldn't want them to think that I'm nosy.

That must the same couple I saw earlier today.

I turn around, pretending that halfway down the driveway I remembered I left something in my car and now I need to go back to get it. I feel like trying to get a better look, but the dimly-lit walkway leading to their front door is too dark.

I open the trunk and rummage in it, shifting things from

left to right. Out of the corner of my eye I see the couple approach. The woman is wearing high heels that clatter on the sandstone paving slabs as she walks; he, on the other hand, moves almost noiselessly. When they get to about twenty feet away from me, I experience the same strange twinge in my chest that I did a few hours earlier. I massage the spot to soothe the pain.

"They'll be here in a month. We have to bump the numbers up. Otherwise, they'll suspect something—that's more than certain," the woman says. Her voice is trembling. "I don't even want to think about what's going to happen if…"

"Shh!" The man hushes her; he's probably noticed me.

I don't raise my head, though it's sorely tempting to take a peek. They're only a couple of steps away. I hear the sound of a car door closing, followed by the rumble of the engine. The couple is pulling out of the driveway. Even though my eyes are still locked on the inside of my trunk, I can sense that they're watching me.

When the Bentley disappears around the corner, I close the trunk with a bang and head inside. A hot bath is all I'm dreaming about right now.

It usually only takes me a minute to fall asleep when I'm exhausted, but tonight I can't pass out. My mind is overflowing, swirling with chaotic thoughts. Through them all, I can't get rid of one single question: *Who are my new neighbors?*

CHAPTER THREE

I WAKE UP THE NEXT MORNING with a small headache. I need to grab a cup of coffee with a splash of my favorite soymilk to make myself feel better. On Wednesdays I break my everyday hurried routine because my classes start late in the afternoon; I don't have to rush anywhere. Unlike Maddie, who as a high schooler needs to set off to school every day at seven-thirty.

When I come downstairs, my cousin is already bustling around the kitchen, opening all the cabinets, drawers and the refrigerator in her attempt to compose a super nutritious yet low-calorie breakfast. Lately she's nuts about cutting down on calories because her prom is in exactly one month. She wants to be able to put on a dress one size smaller than her current four.

"You're going to vanish," I say at the sight of her packing Belvita cookies and half a grapefruit into a Tupperware.

"I'll be fine." She places the plastic container in her backpack. "Are you joining us in Portland this weekend?"

"No. I accepted Charlie's invitation to Emily Meyer's

birthday party, remember?"

"Ah yeah. It totally slipped my mind." Her big eyes flash with disappointment. "Is Rach going to be there too?"

My best friend and the birthday girl don't get along, so it would be a miracle if Rach went.

"No, I don't think so. She has other plans."

"But Matt will be there, right?"

My heart speeds up simply from hearing his name. "Maybe."

"Too bad you're not coming with us… but have fun."

I agreed to be Charlie's date only because I've been secretly counting on Matt showing up at the party. I've been infatuated with him since I saw him for the first time at the school cafeteria a year ago. He'd be perfect if not for one major flaw: a chain of girls in his wake who, like me, have a crush on him and strive to find a ploy that will attract Matt's attention. I'm slowly getting to the bottom of my list of tricks, and I know that if I don't come up with an innovative idea soon, I'll end up in the ranks of those who only attempted, not the ones who actually succeeded—not that there have been many of those!

I'm going to the birthday party to increase my chances of sparking Matt's interest. I'll miss shopping fever in Portland with my Maddie and Cynthia, but I don't regret it. Two days of wandering about a big mall, probably with a stop to watch one of the latest releases at the movies, and maybe dinner at a sushi bar can't hold a candle to the guy of my wildest dreams.

Maddie opens the refrigerator to search for her beloved organic orange juice. Her morning wouldn't be the same without a glass of her favorite drink.

"Do you want some?" she asks, but more out of politeness than to actually serve me some; she knows the only two things I drink are coffee and water.

We hear the sound of a car outside. My cousin, to satisfy her inborn curiosity, closes the fridge and scoots to the kitchen window.

"That's them!" she whispers, as if they could hear her.

"Them?" I frown.

"Our new neighbors, I mean," she replies, overly excited. "Have you seen him yet?!"

I haven't, but I can tell that his appearance ignites fiery passion in my cousin. She glows from the inside out, and I can even see pink in her cheeks.

"The woman he's with is a damn lucky one. She isn't bad-looking either."

Maddie's reaction to them intrigues me, makes me wonder what's all of the fuss about. I hurry to the window to evaluate the couple myself.

He's standing with his back to me—I can only tell that he's tall and muscular—but I have the perfect view of her. She's a woman of unconventional beauty; I'm guessing she must have some Armenian roots. I'd give her age as around twenty-six, maybe twenty-seven. She looks very vintage in her black Delores swing dress, highlighting the curves of her hourglass figure. Her dark, wavy hair perfectly complements the look. "Those two are a perfect match for each other, don't you think?" Maddie says with a barely audible sigh.

"I haven't been able to see his face yet," I reply, and fix my gaze on the man. I carefully follow him with my eyes while he goes up the stairs leading to the porch. Unexpectedly, he stops and remains motionless. As I look at his back, the uncomfortable pain in my chest flares up, but this time it's even worse than before. I place my palm on my chest and start to breathe faster and heavier, squeezing my eyes shut.

"Is everything okay?" Maddie lays her warm hand on my shoulder.

"Yeah, I'm fine, it must've just been a nerve pain." I look back at the man, and realize with a shock that he's now facing us. For a fraction of a second our gazes lock; my pulse jackknifes. "Oh my God!" I say, and instantly recoil in shock as if the window was on fire. In my haste, I hit the table behind me with my hip and curse it underneath my breath. Now not only does my chest hurt, but my leg too. "He noticed that we're staring at them."

"Great." Maddie facepalms. "Now he must be thinking that we're nothing but nosy gossips," she whines. "And there goes summer barbecuing with them. What a shame."

"I'm okay, by the way," I say sarcastically.

"What do you think about him, though?" She totally disregards my incident.

"I don't know. I looked away the second our eyes met—I didn't have time to take him in properly," I snap, rubbing the spot on my chest; the pain is lessening. Something strange is going on with me, and I can't understand what it is.

I float through the rest of the day. In the evening, I bring home my best friend, Rach, who I expect to help me create a killer outfit for Saturday night. She's a fashion virtuoso with a good eye for putting splendid outfits together. I know that if I surrender my looks to her, I'll have nothing to worry about.

"Do you think I should wear a dress or pants?" I ask Rach, who's intensively examining the entire collection of clothes I've pulled out from the closet and which, in my opinion, are suitable for the occasion. My bed is now covered with pieces of clothing including three airy summer dresses, two pairs of jeans, a pair of linen pants, and several blouses and tops.

"Honestly?" She makes a sour face as if instead of a pile of clothes, there's a dead squirrel lying right in front of her. "No offense, but these clothes are boring." She tosses me a pitying look through her classy Ray-Ban eyeglasses. "What I see right now is some junk for old women. We have to go to the mall."

"Say what?" I'm not sure if she's kidding or dead serious.

"Zara… A floral midi dress?" She snatches my purchase from about three years ago. "Or that one?" She points at a brown dress right next to her. "No neckline, dull color. It's perfect for a nun, but not for a girl whose job it is to seduce the biggest heart-throb at university," she adds in a gum-chewing-girl manner, which aggravates me a bit.

"What?" I say, a bit resentful. Rach can be very blunt,

and I know that about her, yet I still take her words personally.

"Oh my goodness, you know what I mean." She flings the flowery dress onto the pile. "None of these things pass my seduction style assessment test. You failed, honey." She crosses her arms over her chest and leans against the windowsill. "But you still have a chance to take the test again."

"Thank you, professor, but my financial situation—"

"What's a couple of bucks compared to the satisfaction that comes from being the most desirable object at the event?"

Which is what Rach is every time she shows up somewhere.

"I'm not sure…" I wage an inner battle.

"You are." She winks at me. "Tomorrow afternoon we're going to Salem. Even if it means I have to tie you up and drag to the store by force, I swear I'll do it. So you'd better be a good girl and make it easy on the both of us," she warns me.

"Well, I guess I don't have a choice, as usual."

"Exactly," she reassures me, and gives me the slyest smile, which suddenly vanishes as she's thunderstruck by something she's just seen outside. "Zara!" Her reaction is so passionate that it makes me think she must've spotted a UFO landing in my yard. "Get over here, right now!"

"What's the matter?" I spring to my feet.

"Quick!" She rushes me with a hand motion.

"Did you see a unicorn or something?"

"There's the most gorgeous guy I've ever seen in my whole life standing in front of your house!".

"Aw, yeah," I stop halfway and say with no enthusiasm, "that's my new neighbor."

I feel like peeking out, but after this morning's incident, I don't want to risk him catching me watching him again.

"Seriously, girl?! Damn! To hell with Matt! You have something one-of-a-kind living next door!" She glues her forehead to the window glass. I hope she doesn't start drooling.

"A thing? Rach, really?" I've never liked her tendency to talk about men like they're objects.

"In the sense that… Well… Matt is attractive, no doubt, but the guy outside… Holy shit…"

I burst her bubble. "He's taken. And you'd freak out at his girlfriend too. She's hot."

"Oh well…" She pouts. "Maybe one day he'll dump her."

"You wish, huh?" I smile and shake my head.

"Me? Of course not!" She winks at me and helps me put the clothes away.

* * *

Thursday means another hectic morning filled with haste. I don't know why I never get up right when the alarm goes off. Every single time, I stall the moment of getting out of bed to the max and as a result, when I finally do, I have to rush at breakneck speed to get ready to leave. Guilty as charged.

I run downstairs to the kitchen. The aroma of freshly-brewed coffee spreads through the entire first floor. When I clear the door, I come across my aunt wearing a blue mask, looking like a Smurfette. She's settled back at the table, performing her daily routine: catching up with the local news.

"It's unbelievable." She puts down the newspaper and transfers her gaze to me. Her face is taut, yet that blue color all over it makes her look comical. I turn around and grab a bottle of water, stifling a giggle. "Two days ago someone broke into the Reynolds' house, and three days before that into Mrs. Gonzales's. Plus, Molly told me the other day at work that when she was stepping out of the house to get rid of some papers for recycling, there was some suspicious-looking man hanging around her property. She called the police, but it was too late; by the time they arrived, the stranger was long gone." She takes a sip of her delicious-smelling cappuccino, which leaves foam on her upper lip.

"Apparently we live in a sketchy area," I reply, mostly out of politeness and to let her know I'm listening to her. Frankly, I don't really care about the statistics of break-ins at the moment; I'm trying desperately to remember where the hell I put my notebook, which I need to take with me today.

"It didn't use to be like that." She sighs. "Considering that all these recent break-ins have taken place practically right under our noses, I've taken very basic precautions, just in case, and I've changed the code to the garage door. From now on, instead of your birth date, you should enter May 22nd, which is the date of the end of my first marriage. I think you should jot it down—you never know when you might need it." She flips to the next page. "It's no big deal, I know, but I watched a show lately where the hosts were suggesting that robbers usually use the garage to break into the house. It actually made sense to me."

It's ludicrous how suggestible Cynthia is. She always buys into everything they show on TV. All that happens on the other side of the screen is an undeniable truth to her. If, in one her favorite shows, somebody claimed that the most effective way to discourage potential burglars from coming to our house was installing a scarecrow next to the front door, she'd do it.

"I'll remember it; piece of cake. Plus, what if I wrote it down and someone found it? I think it's better if I just store it in my memory."

I rarely use the garage door to get into the house anyway—I don't even park my car inside because there's only space for one vehicle, and the privileged one isn't my Golf, but Cynthia's Mercedes.

"Changing the subject"—my aunt folds the newspaper and puts it away—"tonight Maddie and I are going to the hair salon. Would you like to join us, sweetheart? I have one extra coupon and still can make an appointment if you feel like it."

"Thank you, auntie, but right after school I'm going

shopping with Rach. I need, as she put it, to stock up on some clothes that don't look like they're from the medieval ages and won't make me resemble a 'tigercow', which is a woman in her forties, frustrated because of her age and very limited sexual popularity, in case you didn't know."

The moment the words come out of my mouth, I already regret uttering them.

"Do you think that a forty-year-old woman can't be attractive?" she asks, her tone slightly insulted. Sometimes I forget that Cynthia is in her early forties, and, after three divorces, has already stopped hoping to meet her prince one day.

"When you look like you're thirty, of course you can be," I blurt out.

I find the notebook on the windowsill, grab it and throw it into my purse, kiss Cynthia goodbye on the cheek, and leave before she can add anything to our awkward conversation.

This fine morning I take a bus to school. Rach and I decided that it's nonsense to drive to the mall in two separate cars after class. Even though she only got her driver's license two weeks ago, I wanted to give her the satisfaction of taking us shopping and agreed to her being the driver.

As I amble along the fence, I notice that the Bentley is gone. For some reason I'm a little disappointed. Maddie proudly bragged yesterday about being able to see them up close while coming back from school. She even received a friendly smile from the girl, but neither of them initiated a conversation. I must admit I'm a bit jealous that, even though she blew it, she had a chance to actually meet them. But all is not lost that is delayed.

* * *

After three long classes, totally drained, I get into Rach's tiny car. The Golf that I drive isn't the peak of luxury and comfort, but at least I have enough space to stretch out my legs inside, which is quite challenging in my friend's "little baby", as she calls it. Her vehicle makes me feel cramped, as if I were packed into a can like a sardine. But it's not the tiny interior that freaks me out the most—it's her driving. I have the impression that although she's physically sitting behind the wheel and maneuvering between the other cars, her mind is in a totally different world. She brakes fiercely—the same way that she speeds up—and she shows a total lack of respect toward the 'amber light means slow down and stop' rule. She even runs a couple of red lights and doesn't give way to other drivers, royally pissing them off. She also honks at everybody whenever she feels like it. I see more middle fingers shown to us today than I have for the last five years. When Rach finally pulls into the underground parking lot of the mall, taking up one and a half spaces, I breathe a sigh of relief. The nightmare is over and I'm still in one piece, safe and sound. I feel like I need a drink.

Apparently Rach still has a lot to learn when it comes to driving.

Two hours later, exhausted from walking from store to store and trying on at least ten outfits in each, I'm forced to face the nightmare of Rach on the streets again—this time in the rain. For a moment I have the compelling urge to demand to take over the wheel, but how would I explain it to Rach? I'm not as blunt as she is, and I'd never tell her she's a shitty driver.

Just as I expected: Rach driving a car is a pain, but Rach driving in the rain is terrifying. She drives straight into potholes filled with rain, and changes lanes without signaling because of how tense she is about the raindrops hitting the windshield. At one point, she brakes so suddenly to let a pedestrian cross the street that my purse falls from the back seat onto the floor and all the stuff inside it ends up strewn under my seat.

"I'm so sorry, but I hate driving in the rain."

Tell me about it, I say to myself, but refrain from sharing my thought out loud. I don't want to stress the poor creature out even more.

When we finally arrive at my house, Rach knocks over the recycling bin that my aunt left in front of the house in the morning.

"Oops, sorry, didn't mean to do that!"

"Yeah, yeah, don't worry," I say, eager to finally get out. I don't even want to wait until the rain calms down; the only thing I need right now is to leave this car as soon as possible and pull myself together after that traumatic experience.

I collect all the things from under the seat, grab two

shopping bags with my brand-new purchases in, say bye to my friend and break into a run. I sprint toward my porch, but my furious pace doesn't save me from getting soaking wet. I wave to Rach, who, having made sure I'm on my porch, allows herself to take off.

The only thing that's keeping me now from settling back on the couch in front of the TV, sipping hot cocoa in a dry and cozy house, is the front door I need to unlock. I fumble around in my purse for the precious key in it. Unfortunately, after several seconds I realize that the key is missing.

Damn it! I stomp my feet a couple of times. *I must've left the keys on the kitchen table this morning while searching for the notebook.*

There's no one in the house. Maddie and Cynthia are at the hairdresser's now. The only thing to do in this emergency situation is use the garage door.

A second before my desperate do-or-die run in the pouring rain, an unpleasant feeling spreads in my chest; I realize I can't remember the new code. No sense in going to the garage. I know that the combination of numbers needed to unlock the door is the date of the end of my aunt's first marriage, but that's not helpful at all. I'll have to call her and ask to give me the code.

No sooner do I reach into my purse for my cellphone than I realize it's not there. I rummage through my purse frantically, but there's no doubt that while I was grabbing my stuff in feverish haste, I didn't spot my phone. Rach is probably struggling with the rain on her way home at the moment and isn't even aware that under the passenger's seat lies my cell.

Desperation spikes inside me; I feel homeless. I'm forced to taste the curse of my own recklessness. I should have written the code down instead of assuring Cynthia I'd simply remember it. The rain is pouring down and I can't get into the house to hide from it. I slap the bags on the plastic chair. I feel like kicking it to take out some of the exasperation that has welled in me.

I hunch over on the porch with my hands in the pockets, wondering what to do without a cellphone, house key, and car. Usually I savor the sound of the rain and find it relaxing, but right now it doesn't soothe me at all. On the contrary, with every single raindrop coming down from the sky, my frustration grows bigger. I hate to admit it, but the only solution that comes to my mind is turning to Charlie and asking him for shelter until my family comes back. I wince at the thought, but I can't think of anything better.

I'm about to jump into the rain and sprint to Charlie's house when something steers me away from doing so; I clearly sense someone's presence near me. My skin prickles. I look around and spot my neighbor, sprawled comfortably on a porch sofa. I wonder how long he's been hanging out there. His stretched-out legs, crossed at the ankles, are propped up on the coffee table in front of him; his hands are clasped behind his head. Because of the hood that covers most of his face, I can't tell whether he's gazing into space or asleep.

I freeze, sizing him up; it's just the two of us. Excitement shivers through me, and something flutters in my gut. I can't be sure whether he's conscious of my presence, but I can't stop staring.

Unexpectedly, he twists his head in my direction. I can just make out his eyes in the shadow. When our gazes meet, I'm gripped by a strong thrill. As we stare at each other for a lingering moment, a hot wave washes through me, reaching every fiber of my body; unable to withstand his intense look, I break our eye contact. There's something intimidating about him that takes away my already microscopic confidence.

"Nobody home?" His voice penetrates the slanting rain and reaches my ears.

"No," I answer with a touch of hesitation; I just admitted in front of a total stranger I had nowhere to go.

"Do you need some company?" His voice cuts through the rumbling rain again. "You can wait here."

His question makes my heart hammer. When I raise my eyes back to him, adrenaline immediately starts to fill my veins.

"I… actually…" I mumble, stunned; his offer is tempting, considering that I've been dying to finally meet the mysterious man who has made both my cousin and my friend swoon at the mere sight of him.

But doesn't he have a girlfriend? Wouldn't it look suspicious if she found us sitting together on the porch by ourselves?

I hold my breath and make a spur-of-the-moment decision. "Actually, why not?"

I have a hunch that I'll regret it later, but I take my chances anyway.

CHAPTER FOUR

I SPRINT THROUGH THE POURING RAIN. It only takes me several seconds to make it around the front yard fence and reach my neighbors' porch.

"I'm Zara Logan," I introduce myself, climbing up the stairs. The butterflies in my stomach multiply with every step I take. I'm overly excited, which isn't like me. I usually keep my cool, but this guy seems to overturn all my level-headedness.

"You have a quite unique name," he says, taking off the hood. It immediately becomes clear to me why the other girls were swept off their feet when they saw him for the first time.

He has tousled, raven-black hair; his face is strong with pronounced features, angular cheekbones, and a sharp jaw. Up close he seems oddly familiar, as though I've seen him somewhere before, and not only through my kitchen window. I fix my eyes on his soft lips, which are dangerously captivating. But what entrances me the most are his extraordinary, ocean-blue eyes.

For a swift moment, I'm lost in a mystical depth of his eyes, but I manage to finally strangle something out. "My real name is Zahara, but that sounds even worse."

At my comment, his lips curl up.

"Dorian Hatch," he says. "Do you want to join me?" He makes some space for me on the sofa.

"Sure," I say brightly, pretending that I'm as cool as he is.

As I approach, he quite openly studies me. I daintily sit down next to him, tension creeping up my spine. No sooner do I touch the backrest than I'm struck with his scent. I've never smelled anything like that before. If someone were able to fumble through my brain in order to find the one smell that would have the power of leading me into any temptation, it would be exactly the one that Dorian is emanating. It's masculine but soft, with some spicy notes. I inhale it deep into my lungs and relish it.

"Nice to finally meet you," he says, sinking into the cushions. He's far more comfortable than I am.

"How do you like this neighborhood?"

"It's nice. Very peaceful." His voice is deep and low, every word pronounced with an unusual precision.

"I'm glad you like it."

My mind is like a blank page. Socializing is my big weakness. I've never been good at small talk, especially with handsome guys. I don't even know what to ask him about and how to direct our conversation. He takes the initiative—thank God.

"Does it happen to you often?"

"What, forgetting my key or chatting with a stranger?"

"Which one do you think I mean?"

I fidget on the sofa. "Actually, both are happening to me for the first time." I try to control my shaking hands.

"In that case I feel honored that I'm the first stranger you decided to talk to."

"Well, we practically live in the same house, so you're not completely unknown to me. I've seen you a couple of times."

I have the impression that every breath I take puts me more and more at ease. It's such a strange feeling, as if someone is injecting me with an anesthetic. My tensed spine starts to slowly relax, and the adrenalin rush slows down.

"It doesn't change the fact that I may be a secret criminal who's only waiting for occasions like this one," he says.

He makes a good point, but there's not even an ounce of fear inside me right now. "I'm a risk-taker."

"Oh, are you?" He raises his brow in curiosity.

"Nothing ventured, nothing gained, right?" That's something that Rach would say.

A half-smirk spreads on his lips. "How much are you willing to put at stake?"

His question surprises me. "It depends on how much I want what I'm interested in."

Our conversation has taken an unexpected tone. I didn't anticipate that when I decided to join him on the porch. It feels like flirting to me, but I don't want to stop; I want to continue this innocent game of going back and forth.

"Let's say… you're craving something to the extent that you can't concentrate on anything else. Your hunger is so overwhelming that you feel physical pain and aren't able to function until you satisfy it."

His words cause a dizzying current to race through me. *Is it me or has he just described desire in its purest form?*

"I believe that the answer is obvious." I strive to look unshaken, as if our conversation hasn't made my heart speed up again.

"Not until you say it out loud."

"I'm ready to sacrifice anything for something like that."

Dorian gives me a raking gaze. "Now it's clear."

It's so unusual the way he articulates every word, every syllable; so slowly and clearly.

"And you?" I ask.

"Same."

"Has it ever happened to you? Have you ever felt such a desire?"

Dorian doesn't respond straight away. His eyes shift from me to the lashing rain. He seems to have dived into his thoughts, whirling around a particular moment from his past. All emotions are wiped from his face, and I can't tell whether he's remembering something pleasant or rather something he'd like to erase. "Yes, it's happened to me before."

"Was the risk worth it?"

"No."

Dorian intrigues me. Usually when people first meet, they talk about their interests and hobbies, or maybe the weather. They don't touch upon their desires and thirsts right away. Nonetheless, I'm enjoying our little chat, and grow more and more interested in my neighbor. He's very peculiar.

"Why not?" I ask.

"At times, something deludes us in such an irresistible fashion that it's easy to believe that our future life will be meaningless and empty if we don't get it. Trust me," his gaze returns to my face, "the price is irrelevant when one's deepest urges are involved. Man is unable to think reasonably when the object of his desire is right in front of him. He's ready to sacrifice whatever it takes to get what he's longing for." He pauses for a second to analyze my reaction. I'm speechless, carefully listening to every word coming out of Dorian's mouth. "Once in a while it pays off to take a risk, but not always. Sometimes you come to realize that by taking that risk you've made the biggest mistake of your life; unfortunately, now there's no coming back, and, as a result, you need to pay for your recklessness and impulsiveness."

"I don't quite understand," I say, intrigued.

"You won't understand until you experience it yourself."

"Experience what?"

"Such an overwhelming desire that if you don't feed it, it'll drive you insane." His eyes hold me still; it feels like he's penetrating right into my soul with his gaze.

Dorian's scent hits me again with double power. He has

this potent magnetism that pulls me toward him, regardless of the fact that we've just met. I swallow hard. My thoughts are tangled up in his words, setting my insides on fire. Every cell in my body is yearning to experience what he's talking about.

"I want to know what it feels like," I declare, as if Dorian could make it happen right at this second.

My words echo between us. A shutter seems to fall over his eyes. After drilling me with his gaze once more, Dorian frowns, as though he's just noticed something on my face that wasn't there before.

"What's the matter?" I ask, pulling away.

Do I have a massive zit or something?!

"That's strange…" he says; his eyes narrow with a flicker of suspicion.

"What's strange?" I duck my head as an unwelcome blush creeps into my cheeks.

Dorian doesn't bother to enlighten me. Instead he's slowly leaning toward me, minimizing the distance between us. A quiver surges through my veins; he's perilously close.

He flicks my hair from my neck and studies the uncovered area. Prickly tingles go over me as his warm breath touches my bare skin. An explosion takes place somewhere in my abdomen. I can't take this anymore and sit upright. Our eyes meet; he's puzzled.

"How is this possible?" Incredulity flashes across his face.

"What do you mean?"

Our conversation is interrupted by the sound of a car engine cutting through the rain. I cock my head and see two bright yellow spots coming in our direction. I recognize it even, from afar; it's the black Bentley pulling into the driveway. I have no doubt that it's Dorian's girlfriend sitting behind the wheel. The sight of her sobers me a bit.

Dorian is taken, and I need to break out from this weird trance I've fallen into. Preferably even vanish from their porch and never come back.

The girlfriend stops at the garage door, but she doesn't open it right away. I can't see a thing through the heavy raindrops bouncing off the windshield, but deep in my bones I sense her gaze. She's watching us, most likely wondering what the hell a strange girl was doing with her boyfriend while she was gone.

My face flushes with humiliation and anger at myself. *What the hell I was thinking?*

When the garage door finally rolls up and she disappears inside, I rise swiftly from the sofa. "I think I've got to go now." I flatten the front of my sweater.

"Why is that? I didn't notice you finding your keys."

"I don't think your girlfriend is okay with me sitting here with you alone."

"My girlfriend?" He makes a face as if he didn't quite understand the question.

"Yeah, the one who just showed up." I point my head toward the garage door.

"Rita?" He chuckles. "She's my cousin. I don't do

relationships. No girlfriends."

Cousin?! I squint in disbelief. It blows my mind. I need a few seconds for my brain to process this revelation, but when I think about it, I realize that they've shown no sign of being a couple. I've never seen them affectionately hugging, holding hands, or kissing. Somehow this news is a powerful relief; I don't feel out of place anymore. I lower myself beside him again.

"Rita won't have anything against you being here. I even bet she'll come over to meet you," he says.

"I'd love to meet her," I say. "There's one question I need to ask you, though. Since you said you didn't do relationships with girls, does it mean that…" I feel dumb saying it aloud.

He makes it easier on me. "No, I don't date guys either. I'm just not good at long-term relationships. I'm much better at those short but intense ones."

We're sitting closer than before, his thigh pressed against my leg. A shockwave of desire rockets through me, and my throat goes dry. "How intense?"

"There are no words descriptive enough to answer that question. You won't understand until you try it yourself. It's like nothing you've experienced ever before."

It sounds like an offer, but I can't tell if it really is one, or IF it's just my brain misinterpreting his words, giving them the meaning I want them to carry.

"I'm not sure if I'll ever have the chance to give it a shot," I say. Dorian is definitely too close; I feel the warmth his body is emanating. It's hard for me to think straight.

"You might one day."

The moment his gaze drops from my eyes to my lips, a wave of pain suddenly washes over my chest. It comes and goes. I keep it together, not wanting to reveal my sudden indisposition.

The front door swings open. We both turn left to face Rita, who's standing on the doorstep. Close up, her beauty is even more overwhelming. Her face is a perfect oval with a small, charming nose, and soft, rounded, red lips matching the light rouge on her upper cheekbones.

She tosses me a kind smile, and says, "I see my cousin has some company." Rita has a warm and soothing voice. She'd be a great children's book reader.

"It's our neighbor—Zara," Dorian tells her.

"Nice to meet you, Zara. I'm Rita."

The two of them are both unusually attractive, but nothing alike. Besides tar-black hair, they don't share any similar features that would suggest they're related.

"Don't you want to come inside? The weather is awful," she asks, opening the front door wider.

"I don't want to impose," I say.

"It's okay—no problem at all. We love having guests, don't we. Dorian?" She throws him a meaningful look.

"Of course," he replies curtly.

"Come inside, seriously," she encourages me.

"We just met; Zara may be uncomfortable with coming inside," Dorian reminds her.

"It's okay," I say, "I'm fine with it."

"Give us a second, Rita," Dorian demands.

"As you wish." She shrugs unenthusiastically and vanishes inside the house.

"Those two women you live with are your mother and sister?"

"No, they're my aunt and my cousin. My parents died right before my fifth birthday."

"I'm sorry."

"That's okay. It's been a long while. I don't even remember them too well."

"At least you have a couple of family members who take care of you," he says, seemingly trying to comfort me.

"Cynthia isn't my real aunt; she was my mom's best friend. We don't know why, but the whole family turned away from my parents even before I was born." This time it's me looking into space, considering for the hundredth time what might have been so terrible that it made every single member of my family turn their back on my parents. "Families…" I sigh.

"Did you ever try to contact them?"

"I'm not interested in them," I say. My tone is emotionless. "Cynthia told me that she tried reaching out multiple times, but they weren't concerned about me, so why would I bother?" I shrug my shoulders in resignation. "Hey, why were you looking at my neck earlier?"

"I… thought you had a tattoo on your neck, but I was wrong." He fixes his gaze on my neck.

"I do have one, actually."

I spark his interest. His eyes widen. "Where?"

"On my ribs."

"Can I see it?" Something like a flame starts growing in his eyes.

"Umm…" I'm flustered, and I don't quite know what to say. I shouldn't have mentioned the tattoo, but now it's too late. He wants to see it, and I hate chickening out. It's not like it's on my butt-cheek or anything, but still. I feel too exposed on his porch as it is.

"If you don't want to show it to me, that's fine."

"I don't know how the neighbors might react. You don't know them yet, but they can be very nosy."

"Let's go inside then." His lips lift in a smirk. "Didn't you say you were okay with that?"

"Yes, I don't mind—" I wince, feeling a sudden pain again. This time it's a strong enough stab to make me hiss.

"Are you alright?" Dorian places his hand on my arm; the spot he touches immediately burns.

"Ouch!" I jerk away. "Sorry—I just had a nerve pain, that's all," I lie. The pain still hasn't gone away.

"Let's go then."

I get to my feet, unable to sit still anymore. I breathe slowly, trying to calm down my pounding heart. I don't know what's going on with me, but it's the worst possible timing.

Dorian opens the front door and motions me inside. I only ever visited Mrs. McConelly twice while she was alive, so I only vaguely remember how the place looked back then.

Despite that, I'm certain it was nothing like it is now. The layout is more or less the same as our house, but that's all there is in terms of similarities. Our house needs renovation and a breath of freshness, which won't happen in the near future—unless Cynthia meets her fourth husband and he covers all the expenses. This house looks like a cut-out from the Architectural Digest magazine.

We make our way to the living room. Purple walls perfectly contrast with the white L-shaped couch, which adjusts to my body as I settle on it.

"Would you like something to drink?"

"A glass of water is fine," I reply, and I lean back on the pillows. The pain is diminishing.

"Sure." Dorian disappears into the kitchen.

While he's gone, I scan the room again. It's cozy, yet it seems so pristine, as if no one lives here; it's too impeccable and clean. Everything has its own, precise place: I don't see any unnecessary elements that would ruin the harmony here. My attention is caught by a white bookcase across the room with neatly arranged books on the shelves—twenty-five on each. No more or less. The walls radiate emptiness, for there are no pictures or paintings on them.

One element stands out the most: a tall pendulum clock standing in the corner by the window that doesn't match the rest of the décor at all. It oozes with unexplained mystery. Its rod has a snake wrapped around it, facing the dial as if it's trying to climb up and reach it. The dial itself is peculiar too; it displays twelve-hour time markers, but instead of digits, I see sparkling dots that seem to be gemstones. Every single one of them is a different color. Even though the clock is quite interesting, I can't quite grasp what such an antique is doing in this catalogue-worthy modern home.

Dorian comes back holding a glass filled with water and ice. I'm struck speechless at his sight. He's taken off his baggy hoodie and is now wearing only a tight, crew-neck T-shirt. His muscles, rippling under the fabric, quicken my pulse and I hold my breath at the sight of his strong arms, wide chest and firm abdomen. He walks with a nonchalant grace that I can't help but admire.

When he drops down beside me, our closeness makes my senses spiral out of control. His scent is enveloping me tightly with no intention of letting go. It's making me dizzy and confused, but I want to inhale it deep into my lungs, get drugged by it. I can barely fight back the desire to place a million kisses on his bare neck.

I need to stay cool. I just met the guy, I scold myself.

"It's very stylish in here." I say the first thing that comes to mind, pretending that he hasn't just caused an avalanche of dirty thoughts in my mind.

"To Rita's credit."

"Is it just you two?" I take a sip of water. The gentle coolness goes down my throat and slightly quenches the fire inside me.

"I have a brother, but we haven't spoken for many years. Our paths…" He hesitates. "Let's say they've split and gone different directions."

"What about the rest of your family?" I take another cooling sip. "Do they live in a different state?"

Dorian's expression clouds over. "I don't like talking about them." I sense that he'd rather avoid the subject. "Don't you have something to show me?"

"Here in the living room?" I ask blankly.

"Why not? Rita's upstairs and won't come down unless we set the house on fire," he assures me, and slides his gaze down from my eyes to my lips. "You have nothing to worry about."

It shouldn't feel like a big deal to show him my tattoo—after all, a number of people have seen it before—but with Dorian it's different. I've never had such a gut-wrenching reaction to anybody in my whole life. Not even to Matt. Dorian's presence excites me too much.

I pull my shirt out of my jeans with one swift movement and bring it up to the under band of my bra, revealing the tattoo. It depicts two butterflies separated by a ribbon, each of a different color, with black tribal swirls and ornaments on their wings. What makes it unusual is where the tattoo is. It starts on the left side of my ribs, curves up, vanishing under my bra wing, and then emerges again right underneath my armpit. Whoever wants to see the whole masterpiece has to take a peek under my bra. There have only been three people who have had the honor of admiring both butterflies.

Dorian leans forward to take a closer look. He takes all my personal space away, but I don't mind. His face is so close to me that I can feel his breath on my bare skin, and

I'm immediately covered in goosebumps. His unruly hair, right next to my hand, calls for me to run my fingers through it. I freeze; my lips go dry. Dorian studies my tattoo thoroughly, his eyes full of attention, fascinated.

"I love this part." He puts his index finger on the wing of the bigger butterfly. "A butterfly," he says, and runs his finger all the way up to the bra, where he stops, causing my pulse to leap through my veins. My breath falters in anticipation of what he's going to do next. I can clearly tell he's being eaten by curiosity about what the whole tattoo looks like, but he doesn't let himself go any further.

He looks back up at me, causing a wave of sensations to wash over me, starting in the spot he's just touched. Never in my life has anybody looked at me the way he is right now. It's an extremely sensual yet tactful request to allow him to cross this intimate border.

"Do it." I can't muster more words.

I place both hands on the front of my shirt, holding my bra in place, when he undoes the latch on the back. With his warm hand, he pushes away the wing that is in the way, uncovering the rest of the tattoo. Pure lust detonates inside me; I'm hungry for his touch.

Where are these desires coming from?

"Interesting," he says suavely. "Was it your idea?"

"Yes. I wanted the design to be sort of a mystery. The visible bit is a prelude to something much bigger. At first glance, you only spot a little creature and a piece of ribbon, but when you eventually see the whole picture you realize it shows two butterflies."

"They're facing each other, yet are separated by the ribbon." He seems even more riveted than before.

"The ribbon symbolizes a boundary. A boundary that can't be crossed."

"Why?" he asks.

"Because, let's say, it may end up poorly."

Dorian sits upright and helps me fasten my bra. Our faces have never been closer than they are now. His scent shoots through me; his glittering eyes make contact with mine, leaving me dazed. I look down to his mouth. Those lips look like they would be a sweet pleasure to kiss. My heart is pounding so loud that I'm almost sure Dorian can hear it.

"You said you were a risk-taker, so where does the tattoo symbolizing boundaries that can't be crossed come from?" he asks quietly.

That closeness is killing me, taking away my capability of forming a coherent thought. I have every intention of answering his question, but an excruciating pain around my heart prevents me from doing so. The agony forces me to double over, and I start to cough. It feels like something's ripping my chest out from the inside. The pain is three times as bad as before.

"Zara?" Dorian draws his eyebrows together, seeming concerned. "Are you alright?"

The pose in which I've frozen suggests that I'm not really. I put my hand on my chest and breathe deeply, striving to get some air into my lungs. There's no way he doesn't notice that my face is contorted with pain.

"I don't know." I'm confused and ashamed. It's too humiliating to admit that I have the worst chest ache of my life and I'll die if somebody doesn't ease the pain within the next minute.

All of a sudden, to my clouded mind comes the sound of a car outside, and then the opening of a garage door. It's my aunt's Ford. I'm rescued.

I can't think straight. All I need is my dark, quiet room with my big bed, far away from everybody and everything.

I get up abruptly, and dart toward the front door without even explaining my weird behavior. Right now I'm genuinely certain I won't make it to tomorrow.

Disoriented, I leave Dorian's place, and a minute later, I bang on my front door like I'm insane. Cynthia opens it and throws me a biting comment about waking the dead in the cemetery two blocks away, but I don't really care at the moment. I storm upstairs to my room, lock the door and throw myself flat on my bed. I squeeze my eyes closed and pray that I'll be able to open them again.

CHAPTER FIVE

'M IN THE WOODS. It's dark. The freezing air prickles my lungs as I breathe. My soaking wet clothes are stuck to my skin and make me feel uncomfortable. A shiver runs through me.

I glance around, but I see nothing familiar. I don't know where the hell I am, but I have a sense of foreboding. An inner voice orders me to flee. Fear builds up in me. Heedless of the slimy ground and mud, I race off, but I don't make it too far; a few seconds later I stumble over a protruding branch and fall flat on the ground. As I try to lift myself back up, a reek suddenly hits me—a pungent smell of rotten meat that makes me feel queasy.

Is it death?

Adrenaline spikes in me. My body is in full fight mode. *I can do it. I can find a way out of this place.* As I strive to get up, I feel that something is restraining me. My legs are tied up; I can't move them. I kick and scream in a pounding frenzy, desperate to stand up, but I struggle in vain. It's only now that I realize what the obstacle is. A snake, wrapped around my ankles. It flicks its forked tongue in and out rapidly in my direction. It seems to be able to taste my fear in the air.

The snake constricts tighter viciously. I feel it spiral up to my knees. Fear paralyzes me. Its head is getting closer and closer to my face. The hissing sound grows louder. I close my eyes, ready for the worst.

ZARA...

I hear a man's voice, which seems to come from inside my own head.

ZARA...

The low, rough voice echoes in my head again.

"Who are you?" Somehow, I manage to put those three words together and say them out loud.

The moment the questions passes my lips, I feel a hot fleeting touch of wind on my neck. It's a strange experience because it's burning yet pleasing at the same time. I thirst to feel it again.

I KNOW WHERE YOU ARE.

Again, the same sensation. A gentle lashing of hot air on my neck. It's like a living flame, but I don't feel like putting it out. I don't want to deprive myself of the pleasure. It's slowly wrapping around my throat like someone's gentle hands. I open my eyes and look down; there's no trace of the snake that was twined around me before. I'm free! But to my surprise, an unbearable coldness spreads from my feet and travels up through my veins, reaching my knees, thighs, hips, abdomen.

"Stop!" I scream. "Stop!"

The biting iciness doesn't go away. On the contrary, it climbs further and touches my chest. When I exhale, I can see my breath in front of me. It's freezing. Finally, even the warmth on my neck disappears.

ZARA.

I lift my head up with difficulty. There's a man in the distance, and though I have no reason to know him, I instantly feel certain that it's the same man who's been haunting me in my dreams. He's leaning against a tree and looking at me. I can't see his face because he's wearing a hood.

ZARA.

I hear my name for the fourth time. It's him. It's his voice I'm hearing in my mind. I want this man to come over to me, but he remains still. I strive to get up from the ground, but I'm too weak. Some invisible force is keeping me glued to the ground. The man and I stare at each other. A weird thrill comes over me; it's not fear, it's something much stronger. I'm still motionless, as if someone's buried me in the sand. I'm incapable of moving my limbs.

"Who are you?"

I WILL COME FOR YOU.

Suddenly my throat tightens. I can't catch my breath; it feels like I'm having an asthma attack. I choke and panic, gasping without getting any oxygen. In my mind I beg him to help me, but he only observes me struggle passively. I'm losing consciousness. I'm *dying* and he's watching me…

I wake up drenched in cold sweat, my heart slamming against my ribs. The room is dark. The digital clock on the nightstand says it's three eighteen in the morning. I'm lying on the bed, fully dressed.

What happened? Why aren't I in my pjs?

It takes me a good while to recollect the events that took place before I passed out. When I think back to how the visit to Dorian's ended up, a blaze of embarrassment washes over me.

I sprang to my feet and raced outside like a maniac!

At a snail's pace, I sit upright. All the pain that was ripping my chest apart earlier is now gone. I touch the spot where I have a little lump. It's never bothered me before, but now I'm seriously considering a visit to the physician's to ensure it isn't something serious.

I switch on the bedside lamp, which sheds a dim light on the room. Hauling myself up, I trudge over to the big wall mirror beside the door and stand in front of it. I gaze at a girl with tousled hair and a pillow mark on her cheek. My bony face and dark under-eye circles make me look sick.

My appearance leaves a lot to be desired.

My stomach clenches when I wonder how much the odd incident several hours ago has colored Dorian's opinion of me. It must be bad. I owe him an explanation and an apology.

For the time being I can't do too much about it, so I simply change into my pajamas and go back to bed. I stare at the ceiling with my thoughts revolving around Dorian. I can't understand the peculiar effect he has on me. I've never felt such a burning, profound desire smoldering in me before. When I was with him it was consuming me, setting my insides on fire. A visceral need to be close with Dorian. Simply by thinking of him I already feel the warmth building up inside.

With my head bombarded with hundreds of thoughts, it takes me an hour and a half to fall back to sleep.

* * *

Another morning race in my attempt to be on time to school. As is my weekday routine, I shower, get dressed, and have breakfast in a hurry. Everything seems normal, but this morning my leaving the house in a rush is interrupted by Cynthia blocking the front door with her bony body. Her expression is as hard as stone.

"Don't you have something to tell me, young lady?" She tosses me a meaningful look.

"Not really." I shrug one shoulder.

"No?" Her voice whips. "How about last night? What was that supposed to be?"

"What do you mean by 'that'?

"For starters, you shut the front door right in my face, and when I said I wouldn't pay for it to be repaired, you threw a loud 'I don't give a shit' at me. Then you ran upstairs, barricaded yourself in the bedroom, and didn't come down despite me calling you for five minutes straight!"

I immediately blush and rub the back of my neck. Such

behavior doesn't sound like me at all. Why would I offend my aunt? For a second I even think that Cynthia might be just kidding, but her serious expression suggests otherwise. I try to stay cool-headed and say the first thing that comes to my weary mind.

"I'm really sorry. I didn't mean to behave disrespectfully in any way. I just… I had a huge argument with Rach; it was really bad. It'll be some time before we make up, for sure. I admit that I shouldn't have taken my frustration out on you. It wasn't fair at all."

"Are you telling me that you and Rachel aren't talking?" She raises her eyebrows in disbelief.

"Yes—she made it very clear she didn't want to see me again," I confirm. It's unbelievable how easily lying comes to me.

"Hmm, that's interesting… isn't that Rach's car pulled into our driveway, waiting, I believe, for you?" she says sassily, and points her index finger at me.

This takes me by surprise. We didn't talk about her coming to pick me up, which makes my current situation even more complicated than it already is. Cynthia only sends me a frosty look, shakes her head, and strides away from the door.

"We're not done here yet," she informs me.

In this house, there's one golden rule: be honest, no matter what. My aunt has forever hammered away that the worst truth is better than the smallest lie. In my defense, I myself don't quite understand what's going on either, so how can I explain it to anybody?

The morning breeze cools down my temper a bit. I don't feel like killing the unsuspecting Rach for showing up unannounced anymore, but I'm still irritated.

"What are you doing here, for God's sake?" I grumble as I get into the car.

"You left your phone in my car yesterday." She brandishes the cell inches from my face. "I thought you'd appreciate it if I dropped it off first thing in the morning, because we won't see each other later. I called your aunt last night, but when I asked her to give you the phone, she told me you were locked in your room."

Fuck! If they've talked, I'm in real trouble. They adore one another and whenever they have a chance to talk, they do so thoroughly. Sometimes they're on the phone for close to an hour. I can understand that; Cynthia is a great listener. Although she can be judgmental, she's at least there when we need to talk to her. Rach's mom, in spite of being more laid back than Cynthia, is too busy to carve out time to chat with her daughter. She's barely ever at home.

"Did she say anything else?" I demand.

"Not really, we just talked for a minute or so." She shrugs. "So what? Why did you hole yourself in upstairs?"

"What did you talk about?" I'm persistent.

"Nothing in particular. I only told her we went shopping, and obviously how stunning you look in your new dress. You look really gorgeous, honey! Then I mentioned something about that ridiculous cashier…"

At this point, I stop paying attention to her words. Firstly, I tell myself off in my head for how seriously I have betrayed Cynthia's trust. Secondly, I rack my brain to try to remember where all the things I bought even are.

Rach is relentlessly badgering me to reveal what I was fuming about, but I'm stubborn and tell her to drop it and leave me alone because I'm not in the mood to talk about it. She's starting to get on my nerves, and I'm inches from blowing up at her.

"What if I list all the possible things that you might be angry about, and if I get it right, you'll tell me?" she suggests, proud of the smart solution she's just come up with.

"I said no!" I lose my cool and shout. She can be so stubborn.

"Okay, okay. There's no reason to be rude and raise your voice, Zara. I'm sorry I came here to make it easy on you. What a terrible friend I am." She shakes her head.

Rach makes me feel bad, but she's right. I'm not being fair toward her. I'm angry because she contributed to my lie coming out, but how could she have predicted my confrontation with Cynthia? We drive in silence for the rest of the journey.

When we finally get to school, there's no way I'll make it to my first class on time. With all those tardies, what if I need to repeat this semester? I'm so disappointed in myself that it makes me see red.

I'm too angry and frustrated to master an apology for my rudeness, so I toss a simple "See you later" to Rach.

Maybe Professor Sullivan will be unusually understanding and forgive me being thirty minutes late.

* * *

When I'm back at home, Maddie and Cynthia have already gone to Portland for the girls' weekend. They've left me a note on the kitchen table: *Going to Portland, back on Sunday around 6pm. Love you.*

Rach hasn't spoken to me since this morning. I don't blame her; if I were her, I wouldn't want to call my friend who gave me attitude last time we spoke either. I'm aware that I'm the one who screwed up. Neither she nor my aunt deserved to be mistreated. All the emotions I've recently experienced and the frustration coming from them are my problem—they have nothing to do with it. I have no right to take it out on the people closest to me.

I reluctantly grab my cell phone, but I stop myself from dialing Rach's number as it crosses my mind that she's most likely hanging out with Sara and Natalie, her besties from college. The last thing I want to do right now is disturb the Friday night fun they must be having. Not everyone has a boring evening by themselves like I do.

Instead, I check my inbox, where I find two unread messages from Charlie.

Charlie: Hey girl, are you ready for the party tomorrow? Got an outfit yet?

I didn't respond to that text, so he sent me another one twenty minutes later.

Charlie: What time would u like me to pick you up, beautiful?

I throw myself on the bed, fixing my eyes on the ceiling. Replying to Charlie or calling up Rach seems like too much of an effort right now. I don't even have the energy to go downstairs and put on a TV show. At the thought of the birthday party tomorrow, my guts are twisting. I accepted Charlie's invitation only because Matt was going as well, but currently I truly regret my decision to go. I'm so sluggish that I could spend the whole weekend doing absolutely nothing, without even getting out of bed.

What am I, seventy? Why has there been so little life in me recently? I should at least take advantage of the fact that I'm home alone and throw a house party or invite my girlfriends for a sleepover.

I roll over my back and close my eyes. Immediately, in my mind I see Dorian.

I recall his handsome face, then his blue, hypnotizing eyes and his strong, chiseled body. I take a deep breath at the memory of his irresistible, overwhelming scent. Finally, I reconstruct the moment when he touched my skin. The flashback of him sliding his finger along my ribs sets me on fire.

I bite my lips and place my fingers on the same spot that

Dorian touched yesterday, imagining that it's his hand gently playing with my bra right now. I put my other hand on my stomach and brush my skin with my fingertips, climbing higher and higher until I reach my neck. I can picture him lying right next to me, caressing the sensitive spots on my neck. Dorian moves his face close to mine, but he stops inches from my mouth, keeping me unsatisfied, working up my appetite. I feel his warm breath on my parted lips. His tongue runs over my lower lip, causing chills to rush over me. He plants dozens of soft kisses on my chin, neck, and collarbone. As he explores my body with his lips, my desire flares up. A volcano of passion roars through me. There's so much built-up tension that I need to release it somehow, otherwise I'll erupt.

BANG!

I startle as something explodes loudly and open my eyes. My room is enfolded in darkness. At first I think the light bulb has burned out, but the moment I leave my room and turn on the light switch in the hallway, I realize that the fuse must have blown because there's no electricity in the whole house. I have no idea where to look for the fuse box.

I hate the thought of looking for it throughout the house because I am, for some reason, terrified of being home alone when it's dark. It's most likely a side-effect of all those horror movies I binge-watch. Every time the fuse box blows in a movie, someone is either killed, wounded or possessed. Watching scary scenes on the screen while sitting comfortably on the couch and eating popcorn is one thing;

being alone in the dark is a different ballgame.

My stomach roils, and I swallow hard. I have to handle the situation; I'm the only one at home for the remainder of the weekend. I don't even remember where I put my cellphone to use its torch function. Luckily, in my closet I always keep a spare flashlight just for this kind of situation. I push the button on it with a wobbly finger, praying it's not broken. Luckily, it's working, but the battery is about to die. I sigh, frustrated.

My imagination has been activated, and I can't focus on anything else other than the idea that at any moment some vicious thief will break into my house and attack me. The only weapon that I have on me is this little flashlight, which wouldn't pass the "knock the burglar out" test. At most I could bruise him—maybe.

I look around the hall. Even the faces of people in the pictures on the walls seem to be ferociously distorted in the dark. They're staring at me with blood-thirst. My limbs begin to shake as I move along, holding on to the wall. I need to think straight, but it's hard when my body is in fight-or-flight mode.

Fear and helplessness push me to make a desperate move. I head out to knock on my neighbors' door to implore Dorian or Rita to help me. The embarrassment generated by yesterday's incident isn't enough to prevent me from begging him for rescue.

I only make it halfway down their path when the door opens. I see Dorian looming in the doorway, and my heart speeds up. I feel a lump forming in my stomach and dryness in my mouth. He's wearing a black, skin-tight button-down shirt, which perfectly emphasizes his muscular form, matched with gray, low-rise straight jeans. He looks breathtaking. I stop dead in my tracks, unable to move even an inch. His outfit makes me assume he must have some commitment and is heading out just as I'm about to ask him for a favor. It doesn't seem like perfect timing. I feel like turning around, but it's too late for that.

He spots me. "Zara?" My pulse skyrockets.

"Hi." I blush. "I wanted… I need... Are you leaving?" This incoherent blend of words comes out of my mouth . I feel dumb.

"Why? Do you need anything?"

Does my face look that desperate?

"No… I mean, if you have something arranged, I wouldn't like to mess up your plans."

"What's the matter?" Dorian goes down the porch. With every step he takes, my pulse spikes again.

"For some mysterious reason my fuse box has blown. I'm all alone in the house and have no clue where to find it or how to fix it."

"And you came here to ask me to help you out with that?"

"Yeah, roughly speaking." My deadly fear of the dark I leave unspoken.

Dorian doesn't hesitate. "Lead the way."

We walk shoulder to shoulder, and, to my surprise, Dorian doesn't rush me, regardless of his previous engagements.

"Are you okay?" he asks.

"Yup," I answer. I owe him an explanation, but until he asks me any specific questions, I'd prefer to avoid the subject.

"Last night you rocketed out of my place. Why was that?"

I knew it was coming.

"It dawned on me that I'd left the stuff I'd just bought on the porch. I'm not sure if you're aware, but there's been a decent amount of thefts in the area. That's why I didn't waste even a second." What a stupid and unbelievable excuse. I feel like curling up and dying.

"Why didn't you come back?"

"My aunt was back from the hairdresser's, and I was able to get inside, so I thought why bother you any longer? I'm sorry I didn't even say goodbye, though."

"You weren't bothering me." When he says that, I feel a warm glow flowing through me.

"Anyway…" I don't want to dwell on the topic. "Do you know where the fuse box is?"

"We need to go to the basement," Dorian informs me as we go into the dark house.

"I have a flashlight." I switch it on, but it sheds so little light that even a candle would be more useful at the moment. "Well, better than nothing."

"Turn it off." He pulls out his cell phone from his pocket and immediately turns on the flashlight on it, which brightens the whole foyer. "Now at least we can see something."

I'm much more confident having someone with me. We make it to the basement door and I open it. Beyond is a narrow staircase, wooden steps descending into the dark. Even though a cold basement isn't the most romantic place to be, the awareness that it's just the two of us in the house makes my stomach flutter.

I lumber right behind Dorian, running my hand along the cold wall for balance. I have the impression that his scent is pulling me after him like an invisible thread. I inhale it deep into my lungs and let it go to my head. I need to be careful not to miss one of the steps and end up tumbling all the way down in front of him.

The basement is small, but Cynthia has managed to pile up a lot of clutter in here anyway. There is an old TV up against the wall, a lawn chair, dozens of shoe boxes, pots and pans, a coffee maker and a bunch of other junk. Everywhere is dust.

"Do you have a tenant living here or something?" Dorian asks, shining the flashlight on the items scattered all over the basement.

"I'm starting to wonder myself."

"Do you see that little box by the ladder?" He directs the light to a steel square on the wall.

"Uhm…"

"That's the fuse box. Bear it in mind for the future."

"I want to forget, because then I'll need to ask for help again."

I don't even know why I said that. It's hard to keep myself in check with Dorian next to me. His presence triggers some puzzling chemical reactions in my system that cause millions of hormones to buzz through me, making me think and say things that I shouldn't.

"Oh, will you?"

"Yeah. Nothing wrong with that, right?"

He fixes his eyes on my face with the deepest attention, as though he's trying to read something from me. "Absolutely nothing."

It's incomprehensible to me that we only spoke for the first time yesterday. Not only does it feel like we've met before, but also as if we know each other very well. There's something familiar about him that gives me a peculiar sense of peace and comfort. I'm curious to know if he shares the feeling.

As I thoroughly study Dorian's face, he suddenly turns the flashlight off. We're shrouded in shadow. I swallow hard. Tension hangs in the air, both scary and exciting.

"Why did you turn off the light?" My eyes haven't adjusted yet, but I don't need them to realize how close Dorian is standing; his body is beaming heat straight into me.

"You know all too well," Dorian whispers, inches from me. His scent wraps around me from every direction, and I'm locked in. I can't get away, but I don't even want to.

"I do." Pure lust washes over me, and I part my lips in anticipation for a kiss.

Instead of the soft touch of his lips, I feel a wrench. Unexpectedly, Dorian grabs me by my wrist, which jerks me out from my erotic trance. Freezing cold embraces the skin on my wrist where he's holding tight. An unpleasant chill travels up to my elbow then to my arm. The left side of my body feels as if it's been thrown into arctic water, and it's stabbing me like a thousand needles.

"What the hell are you doing?!" I strive to extricate myself, but in vain; his grip is too strong. "Dorian, what are you doing to me?"

He doesn't even budge, but grasps my other wrist and pushes me toward the wall behind me forcefully. He lifts both my hands above my head, making it impossible for me to move. I don't understand what's going on.

"Who are you?" he demands, standing no further than an inch from my face. His voice is high-pitched; he's not kidding.

"My name's Zara Logan. Born and raised in Keizer. I'm in my third year of psychology studies, I work at Walgreens and live next door to you. What else do you want to know?" My voice trembles.

Does he think that I'm lying? But who else am I supposed to be? A spy? Or maybe an undercover agent?!

"Why can't I see it?"

"What's *it*?"

He squeezes my wrists even tighter. The biting cold piercing my arms is unbearable. My fingers feel numb. Dorian doesn't say another word; instead we stand suspended for a lingering moment. His rapid breathing is the only sound reaching my ears. Even though I'm defenseless and subdued, I still don't believe he's a menace to me. I'm not frightened. I'm confused.

All of a sudden, I feel a warm spot in my chest. The warmth is gentle—it feels like a single sunray falling somewhere around my heart—but with every passing second, it's expanding like a bubble. When my entire chest is full, and it seems that there's no more space in me, it explodes into thousands of tiny flickers spreading through my body. A hot wave courses through me, causing Dorian to spring back.

The basement is lit up by a couple of light bulbs arranged in a row on the ceiling that turn on by themselves. Miraculously, the electricity has come back on without us doing anything. *But how is that possible?*

Pure disbelief is etched on Dorian's face. He tosses me a suspicious look, apparently deeply reflecting on something, then says, "There you go. Your electricity is back!"

Having pointed it out, Dorian swings around and makes his way to the stairs without bothering to say anything more.

"Hold on!" I scuttle after him and grab him by his shoulder. He can't just walk away like that. He owes me an explanation for the whole incident. "Can you explain to me what is this all about? You just hurt me, in case you didn't notice!"

Dorian slowly turns around. His face is indecipherable. "If you really don't know what's going on, then let's keep it that way. It's better for you." He takes my hand off of his shoulder and climbs the steps.

I stand, stunned, for a good moment after he vanishes from sight. It gets through to me that most likely, it's not a doctor I need to help me with my weird chest pains. Dorian obviously knows something, and I'm going to find out what it is.

CHAPTER SIX

SATURDAY HARDLY EVER MEANS sleeping in. To me, it almost always means a morning shift at Walgreens. On my break, I usually browse through social media to keep myself updated on what all my friends, who don't have to moonlight on the weekends, are up to. Today, however, when stuffing my face with a turkey sandwich, for the first time in forever I don't even bother to pull out my cell phone. My thoughts are twisted up in last evening. I can't come up with any logical explanation for what happened.

What was the 'it' he couldn't see?

Why did I feel that freezing cold in my wrists when he grabbed them?

What was the deal with the miraculous way the electricity came back on without us even touching the fuses?

That enigmatic man is intriguing me more and more. I get a thumping headache from all these questions.

I eventually look at my phone and see an unread message from Charlie.

Damn it, the birthday party's tonight. I sigh with

frustration and put the phone back in my purse without even reading the text.

* * *

Charlie is supposed to show up at six. I have a little bit over an hour to get ready. I can count on neither Maddie, who's with Cynthia in Portland, nor Rach to help me prepare myself for the event. The latter is still angry with me, and unless I do something about it, the situation won't change. After the birthday party, I should finally get myself together and make up with Rach for my awful behavior.

Without wasting time, I put on my latest purchase—a knee-length raspberry cocktail dress. It emphasizes my slender calves without uncovering too much of my body. The fabric fits my figure perfectly: it isn't too tight, making me look like I borrowed it from Maddie, nor is it too loose, making me look like I've lost twenty pounds and haven't updated my wardrobe yet. The outfit isn't that innocent, though—the neckline is pretty deep and reveals my cleavage. I don't feel particularly comfortable in it, but when Rach saw me wearing it, she wouldn't let me leave the store without purchasing the dress. She can be very persistent.

Now it's time to fix my messy hair. I decide to go for a knot bun that I keep in place with bobby pins. I top it off with a silver barrette. Finally, I put on my little pearl earrings, which Charlie gave me two years ago for my twentieth birthday. Even though I nurture no deeper feelings for him, it's a nice thing to do considering he's taking me with him.

When I glance in the mirror to see the final effect, I'm pretty happy. I look better than I expected. Preparing myself on my own has some advantages: Maddie has the tendency to go overboard with makeup, whereas Rach is always so generous with products in my hair that afterwards it needs at least two weeks to recover.

At six on the dot I hear the doorbell.

"*Holy cow!*" Charlie greets me, his eyes popping.

"What's up?"

"You look like a million dollars, girl." He lightly brushes my cheek with his lips.

"Oh, stop it." I roll my eyes, but I like his compliment.

Charlie looks presentable as well, despite his belly sticking out over his belt. He looks nothing like Dorian, who's shaped like a Greek god, but I appreciate that he's made an effort anyway.

I'm doing it again—thinking of Dorian.

I cast a lingering glance at their part of the house, sigh quietly and fasten the seatbelt while Charlie is pulling out of the drive. Heaviness settles in my stomach on the journey to Salem. I've never met Emily. When I accepted the invitation, I wasn't thinking about who the birthday girl was, but it doesn't matter in the end. I just hope it will all be worth it.

When we pull up in front of the house where the party is taking place, the driveway is already filled with cars. My hands start to sweat when I realize how many guests must be inside. As we move along the pathway, I can already hear loud music, balloons popping and people laughing obnoxiously loud. *What am I even doing here?* I take a deep breath and walk inside with Charlie. This is going to be an interesting experience.

* * *

The first two hours fly by fast and I actually have fun. However, the moment when Charlie comes up to me, asking me whether I'd mind being the designated driver because he feels an irresistible urge to indulge in some whiskey, is the beginning of a disaster. He holes himself up somewhere with his pals and forgets all about me.

That's when the second stage of the evening starts. I make an attempt to have a conversation with some other guests, but since almost everybody is quite tipsy, I practically have no one to talk to. People here can be divided into a couple of groups: miserable drunks (dwelling on their dramatic life stories), crazy drunks (those who yell, jump on the couches, and lock themselves in the bedrooms for an obvious purpose), stiff drunks (those lying down on the floor unconscious), and sober people (out of which ninety percent have already gone home).

As a matter of fact, the only sober ones left are me, two angry girls who've spent the last twenty minutes searching for their boyfriends who seem to have disappeared into thin air, and a red-headed guy with his eyes fixed on the TV set, watching a Marvel movie. I don't particularly feel like starting a conversation with any of them.

I'm so bored that I can't help but pull out my cellphone and try to level up in Candy Crush. My iPhone is a better entertainer to me than anyone else in this moment. Over the next thirty minutes I get consumed by swapping the jellies on the screen to the extent that I don't notice someone coming up behind me.

"Hey, Zara. I see you're having a great time as well," says a very familiar voice.

"Matt!" I lock my cell and bury it deep in my purse. "Yeah, I'm having a lot of fun. How about you?" I turn around and face his tousled blond curls and snow-white smile.

"I meant that you must be totally bored if you're browsing your phone at a party."

"Oh… my phone. Yeah, I was checking something super important."

Matt raises his eyebrow in disbelief.

I could tell him that instead of voraciously matching tiles, I was looking up the latest news regarding the stock exchange or the presidential campaign. However, I'm too tired for that. "Fair enough," I surrender, "I was playing Candy Crush."

Matt laughs, showing off the cute dimples in his cheeks. The last thing I want is to pretend to be somebody I'm really not. I'd rather be honest.

"Who did you come here with?" he asks, gazing around the living room. He seems perfectly sober and alert.

"With Charlie Robinson, but you won't find him here."

"Why?"

"I haven't seen him for almost two hours, so good luck with that."

He's standing only two feet from me, but I don't feel intimidated. It's unusual. After all, for a couple of months I've had a huge crush on Matt, and never had a tiny bit of courage to come closer than a safe ten steps away from him. I always preferred admiring him from afar. Now here we are, standing next to each other, and I don't experience even a little pulse jump. Is that because of Dorian? Has he overshadowed my infatuation with Matt?

"I'm sorry to hear you've lost your date."

"We're friends," I feel the urge to clarify right away. "He apparently brought me here to have a designated driver that will take him home when he's incapable of standing on his own feet." It's meant to be a joke, but I have a hunch that it's going to be the exact scenario in a little bit. "Where's your date?"

"I don't have one."

Of course. I forgot that Matt is almost impossible to capture.

"You're your own designated driver, then." I smile. "Unless you're an Uber fan?"

"Not at all. I don't drink."

"Why?"

"I don't want to ever lose control. I've seen people who have, and it was no fun."

"How responsible."

"Perhaps."

I'm genuinely surprised that such a popular guy as Matt doesn't drink at all. However, now that I know he hasn't had a single drop of liquor, I suspect that the reason he's approached me is the lack of other people who look like they're still able to handle a conversation. For a second there I thought that maybe it was the charm of my dress that attracted him. Nevertheless, I'm thankful for his company. At least now I have an actual person to look at, not a screen full of tiles.

"You study psychology too, right?" I ask.

"Yeah. I think I've seen you at school a couple of times."

Only a couple of times?! I've seen you at least a thousand times.

"If I hadn't taken a gap year, we might have had some classes together," I say aloud.

"Why did you take a gap year? If I may ask."

"I just needed some time to figure things out," I say, and grab a pretzel from the bowl.

"Nothing wrong with that." He also reaches for a pretzel. "I was considering doing the same thing, but in the end I changed my mind."

The conversation with Matt goes very smoothly. It's my favorite part of the entire evening. Unfortunately, we only have ten peaceful minutes to speak before our chat is abruptly interrupted by Charlie appearing out of the blue. He staggers through the living room in our direction. He almost trips over an empty bottle of beer on the carpet, but, just in time, manages to grab the couch's arm and keep himself standing.

"Oh my God," slips out of my mouth.

"Hey there. Been a while," Charlie says. His eyes swivel as if he can't see straight.

I wish I could punch Charlie in his drunk face hard enough to knock him unconscious for the next hour so that I could continue my nice chat with Matt without being disturbed. Sadly, what I'd love to do in my head and what I actually do are poles apart. If we don't leave right away, Charlie will probably be swayed to drink the next round of whiskey, which would make him totally unable to stand on his own feet. Then we'd either have to stay here overnight, or I'd have to carry that drunk asshole on my back, which isn't an option because he weighs about three times as much as I do. Clearly, I need to swallow the bitter disappointment, apologize to Matt, and simply leave now.

Thankfully, Matt helps me drag dead-weight Charlie to the car.

"Hopefully I'll see you soon," Matt says after we, not without difficulties, have placed Charlie in the passenger's seat.

He gives me a farewell peck on the cheek and walks away to his own car. I don't buy his words. If he genuinely wanted to see me again, he'd ask me for my number to stay in touch.

What did I expect from a guy who has the power of

driving every girl he meets crazy? Did I think I would rocked his world?

The way back home drags on; Charlie begs me approximately every five minutes to pull over, adding "I'll puke if you don't". His words are remarkably convincing. It takes us almost an hour to cover a twenty-minute stretch of road. But the night doesn't end when we get to our neighborhood.

I pull into my own driveway. My plan is to take advantage of the fact that I'm home alone and give Charlie some time to pull himself together before he returns to his place. If I let him go right away, he'll most likely run into his sick mom and raise her blood pressure with his current state. I don't want her to share Mrs. McConelly's fate—one heart attack in the neighborhood is more than enough for this year. Plus, I know that Charlie isn't normally a drunk. I've never seen him like this before, so I want to make sure he's okay.

"Where are we?" Charlie mumbles, pulling himself up to gaze outside.

"We've stopped by my place for a bit. You can't go back home looking like a zombie; it'll kill your mom." I jump out of the car, go around it and help Charlie climb out through the passenger's door.

"We're going to your house?"

"Yes, my house," I repeat louder, aggravated. "What's wrong with you? Did you smoke something? How come you don't recognize my place? You live two minutes away." I shake my head with irritation.

It doesn't take long before I bitterly regret offering Charlie my help. He fastens himself to me, which I believe is supposed to be some kind of drunken hug, stops in the middle of my driveway and refuses to go further. We stand still for a minute. I'm not especially fond of his odd way of showing me his appreciation. Charlie stinks of booze, mixed with the reek of sweat, and he's trying to touch me in places that he shouldn't. On top of that, I'm pretty sure that we'll lose our balance and wind up on the ground soon.

"Zara, c'mon, I know you feel the same way about me," Charlie says, treating me to his funky breath. He's slurring, but I can understand what he's saying.

"Charlie, I'm begging you, don't be pathetic, and stop making a laughing-stock of yourself." I try to push him away, but he's too bulky for me to move him even an inch.

"Somebody's pretending to be unapproachable. I love it." He slides his hand down to my butt; I feel like vomiting.

"If you don't get off of me, I swear I'll yell!" I warn him sternly. "What's wrong with you?!"

"Don't even think that I'm going to let you go, sexy." He smirks. "Do you know what I'd love to do to you?"

Thank God I don't *know what's lurking in his loaded mind.*

"Stay away!" I cry, once I realize he's leaning toward me to give me a disgusting kiss. "Charlie!"

Right as I'm about to kick him between his legs, I hear a voice coming somewhere from behind us. "Hey! Everything alright here?"

I recognize that deep voice. I look up and see Dorian standing on the porch, facing us.

"None of your business!" Charlie snarls. "Everything's fine!"

"Nothing's fine!" I disagree loudly, still striving to loosen his grip and shake myself free.

"Is he being disrespectful?" Dorian doesn't wait for my response, but immediately scoots down the steps and around the fence. His glare burns through Charlie. I let out a huge breath; he showed up at the perfect time—right before Charlie placed his obnoxious lips on mine.

"Back off, dude!" Charlie's voice is seething with anger. "You're butting in between me and my woman!"

"I'm not your woman—"

No sooner do I say it than Dorian seizes Charlie's hands, freeing me from his grasp. He traps his arms and twists them behind Charlie's back, entirely disarming him with one swift move. Charlie doubles over in pain. I don't feel any mercy, though—I'm fuming.

"What the hell, man?! You're gonna break my arms!"

"I don't think you heard it, but Zara clearly asked you to get away from her," Dorian says calmly.

What an interesting twist of events. Last night *I* was trapped by Dorian's strong grip, and tonight he's turned out to be my savior.

"Let go!" Charlie writhes in pain.

"Now you be a good boy, go home, and leave your friend alone. Understood?" Dorian clutches Charlie's hands even tighter. Charlie hisses. Dorian uses just the right amount of ferocity; he doesn't let himself get carried away.

"Okay! Okay! Fiiine… Jus… lemme go, man," Charlie stammers.

Dorian releases him with a shove, then turns to me. "Are you alright?"

"Yeah." I give Charlie the most disdainful look I can manage. "I should take him home. He can't take two steps on his own. He wouldn't even be able to crawl there right now."

On no account do I want Charlie near me in my empty house, but it doesn't feel right to just leave him like this, no matter what stunt he just pulled.

"I'll help you." Dorian slings Charlie's arm over his shoulder, despite Charlie's resistance; together we carry him to his front door.

All the lights are off but the one in the kitchen. Mrs. Robinson must have been waiting for her son. Heaviness centers in my chest as I ring the doorbell. Last year she had a stroke, and the left side of her body has been paralyzed ever since. She's been struggling every day to get by, and her son doesn't make it easier on her.

When the door opens a crack, I see a short woman peering at us through the slit. When her eyes land on Charlie, she's taken aback. She tries to say something, but no sound escapes her throat. The door opens wider, and a chubby lady with cheeks that blend into her neck stands in the doorway. It's Charlie's aunt. I haven't seen her since I was a child.

"Jesus Christ," is all she's able to utter.

"Hi, Auntie Jess," Charlie says, at which her temper flares. She grabs him by his shoulder, pulls him forcefully inside, and shuts the door with a bang right in our faces.

"I guess we're done here," Dorian says nonchalantly, like he didn't just see the terminator.

"Thanks for your help," I say while we're briskly walking back. "You didn't have to do it."

"Don't mention it. Do I want to know how it came to this?"

"It's a long story." I'm grateful that he lets the subject rest and doesn't ask me to tell him. I just wish I could erase it from my memory forever.

A silence hangs in the air between us. The unexplained course of our last encounter is like an invisible wall, parting us. I hate unresolved matters, so I gather all the courage I have and say, "Dorian, it's a bit weird that today you helped me, but yesterday *you* were the one who attacked me."

"There's nothing to talk about." His voice is gruff. "You'd better go straight to bed; it's late. Anyway, I'm actually heading out somewhere and don't have too much time."

I'm not happy with his reaction, but I can't make him talk. "A date?"

"Do you really think I'm going on a date in the middle of the night?"

"Why not?" I shrug.

"I already told you—I don't date."

"Right! It totally slipped my mind." I slam my forehead. "You never make any exceptions?"

"No."

"Are you sure?"

"Why?" Dorian asks, as we finally reach my lit driveway.

"Curiosity, that's all."

"I already gave you the answer. Have a good night, Zara."

"Night, Dorian."

He walks away toward his Bentley. His approach to dating is weird. He treats it like some kind of a taboo that should never be brought up.

There must be a reason for that.

"What about those intense relationships, then?" I allow myself to ask, more loudly to make sure he hears me.

"What do you mean?" He unlocks the car, but doesn't get in yet.

"What if I'm interested?"

"Are you?"

"Perhaps…"

"You are," he says, with no doubt in his voice.

"Let's say that it sounds interesting to me." I attempt to sound seductive.

Dorian walks around the car and stops by the driver's door. He opens it wide, but before disappearing inside, he looks at me and says, "You're not fit for that kind of relationship."

What does he mean by not fit? Do I not look good

enough? Are my legs too short—is my butt not perky enough?! Or maybe I seem like a good girl who doesn't ever go bad...

"Why?" I do my best to sound casual, but the outrage emanating from me is too much to hide.

"Take my word for it."

"But—"

"It must remain the way it is," he cuts in, getting into his car.

"But last time you said—"

"Goodnight, Zara." He's done it again: just shut me down. "Don't ask any more questions." He closes the door, but rolls down the window as he pulls out of his driveway.

When he's driving past me, I can't bottle it up anymore and simply say, "You're strange, Dorian."

"You have no idea how strange." He stops the car for a second and looks me deep in the eye. "And we'd better leave it at that."

"I want to know," I tell him as the window starts rolling up.

"No, you don't," he assures me, and finally drives away.

"I'll find out anyway sooner or later," I say to myself, turning to go inside.

Rita has been watching us all along, presumably thinking that I don't realize she's been standing at the kitchen window. Ignoring her, I return to my house as if the last twenty minutes never happened.

CHAPTER SEVEN

FOR THE NEXT WEEK, I don't have an opportunity to speak with Dorian. We keep missing one another. I often see him driving off as I look through the kitchen window before I leave for my morning classes and hear him come back when I'm already in my bedroom, getting ready to turn in. There's no way we can talk unless I take the first step—which isn't happening after what he told me last time we saw each other. Admittedly, once we sort of run into each other, but Dorian only raises his hand to greet me from afar and vanishes into his part of the house, without coming up to me or even asking how I'm doing. The questions I have about him must therefore go unanswered for the time being.

We've only interacted with each other a handful of times, so I can't exactly count on any special treatment from him, but I still can't get rid of the impression that the incident in the basement has affected Dorian's behavior toward me. I feel like he's ignoring me on purpose.

On Monday the May weather is beautiful, so I decide to pull out my dusty bicycle from the garage, wipe it down, pump the tires, and hit the road to work. The ride is easy; the only catch is the way back—after dark, which I don't take into consideration when I mount my bike and head out.

When I leave work several hours later, the sun has already gone down. Murky clouds have covered the stars and the moon, making the night inky dark. The road is mostly lit by streetlights, but there are some stretches with limited visibility, and as I head to my place a hazy, ominous feeling accompanies me. Darkness always does that to me. To keep my mind busy and prevent my vivid imagination from kicking in, I listen to some upbeat music. I even start to sing. If there were any harassers in the area, they must be all gone; my shrieking would drive away even a deaf person.

The music is swirling in my head, and I get so lost in the rhythm flowing through my headphones that I don't notice a pothole in the road. My front wheel falls into it with a crash and jerks me to a stop. In a split second, the world spins before my eyes as I fly over the handlebars. My left side slams against the asphalt. Acute pain shoots through my arm, taking my breath away.

For an instant, time seems to stop. I can't register what's just happened and how I wound up on the ground with the remains of my bike next to me. I sit upright. The streetlamp looming above me illuminates the useless remnants of my transportation. The front tire has blown, and the wheel is all bent out of shape; on top of that, the handlebars are twisted at an odd angle. This bike will need some serious repairing if I ever want to ride it again. My body feels like it's bruised all over, and I can taste blood in my mouth. My brain slowly starts processing the course of events that have contributed to my current state. *I had a bicycle crash.* In a daze, I check myself to make sure that all my limbs are still attached. Since I don't see three bikes, I can get up to move it off the road.

As soon as I try to lift myself up, the excruciating pain throbbing in my shoulder hits. I'm unable to get up. I need someone to get me out of here.

Unluckily, my cellphone is inside my purse, next to my bike, beyond my reach. I can only dream about dialing anybody's number. I can't even call 911.

God damn it!

I want to cry from pain and despair. There hasn't been even a single car driving past me over the last couple of dragging minutes. This route is rarely frequented—in fact, that's why I used it in the first place. I thought that the less traffic there was, the safer I'd be. In my wildest dreams I didn't expect to have an accident. Now it dawns on me that the fewer travelers, the smaller the chance of me being rescued. In other words, I'm screwed.

My shoulder is clamoring for a painkiller. I squeeze my eyes and clench my jaw, as if that's supposed to help me deal with the radiating pain. I flop onto my back and lie still. My breath is shallow. The accident must have been more serious than I initially thought.

I have no idea how much time has passed; I'm drifting in and out of consciousness. Maybe a minute, maybe two hours. When I finally see sky-blue eyes inches from my face, at first, I think that it's just a hallucination caused by a blow to my head. Then I hear a familiar voice.

"Zara?!"

It's Dorian.

"Am I dead?"

"You're not dead, you just had an accident." He helps me slowly sit up.

"What are you doing here?" I'm a little confused.

"I was passing by when I noticed someone lying on the ground with a broken bike next to them. That was enough to make me stop. It was only when I got closer that I recognized you."

Of course. If there was anyone who'd choose this isolated piece of road to drive, that would be Dorian. It fits his persona perfectly.

"I should take you to the hospital; you might have broken something," Dorian says, looking at me holding my shoulder.

"How long have I been here?" I rasp.

"I have no idea. You must have passed out. You need to be checked by a physician—let's go."

As he's about to help me stand on my feet, I gently push his hand away. "Take me home, please. My aunt will take care of me. I don't want to be a bother to you."

"You're not a bother."

"I don't even have all the documents on me now. I left them in my other purse."

"You're not being serious. You may have concussion.

There's no time to waste." He gingerly sweeps me into his arms as easily as if I weighed nothing. I wrap my good arm around his neck.

"I truly hope you didn't have any special feelings for that one," Dorian says at the sight of what used to be my bike. From a distance it doesn't look that bad, but when we're two steps away, I notice more damages than just a blown-out tire and messed up handlebars. This thing is ready for the scrapheap.

To make matters worse, the contents of my purse are strewn all over the street. Dorian accidentally steps on the tampon that fell out of one of the compartments. I also find my cell phone with a smashed screen, some raspberry hand sanitizer, my wallet, and more junk.

"I'll pick this up myself," Dorian announces.

Only now that he's carrying me to the car do I realize that the pain has greatly diminished. It doesn't take away my will to live anymore. Maybe I'll be fine without going to the hospital at all.

Dorian is holding me close. Aware of his strength and warmth, my body immediately reacts, and I slide my gaze down to his lips. He seems not to notice, or maybe he's just ignoring it.

He places me in the backseat, buckles me up, and goes back to pick up my stuff. As I watch him through the windshield, I can't shake the feeling that I do know him from somewhere other than the house next door. Even though we're technically strangers, I know that I'm safe with him; there's nothing to worry about when he's close. It's the third time he'd helped me in need now. Dorian is my savior.

When he gets into the car, all the dizziness is gone. I can think clearly again.

"I actually don't feel as bad as I thought. I can definitely go home first."

Dorian turns in my direction and gives me a questioning look. "Are you sure? You didn't look that good when I found you."

"I'm sure."

A shadow flits across Dorian's face, his expression serious. "Are you scared of me?"

"Not at all, but I started to feel like I should be after the basement incident."

"Just forget about it," he says curtly.

How can I forget about something like that?!

"You're intriguing, not scary, to me."

"Intriguing," he repeats slowly. "And you know what you are?"

"No, tell me."

"You're an enigma."

At first, I think I misheard him. "Enigma? But there's nothing mysterious about me. My life is boring."

Something intense flares in Dorian's gaze. "There's more than you think."

He turns on the engine, and we drive off in silence.

CHAPTER EIGHT

THE RIDE DOESN'T LAST LONG, as my accident took place only three miles away from my house. Dorian helps me get out of the car. I wrap my arm around his neck again, but this time he slides his hand down my spine and helps me hobble along the pathway. Even though I'm injured, I still enjoy his solid frame.

The house is dark. There is no sign of anyone inside. Only now do I recall that Maddie's out on a date with the new object of her desires, whereas my aunt is hanging out with one of her besties. Neither will be home within the next hour. My house is empty at the worst possible moment. But who could have predicted that I'd run into the only bump that exists on the Walgreens-Keizer road section and would need medical intervention?

"Damn it!" I cry in the foyer.

"I'll say it again: I can take you to the hospital."

I detest hospitals. I've given them a wide berth since my appendix surgery. It was such a traumatic experience for me that as an adult I'd need to be dying to show up in one—not to mention the fact that I'm wondering if my shoulder has already bounced back. The piercing pain that developed right after I ended up on the ground has calmed. Now I can only feel a slight pulsation in the injured area.

"I don't know what to do. My shoulder is doing better. The pain seems to be fading." I look at him. "Isn't that weird?"

"Your body has produced a tremendous amount of adrenaline that's probably dulling the pain. Besides, it's not only your shoulder—are you sure you didn't suffer a severe head trauma?" Dorian pauses and draws his eyebrows together. "Rita could examine you. She's a registered nurse."

"Why do you even care that much?" I ask suspiciously.

"I found you, so I want to make sure I didn't drop you off at home with some severe brain damage and leave—but apparently you're too stubborn to let someone help you."

I feel bad and quit my sharp tone. "That's very considerate of you, but it can't be that serious. I don't even have a headache."

"Fair enough, then; I'll see you around." He waves his hand in farewell and opens the front door to leave.

"Wait!" I grab his shoulder. "I'll go with you."

Although I'm fine walking by myself, I lean against Dorian on the way to his place anyway. I enjoy his wide shoulders too much to let such an opportunity slip.

When we step inside, the first thing I do is look at my reflection in the horizontal mirror in their narrow hallway; even from afar, I almost scare myself to death. I can see multiple abrasions and bruises all over me, torn shorts, a dirty T-shirt, a cut lip, and a bleeding elbow.

No wonder Dorian couldn't believe that I'm doing just fine.

"I was waiting for you." I hear an antsy voice coming from the living room. It's Rita.

"We have a visitor," he says right away, as if he's signaling to her to be alert and keep her mouth shut in case she says something I'm not allowed to hear.

"Zara!" Her tone becomes friendlier at once. "It's so good to see you again."

Her grin, though sweet, contains some odd quality. It seems like only her mouth smiles, not her eyes. I haven't seen her for less than two weeks, but there's something strange about her. Rita's lost her vibrant charm. Her face is paler, and she has dark circles under her eyes. Her tension is almost palpable. I get the impression that she urgently needs to discuss something with Dorian, something that can't wait, but my presence bars her from going ahead.

"Zara had an accident."

"Oh my God," Rita exclaims, looking at me more closely.

"I fell off my bike. All my relatives are out of the house and Dorian said you could help me determine whether or not I need some medical intervention."

"You should've gone to the hospital straight away—you may have concussion!"

"Yeah, we've already gone over that," Dorian says, and pulls me toward the couch. "Zara is very unwilling to be taken to the hospital unless it's absolutely necessary."

She keeps a poker face, but it's visible to the naked eye that Rita is waging an inner struggle with herself. On the one hand she seems eager to help; on the other, I can't help thinking that she'd love to ignore me and drag Dorian upstairs to talk to him about the issue that's bothering her. If I'm able to notice her distress, so must Dorian. It's obvious to me that he's the only person who can put her mind at ease, yet I can't see him doing anything to bring her relief. Instead, he sits down beside me and thoroughly checks out my face. He grasps my head with his hands and gently twists it left and right, inspecting me thoroughly.

"Does it hurt?"

"No."

"You have a quite deep scratch on your cheek."

"It may leave a scar," Rita says, marching to us. Apparently, she's decided to bottle up her need to talk to Dorian for as long as I'm at their place. "I'll be right back." She strides out of the living room.

"I'm sorry for being so stubborn."

"Stubborn is an understatement." His hands release my face. "You're a character."

Dorian continues to study me. It seems like he can't tear away his gaze from me. He's closer than ever. A pleasant spasm runs down my spine. I slide my eyes from his blue eyes down to his lips and then further to his chest. Dorian's black T-shirt, which perfectly highlights each muscle, triggers an avalanche of sinful thoughts in my head. In my attempt to resist them, I move my eyes back up to his neck, and then I notice it—a thin silver ball chain necklace. I can't tell whether it has a pendant or not, because the bottom part of the necklace is underneath the T-shirt.

"You wear a necklace. Is it a memento?"

Dorian grabs a little rectangle that's visible beneath the fabric as if he's making sure it's still safe on him.

"Yes and no."

"What does that mean?"

Our eyes lock. I can't escape the feeling that he's looking into my soul, trying to spot something deep inside me. My body tingles.

"I didn't receive it from anybody special, but it reminds me of something significant."

"What's that, if I may ask?" My eyes travel up to his full lips, which tease my imagination again. I'm curious to know how they taste.

"I can't tell you that."

Same old, same old, I think to myself with bitter disappointment. "Why are you so mysterious?"

"Don't ask me any questions," he commands. "It's better this way."

"Can I at least see the pendant?"

Dorian pulls out a flat silver rectangle, resembling a military tag.

"Can I take a closer look?"

"You can."

I lean forward to have a better view. His pleasant,

masculine scent hits my nostrils, sending a heat wave down to my abdomen. I'd never mistake this smell for anything else.

I take the necklace in my hand. I can feel Dorian's warm breath on my forehead while I examine the pendant cautiously with my curious eyes. It's shiny and polished, and engraved with the number *2001*.

"Does this number have a special meaning to you?"

"No." He pulls away from me as though I just said something bad.

"Then why have it?" My gaze drifts to his face.

His eyes become hazy. "It's just a random set of digits."

Dorian squeezes it in his hand and places it back under the T-shirt, so I can't look at it anymore. I'm sure that this is his way of discouraging me from asking further questions, but I'm not done yet.

"Didn't you just say it was to remind you of something significant, though?"

"You don't need to understand *everything*," Dorian says with a taut face. I find his answer quite rude, but I strive to seem unfazed.

Eventually Rita reappears, clutching a first aid kit. She takes Dorian's place beside me and shines a pen light into each of my eyes to check the reaction of my pupils, measures my blood pressure, and cleans the bleeding wounds with some stinging liquid.

"Did you lose consciousness?" she asks.

"I think so."

"Do you have a headache or feel nauseous?"

"No."

"Okay." Rita regards my shoulder for a moment and then continues her interview. "I'm assuming that you fell onto your shoulder. You were holding it when I first saw you."

"Yes."

"Alright, let me take a look at it." She pulls herself up to me. "The most common result of a fall is a clavicle fracture. You also might've dislocated it, but honestly if that were the case, you'd be writhing in pain right now." She gently lifts my shoulder up and then adds more pressure at the end of the range of motion. "Does it hurt?"

"Not at all."

"Okay." She puts it back down. "Can you lie down, please?"

I do as she says. Rita bends my elbow to ninety degrees and moves my arm out to my side, then rotates it. "Do you feel like your shoulder is about to pop out of joint?"

"No."

As she's examining me, I can feel Dorian's gaze still fixed on me. He seems deep in thought, distant, trying to figure out or understand something.

"Well," Rita continues, "it's not swollen and doesn't look deformed, but still, sometimes it's difficult to tell whether or not a bone is broken without medical equipment. It's up to you, but I'd go to a specialist anyway."

"I don't think that'll be necessary." I lift myself up. "In the beginning I was certain I'd broken it because of the agonizing pain, but now…" *How to say this*. "The pain has gone all by itself."

"What do you mean? It doesn't hurt at all?" Rita frowns.

"I know it sounds crazy, but yeah, I'm fine."

A glimmer of incredulity shines through her eyes. They both stare at me, baffled.

"Zara, you didn't stumble over a stuffed animal in your bedroom, you had a *bicycle crash*," says Dorian. "Look at your elbow! It's…" 'His voice trails off as he grabs my elbow and looks at it. "Okay, it's not that bad after Rita disinfected it, but your face…" He lifts his eyes up to my cheek and pauses again; not a single word comes out of his mouth.

Before I can say anything, he sits down next to me and runs his index finger down my cheek, touching the same spot Rita rubbed some smelly cream into no longer than five minutes ago. An intense astonishment touches his face.

I wince, and my heart jumps to my throat; I suspect the worst. After all, Rita said that the scratch might leave a scar. "Does it look that bad?"

Do I look hideous? Do I look like Freddie Krueger?

"Umm…"

"Dorian, say something!" I beg with desperation.

"Everything will definitely heal," he says tersely.

"Will I have a scar?" I can hear my own pulse banging in my ears. I'm terrified at the thought that I could have a huge mark on my face.

Rita and Dorian exchange mystified glances. I'm not

sure what's going on, but a shiver of panic surges through me. Without waiting for them to finally enlighten me, I abruptly get to my feet and dash to the mirror in the hallway again. I pull my nose as close to the smooth surface as possible. I stare at my reflection, and see… nothing unusual.

There's not a single scratch or any other damage to my skin.

Stunned, I sprint back to the living room. My eyes wandering from Dorian to Rita, I ask them, "Didn't you two mention a huge wound that would leave a scar on my face?"

"I'm sorry; apparently it was just my imagination." Rita doesn't look me in the eye. She's clearly lying.

"How about you?" I transfer my eyes to Dorian. "Do you also see things that don't exist? Or maybe there's something that you don't want to tell me?"

I try not to sound rude, but it's difficult; there's something untold in the air, something they don't want me to know about at any cost, and it frustrates me. I keep in mind that, after all, they did try to help me, and whatever strange occurrence has taken place along the way isn't their fault.

The silence is like a void that should be filled with words, but neither Dorian nor Rita are eager to do so.

"Zara," Dorian finally says, "since you're clearly as good as new, you should probably go home."

Giving me an evasive response is very cunning of him, but it doesn't satisfy me at all.

"Exactly," Rita puts in. "There's nothing to worry about. You might still be in shock, but that's it." Her eyes are still anchored to the floor.

What a sudden change of heart for somebody who a few minutes ago tried to convince me to visit the hospital with a possible concussion.

I open my mouth to protest, but stall as I notice something that makes my voice stick in my throat: Rita's neck. She's wearing a thin chain with a silver square hanging in the center, exactly the same as Dorian's. It generates a number of questions in my head.

They can't just put me off like this. A pulsating knot within me demands to know what's going on.

"I'm not going any…" I can't finish what I have to say; out of the blue I feel light-headed and woozy. My mouth goes dry and my limbs go limp, like a marionette. I'm losing my balance. The world viciously whirls around.

What the hell is going on with me? Did they drug me? Impossible—I didn't eat or drink anything.

"Zara?" Dorian's voice is the last thing I register before darkness falls.

CHAPTER NINE

MY EYELIDS ARE UNNATURALLY heavy, but I manage to finally open my eyes. Someone has covered me up with a woolen blanket. I sit up and survey my surroundings, disoriented. My vision is still blurry, but I recognize this modern room. A tumble of confusing feelings assails me. I'm at my neighbors'.

But what am I doing here?

That's right; I had an accident.

But hold on—where have they gone?

These and a couple of other thoughts roll through my mind when I eventually come around. I have no idea why I even passed out. Perhaps it was the adrenaline crash after the accident that knocked me out.

As the seconds go by, I recall more and more from before I lost consciousness. Dorian and Rita are *hiding* something from me.

I slowly pick myself up off the couch; for someone who's just been through an accident, I do so quite deftly. I feel like new, as if the incident didn't take place at all. I still can't believe that I've healed that fast.

I look around, but there's nobody here. The only sound that reaches my ears is the continuous whir of a pendulum swinging back and forth in precise intervals. I tiptoe to the kitchen. There's no sign of a living soul either. I'm alone on the first floor.

I'm about to call Dorian and Rita, but then bite my tongue. I have a better idea. They must be upstairs; I doubt they would have left a stranger alone in the house—a fortress of their secrets. I bet they're going over the matter that was bothering Rita so much that she was ready to reject me in my time of need. I can't miss such a unique opportunity. If I don't sniff something out myself, those two will never tell me what's going on here. It's either now or never.

I sneak up to the stairs, and quietly climb the steps. I stop halfway, listening intently to the sounds coming from the second floor. I can hear vague voices; it must be them. Driven by my curiosity and a pinch of adrenalin, I keep ascending the steps. The fourth step from the top creaks when I put my foot on it. I freeze, my stomach clenching, and hold my breath. Dorian and Rita carry on with their conversation, so they can't have heard anything fishy. I breathe a sigh of relief and advance further, shifting my weight to the right to avoid making that sound again.

With my heart beating a hundred times per second, I traverse the few remaining stairs. I press my back against the wall and skulk along the corridor. Their conversation becomes increasingly clear as I move forward; I pause, listening carefully to establish where exactly their voices are coming from. They must be in the room on the left-hand side right by the table with a Chinese vase on it.

Their fuzzy carpet muffles my steps, as I make it to the slightly ajar ebony door. They're not speaking loudly, but clearly enough that I can catch what is being said.

"I'm sure they suspect something," Rita says, flustered.

"They can't possibly. How could they?" Dorian says. His voice is calm, as though he's trying to steady her.

"Because of that!" Silence falls; she must be showing him something to prove her words.

"It happens sometimes."

"Not for three months in a row! We need to do something about it; that's why we moved here, right? I hate to think of all our plans being ruined."

I'm intrigued. My heart is pounding madly as I take one more step forward. I don't want to miss even one word.

"Yeah, I know," Dorian says indifferently; he's the stable one in this discussion.

"That girl, Zara—did you choose her?"

"No. I planned to at first, but it can't be her."

My eyes and mouth freeze wide open. I'm totally stunned. They are talking about *me*.

What plan did he choose me for?

"Why not her?" Rita demands.

"Because I can't see her at all."

"What?! That's impossible!" This time pure fright is audible in her tone. "Do you think she is one of *them*?"

"I wouldn't go that far. The girl knows nothing. She even asked me what the necklace symbolized."

"I don't know, Dorian." She sounds puzzled. "You seem to be so unconcerned, and I think she might have only pretended that she was unaware to lull you into a false sense of security. Don't you remember that they're all first-rate liars?"

"I'm aware of that all too well," Dorian says with an unusual coldness in his voice. "She has no clue who we are."

Tense silence envelops the room. Rita is so stressed that none of Dorian's words seem to be able to put her at ease. She speaks first. "There's something odd about her. Did you notice those wounds?"

"Yeah…"

A longer silence falls between them.

"What are you thinking about?" Rita asks shakily.

"We should be going back downstairs."

"You know something," Rita insists.

"No, I don't. I have a theory, but I'm not eager to share until I make sure."

"Tell me!"

"As I said, not until I'm certain." Dorian remains rigid. "Now, let's get out of here. We have two weeks; we must be quick."

I don't wait to discover whether the two will decide to continue their talk for a little bit longer. With my stomach still churning, I retreat as noiselessly as possible. If I get caught eavesdropping, I'll surely pay for it. Those two are hiding something, and both are masters at keeping their secret safe, but I won't be able to rest until I learn the truth. The feeling of being deceived is eating me up from the inside. It's no longer a matter of me wanting to discover the truth; now I simply need to know it.

I leave their house without saying goodbye. The next time we run into each other, I figure, I can say that I called for them, but nobody answered, so I left. It's better this way.

When I take a look at my watch, I realize it's almost eleven o'clock. On my way back, I list all the questions I've had since Dorian and Rita moved in next door. The more I interact with them, the longer the list becomes. Maybe I should start writing things down not to forget about anything along the way.

As I stroll up the pathway, the wind pushes me forward and makes my hair whip around my face. I quickly climb the porch steps and do my best to find the house key in my purse. When Dorian collected my things from the road, he simply threw them all inside, without caring about keeping a proper order. I could knock on the door, but I'm hoping I'll be able to manage to slide inside unnoticed.

My fingers eventually grasp a wooden elephant keyring that Rach gave me as a souvenir after she came back from Africa. A violent gust of wind hits me with such force that I drop the bunch of keys before I even succeed in finding the right one. I squat to pick it up, and it's now that I sense someone's eyes on me. I feel a presence. A wave of apprehension sweeps through me.

I get up, whirl around and anxiously scan the area, but can't see anybody. I swallow hard.

"Dorian?" I yell into space, but I don't get any response.

I wheel again and, at the speed of light, try to find the house key. I finally single it out from the rest. The more I strive to put it in the keyhole, the harder it is for me to make it.

"Boo!" reaches me from behind. I jerk, scared to death; a scream escapes my lips. My heart races like it's going to beat out of my chest. All I can hear from behind me now is hysterical laughter. I don't have to look over my shoulder to realize which moron thinks this is hilarious.

"Are you fucking crazy?! Do you want me to drop dead?!" My eyes are probably blazing amber fire, but Maddie cracks up and couldn't care less about my remark.

When I spin around, I register that she isn't the only one who's having fun. Beside Maddie stands a guy of medium height with a baseball hat on his head. He gives the impression of a cool high-school kid who's fun to be around.

"Hilarious," I say sarcastically, and roll my eyes.

The pattern is the same every time Maddie brings home a new love interest; it frustrates the hell out of me. Her aim is to demonstrate, as she's doing right now, that she has a stunning sense of humor—hence why I truly detest when she invites boys home. It always means Maddie being fake and overly amusing. I have no clue why she does it; she's such a great person the way she really is.

"This is Mike," she says.

"Zara," I respond, without, however, adding "nice to meet you" or "how are you doing" as he's still giggling, which pisses me off. I even go one step further and put her in her place. "Maddie, don't you think that it's a bit late for bringing your friends home?"

"Mike only swung by for five minutes," she says, her face immediately going from amused to serious, even downright insulted. Maddie hates it when somebody points something out to her. According to her, she knows it all, so nobody has the right to pick on her.

When they both disappear inside, I use my tactic of distracted attention—I wait outside a while for Cynthia to focus all her attention on them and make her overlook me slipping in. We still haven't made up after our last conversation. Reopening the subject wouldn't be the smartest decision, since I don't have any better excuse for my bitchy behavior than I did during our last talk. I prefer to avoid her for a tad longer, until she doesn't insist on discussing that anymore.

Several minutes go by; the kitchen lights switch on—they must have moved there. The foyer is empty. It's time to go inside. I place my hand on the handle, but as I'm about to press it, I freeze. The feeling of being watched hasn't gone. I'm still impaled by someone's gaze, even though my cousin and her friend have vanished into the house. My heart lurches.

I turn around to sweep the area with my alert eyes again. Nothing is out of ordinary. I can only see a stray cat trotting on the sidewalk; I don't detect any other movement. The silence of the night is somehow calming, yet a cold shiver travels along my spine. I crack open the front door and jump inside, then double lock the door. I'm safe, but I'm sure someone is still out there, fixing their eyes on my house.

CHAPTER TEN

WHEN I INSPECT MYSELF the next morning, I don't find a single bruise or a scratch on my body that would suggest I had an accident last night. I rotate my shoulder backward and forward. I don't experience any discomfort or pain when I do so.

I can't be that lucky.

I walk swiftly to the window and peep through the chink in the curtains. The Bentley is gone. It dawns on me that I've never even asked Dorian what his profession is. Rita is a nurse, so it makes sense that she leaves early and comes back late, but what about him?

I shrug and trail away from the window, collecting my things, and getting ready to leave for school.

* * *

In my morning class I can barely keep my eyes open. The lulling tone of my Statistics professor doesn't help to keep me awake. Everything feels heavy, and if I don't start doing something requiring active participation soon, I'll drop off.

I stop listening to the old man, who has no talent for keeping his students attentive. My thoughts drift around Dorian and his conversation with Rita. I keep pondering everything I've heard. What did she mean when she asked Dorian if I was one of *them*? What was he going to choose me for? And last but not least, what does Dorian suspect me of?

I knew that there was something peculiar about them from the very beginning, but after yesterday, their mysteriousness has reached a completely new level. The more I think about them, the less I seem to comprehend.

I can't even talk to anyone about them, because who'd believe me?

Maybe Rach...

I feel a stab of guilt at the thought of my best friend. I miss her presence, our girly chit-chats, and even her crazy driving. Even though I feel neglected, I realize that I'm the one who pushed her away with my nasty behavior. The fact that she's been hanging out with her other friends is entirely my fault. I'm aware of that, but somehow, I still expected her to come to me first. She always used to. Has she spoilt me too much?

Since Rach isn't one of those people who holds grudges, all it takes to make her forgive me is inviting her to her favorite Mexican restaurant. Pollo a la crema plus a glass of white wine buries the hatchet. Rach is on cloud nine and eager to talk to me again.

After a mouth-watering meal, we decide to head over to my place to watch our favorite movie *Titanic* for the hundredth time together. Admittedly, a damn cute Leo DiCaprio contributes to our crush on the movie.

While I'm rummaging through the old and worn out DVDs in one of the messy drawers, Rach leans against the windowsill.

"I can't believe that Matt didn't even ask you for your number," she says randomly.

"Really? I'm not shocked at all." I pull out a stack of DVDs and spread them on the floor. *It would be so much easier if Titanic was on Netflix*, I sigh.

"What a jerk."

"There's only one jerk, and his name is Charlie." I shove *Forrest Gump, Green Mile*, and *Dirty Dancing* to the side.

"Don't even mention that name." Rach shivers, disgust written all over her face. "Did Charlie even apologize?"

"I haven't heard from him ever since the birthday party," I say, and push several more titles aside.

"I feel such an urge to walk to his house and shout what I think of him in his face. What a stupid prick!" Her nostrils flare with fury, and her knuckles are white from clenching the edge of the windowsill. Rach has never gotten along with Charlie, but now her aversion has intensified at least three times.

"Better not. What if you accidentally killed him with that bloodthirsty look?" I joke, trying to alleviate the tense atmosphere.

She gives me a forced smile and casts a glance over her shoulder. Her expression rapidly changes; her facial features soften. She's noticed something outside.

"Well, well…" Her tone becomes sultry. "Isn't that our sexy neighbor down there?"

OUR?!

At her words, I feel like springing on my feet to speed over to the window, but I keep myself in check. I don't want Rach to know about my sweet spot for Dorian—at least, not yet. She'd be making suggestive comments and remarks if she knew. I even restrain myself from telling her how Dorian, like a real hero, showed up to save me from Charlie.

"Oh no," she groans, disappointed. "He brought some chick with him."

The word *chick* makes a sharp pang of jealousy erupt somewhere in my abdomen. I stop caring whether Rach will sniff something out or not. In no time, I'm stand on her right. I need to see for myself who this girl is.

When I take a glance at my neighbors' driveway, indeed, I see a blonde walking shoulder to shoulder with Dorian. She's clad in an airy summer dress that reveals far more of her body than I find appropriate. Also, having legs up to one's neck should be forbidden. I could swear she's seductively swaying her hips on purpose. Pure jealousy consumes me while I watch them stroll.

"That's impossible." I don't mean to say it aloud, but it comes out of my mouth anyway.

"Why? Maybe he dumped the other one and found a new

object of affection. You know guys," she rolls her eyes, "they're capable of putting themselves back together pretty quickly after a breakup. Don't get me wrong, though, the one down there can't hold a candle—"

Rach's voice seems to fades. I'm usually good at paying attention to my friend's words, but at this very moment I can't focus on anything else other than what I see in front of me. Even if I wanted to, I wouldn't be able to look away. Besides, Rach doesn't even realize that Dorian and Rita were never a couple. She doesn't know that I've met him and how he affects me. She doesn't understand anything at all.

I purse my lips and glue my forehead to the glass. I keep my gaze on them. I can't believe that Dorian, who *doesn't have girlfriends,* has just taken home a woman. It can imply only one thing: an intense relationship with her. After all, he only has those.

Why did he choose her and reject me?!

A heaviness centers in my chest. It's not my place to feel resentment against him. Dorian isn't obliged to hang out with me exclusively because I want it. I don't even have the right to desire it. We mean nothing to each other. We're only neighbors, and it will always be that way. But will it? Haven't I been silently counting on something more, even though he made it clear I wasn't a good fit?

I try to stay rational, but an edge of jealousy poisoning me robs me of any sense. When I picture those two sitting close beside one another, her feeling the warmth of his body, inhaling the same scent I'm addicted to, and him caressing her skin with his soft touch, my insides twist. I feel like something that belongs to me has just been stolen. Pain squeezes my heart as I draw the curtains testily.

"…Unless she's just his friend, then I'd be able to understand." Rach is finally done with her extended rant. I feel bad I wasn't listening to her more carefully, but my brain shut down once I saw Dorian.

"Doubtful," I reply, walking away from the window. I can't bear the torture of watching them together anymore. "Where was I? Oh yeah, I have one drawer left to check out." I try to sound casual.

"Don't bullshit. You have a crush on him!"

"I beg your pardon?" I turn my back on her so she can't see my cheeks burning.

"You were snapping your fingers and blinking much faster than usual. You only do that when you're really angry."

"Here we go!" My hand rests on the DVD box with the faces of Leonardo DiCaprio and Kate Winslet above the bow of the transatlantic liner on the front cover.

"Now I'm positive, because you've changed the subject."

Why the hell does she know me this well?

"Rach, give me a break." I grow embarrassed.

"I thought we shared everything with each other."

Everything within reason.

"There seriously isn't anything to talk about," I say, and open the plastic box. "Ready for the show?"

"Sure," she mumbles, displeased, but she sits next to me

on the carpet anyway, grabbing a bag of popcorn that we made in the microwave. I honestly can't even think of touching it right now. My stomach is twisted inside out.

I hate him echoes in my head every time I imagine what Dorian and the blonde might be doing. I don't even pay attention to the movie.

* * *

The next morning means my routine rush to be at school on time. I turned in late last night, as *Titanic* lasted forever. Even Rach gave up and drove back home halfway through the movie—right after the love scene in the car, which she couldn't miss. After five hours of sleep, I open my eyes feeling like I've just woken up in the middle of the night. I'm lured by the idea of falling asleep again. It's a considerable struggle to haul myself out of bed and get ready for school.

There's still a cumbersome weight on my chest caused by the strange blonde. I can't get the picture of her and Dorian out of my head. A brew of peculiar feelings is nestled inside of me: on the one hand, I want to start crying; on the other, wallop someone, or at least scream at the top of my lungs.

What's wrong with me?

To make matters even worse, when I reach the handle to push the front door open, I stall as I spot through the sidelight window that my neighbor's doorway is opening wide;

someone must be about to come out as well. My stomach churns. For a second I pray that the person who is coming out will be Rita, but my hopes are immediately dispelled. Dorian is the one who has opened the door and, as I feared, he's not alone. The blonde girl emerges from inside right behind him and *seizes his shoulder*. She's drenched in happiness as they cut through the driveway. A smile is permanently attached to her face.

Even from afar I notice that her blonde waves are in a total mess, and her dress is creased. I'm instantly deprived of all delusions that they were just friends. I need to face reality. A huge and painful knot forms in my stomach.

Thank God I haven't already left the house; otherwise, I'd spit venom in that oversweet face.

"You're pathetic, Zara," I say out loud when they screech away.

* * *

My whole day at school is ruined; I relentlessly go back over in my thoughts to the morning, which ends up giving me a nagging headache. I can't even collect myself at work. I fool around in the aisles and occasionally ask a client whether they need any assistance. Finally, to keep my mind occupied I get to organizing the greeting cards that the customers have a tendency to mix. I find a "Happy Father's Day" card among the birthday cards, and in the 'good luck' section I notice a red one congratulating the receiver on their graduation. It irritates me that people will take something from a shelf and not put it back in the right place.

Twenty minutes later, I'm sick and tired of the cards, so I decide to switch to the drug section and pick up some Advil to ease my headache. I march quickly. The pain is violently throbbing inside my skull; I need to kill it as soon as possible. Unexpectedly, I bump into someone who's just appeared from the aisle with syrups and DayQuil products. I drop a pile of cards that were outdated and needed to be removed from the display, but don't bother with collecting them from the floor. First, I need to make sure that I didn't hurt the customer I just trampled.

"I'm so sorry—" I lift my head and cut off my words. My pulse spikes. *What the hell?* "Dorian?!"

"Good afternoon, Zara." He stoops to help me pick up the cards.

"H-hey!" I stammer, not even looking into his gorgeous eyes, fixing mine on the floor. My hands are trembling, and it's hard for me to concentrate.

"I had no idea you worked here," he says, peeking at the name badge pinned to my chest, "Zahara." Even though I don't like my full name, it sounds so sophisticated coming out of his mouth.

"Don't call me that. My parents must've hated me to give me that awful name."

"Why? Zahara means dawn in Hebrew."

"So what? Who names their baby Zahara?" He passes me over all the cards and I move my eyes to his hands, avoiding his face. This cold indifference comes hard to me. "Thanks for the help. Now, excuse me; I gotta get back to work."

No sooner do I get to my feet than my nostrils are struck by his scent, so familiar, stirring me. My legs are rooted to the floor; there's something about him that ensnares me. When Dorian is close, a strong, irresistible desire to be with him comes over me. I just want to gloat over his presence.

"You left without saying goodbye the other day," he says.

"When I woke up, you were both gone. On a side note, I hope you had nothing to do with me passing out?"

"Nothing at all. Rita is of the opinion that you had an adrenaline crash."

"Whatever." I shrug dismissively and change the subject. "Are you just browsing, or looking for something in particular?" Even though his presence causes me to ache, I simply can't leave him.

I notice the paper bag he's holding, seemingly carrying some medicine he just picked up. I can't see what's inside.

"No—I think I have everything I need."

"Are you suffering from something?"

"No. This is for Rita." He clutches the bag a bit tighter.

"Gotcha." I suppress the need to ask what she needs it for.

"Your bicycle is still in my garage; don't you want to pick it up?" he asks, apparently in an attempt to avoid the question I wasn't going to ask anyway.

"Oh my God, it totally slipped my mind. Sure."

"Have you bounced back after the accident?"

"I made it home untouched, so there's nothing to bounce back from."

We go silent. Both of us remember my miraculous recovery, and I take it for granted that revisiting the subject is the last thing that Dorian wants to do.

"I can swing by for the bike today if you're home."

"Today doesn't work, but tomorrow feel free to stop by."

"Okay." Frustration grows in me, and I can't bottle up my feelings anymore. I need to spit it out. "I saw you with a woman yesterday. Are you still claiming you don't date?"

"Yes. I don't date."

"It didn't look like a friendly meeting to me." I don't want to sound accusatory, but rather nonchalant; however, driven by emotions, I can't pull it off.

"Whatever that was, do you think I owe you an explanation?"

I can feel my cheeks flushing. "Apparently not." Another silence falls, but this time my stomach coils. "Dorian, do you realize that since you and Rita moved in, strange things have been happening?"

"What do you mean?"

"You know exactly what I mean," I say, and frown. "The fact that you want to avoid certain subjects doesn't mean they don't exist. The world doesn't work like that. On the contrary, the issues that aren't resolved only snowball and grow bigger."

"What do you want to know?"

That's a good question. I would like to know everything

from the very beginning, but one thing has been niggling at the back of my mind the most, so I finally decide to let it out. "Why do you affect me in such an odd way?"

"How?" He comes one step closer to me, his eyes searching mine. I melt under his intense look; he towers over me. All my muscles tense, but it's a pleasant sensation.

"Just like that."

"Like what?" The corners of his lips go slightly up, and the hint of a cocky smirk creeps onto his face. Those lips look so soft that I'm tempted to kiss them wildly. I ache for the touch of his hands traveling across my body. I wish I could press my body against him right now.

What's going on with me?

"I can't get you out of my mind. I'm unable to stop thinking about you." A scorching heat rushes over me.

Dorian doesn't respond. I could swear that he knows something that he doesn't want to tell me, and it's been hovering between us since we interacted for the first time. I'm sure that it has something to do with the matter that Rita needed so urgently to discuss with him the other day.

He grabs my chin between his fingers and tips my head up so that we look into each other's eyes. "It can't be you," Dorian whispers, "even though I really want it to be."

"What can't I be? Tell me!" I beg. "These secrets are killing me. I want to understand what's been going on with me."

"No, you don't. Trust me," he assures me, and pulls his hand back. He can't seem to look away, though, and we remain locked in a silent mutual gaze as my heart thuds in my ears.

This intimate moment is interrupted by my manager, who has emerged from behind my back and is very suggestively letting me know with her expression that I have spent too much time on taking care of one customer and should help other ones throughout the store as well. Thank God there are no cameras facing us, or she'd have evidence of my longer-than-allowed chat with Dorian.

"I'll see you tomorrow," Dorian says to me.

Frozen to the spot, I follow him with my gaze to the door, which slides closed behind him when he steps outside into the parking lot. I wonder whether I'm ever going to discover the truth that they have both been hiding with such determination.

It's not until much later that I realize my headache disappeared all by itself.

CHAPTER ELEVEN

I CALL IT A DAY PROMPTLY at ten. The first thing I do after leaving Walgreens is catch up on unread messages. Once I unlock my phone, I see four missed calls from Rach and two unread texts, both from her. In the first one she's inviting me over to finish watching *Titanic*. In the latter one, she lets me know that she's going on a date with Brandon Whitley, on whom she's had a crush since seventh grade. I'm guessing it must've been him she wanted to tell me about so eagerly.

I'm about to return her calls, but first I log in to Facebook to take a glance at what's new with my other friends. I come across a message from… Matt! I rub my eyes in amazement and to make sure that I'm not just seeing things.

Matthew Albert Clayton: Hi Zara, I hope that Charlie didn't bother you too much on the way home from the party. I need to tell you that the best part of the entire evening was the talk with you. I'd love to repeat this experience, in a different setting though. Are you up for it?? Have a great day. Matt

I read this short message three more times. Shock flows through me. I've recently classified Matt among the group of guys that would never give me attention, and here you go—a message that clearly is a date proposal.

It's hard to determine whether I'm feeling mostly euphoria, dismay, or distrust right now. I have a suspicion that something is hidden under the cover of an innocent invitation, and that it's not so innocent. Perhaps it's my lack of confidence. Matt, who doesn't date much, has all of a sudden invited me out, so he must want something. Why hasn't he ever approached me before if I'm so interesting to him? What has changed so quickly? Or maybe it's my latest incident with Charlie that has made me so suspicious of men…

On my way home I wonder what I should do. After all, Matt's position in my heart has been gradually taken over by someone else. My pulse still speeds up a tad when I think about Matt, but it jackknifes when Dorian shows up in my mind. Why have my feelings changed so dramatically almost overnight? Not too long ago, my thoughts were preoccupied with Matt every day. Now I can't get rid of the image of Dorian's face. It's like an obsession that I can't control. The more I try, the more it feels like it controls *me*.

Nevertheless, Dorian has made it clear that nothing's going to happen between us, so why shouldn't I just try with Matt anyway? Maybe the old sparkle will light up in me.

I pull into my driveway, but don't rush to get out. I stay inside, staring blankly at my phone screen, mulling over what I should do.

Respond. Not respond. Respond. Not respond.

Someone's laugh cuts through Jon Bon Jovi's "It's My Life" on the radio and reaches my ears, reminding me of the surrounding reality. I lift my head up to look at the source of the giggle. I see Rita walking down the path next to a tall man dressed in a sleek button-down shirt and khakis. The way she walks combines such elegance and sex appeal that I can't help but gawk at her.

They're not alone. Dorian and the blonde whose name still remains unknown to me emerge onto the porch. They follow Rita and her companion to the car. All four of them look impeccable.

Jealousy bursts into flames inside me, burning. I thin my lips and glare at them with reproachful eyes.

Somebody's going on a double date.

I can't stop staring at Dorian. Even the way he moves is attractive; so distinctive and refined that it couldn't be imitated by any other man. *Does she even know how lucky she is?*

As they saunter along the fence, Dorian pivots his head towards me. My stomach lurches when our eyes meet. His expression is emotionless—he doesn't exactly look thrilled at his evening out… unlike the smiley blonde beside him, who's just put her hand on his shoulder in a possessive gesture. I quickly drop my head down, pretending that I'm texting someone, unable to watch them anymore. It hurts too much to be aware that I'm not good enough for him.

At least seeing that has made my decision for me, though. As soon as they vanish from my sight, I type a quick message to Matt.

Me: Hi Matt! Sure, let's meet again! How about Saturday evening?

It takes him a minute to respond.

Matthew Albert Clayton: Sounds great! 7 pm?

Me: Perfect :-) I'll see you soon!

With a sigh, I put my phone back in my purse. What I would give to have Dorian, not Matt, on the other side of the phone!

* * *

I meet with Rach the next day at school during our lunch break. We go to the nearby park, which is our favorite place to rest between classes. There are several benches spaced along the graveled path, but we choose to lounge on the grass, under an isolated tree. I watch the clouds lazily drifting in the sky, listening to Rach updating me on the current state of her love life. Our conversation doesn't resemble a dialogue at all—it's a ten-minute-long monologue. At times I try to chime in when Rach takes a breath, but she does this so quickly that before I'm able to produce a single sound, she's talking again.

"…And then he asks me if I feel like going to the movies, and grab a drink after." She chuckles like a teenage girl. "I *obviously* said yes."

"Looks like you have a date with Brandon and I with Matt," I drawl, more to myself than to her.

"Say what?! With Patterson? Did he respond after all?!" Her mouth opens in an O-shape. "But where did he get your number from? Didn't you say he never asked you for it?"

"He texted me on Facebook."

"And you agreed," she states, as if it's obvious.

"Yeah…" I grab a random stone and fling it away.

"You don't seem thrilled, girl."

We both watch the stone, which bounces off a nearby bench and drops on the ground.

"No, I'm really happy."

Who am I lying to? Her or myself?

"You're a terrible liar. I can tell that something's off."

"Everything's fine."

"Sure it is." She frowns. "Does it have something to do with that neighbor?"

"Don't you even mention him, Rach!" This slips from my lips much louder than it was meant to. "I'm sorry—I didn't mean to be rude. I'm just confused."

"So it is him." Rach rests against the trunk and stretches

out her legs. "Will you ever tell me what's going on? Why do you even care about him?" She turns her face toward me. "Honestly, I thought at first that he was just a hottie you were into and couldn't help but watch through the window every day and drool. But your reaction to seeing him with another girl makes me assume that there definitely must be something more on your side. And if so, I don't get how. He's never even asked you out or anything, has he?"

"I'm not ready to talk about this," I say, then wince. I know that Rach is dying to know more. I feel bad about not spilling the beans, but thinking about Dorian is the last thing I want to do on my break. Not after what I saw last night. It's too painful. "I promise you'll be the first one to know about everything once I get some clarity. Right now, I have one big mess in my head."

"Maybe if you opened up a little bit and released some tension, it would help you clarify things in your head? Don't you think?"

I remain silent.

"You're impossible," Rach says, and shakes her head. "I don't want to be pushy; it's your business, so if you prefer to bottle it up, that's your choice. I only hope you're aware you'll eventually blow up if you don't tell someone." She stops here and lets the subject rest. Instead, she brings up another matter: "Are you up for a double date at the movies? Take Matt and let's all go! We can relax over a glass of something afterwards."

"Why not? I'm sure it's doable."

"I choose the movie!" Rach says, clapping her hands, happy that she's come up with such a splendid idea.

"Sure—as an exception, you have the right to choose." I wink at her. We both know that Rach is always the one who decides what we're going to watch. Her favorite genres are horror and romantic comedy. The combination doesn't make any sense to me, but I never complain, because she usually picks good movies.

"Sounds excellent!" she squeals in excitement.

A few weeks back, I would've been on cloud nine that I'm going out with Matt. But at the moment I'm indifferent. I try to feel enthusiastic, but all I can summon up is a faint smile.

Will this double date help me forget about Dorian?

* * *

On Friday I need to pay Dorian a visit to pick up my bicycle, or rather its remains. Every fiber in my body has been vibrating in anticipation all day for this moment. When I make it to his front door in the evening, my stomach tightens. I take a deep, ragged breath before knocking on the door. When I finally gain the courage to do so, silence greets me. I press the doorbell twice. Still no answer.

Even though the Bentley is gone, all the lights upstairs are on, which implies that somebody must be inside.

Third time lucky, I think to myself, and ring again.

Finally, my waiting pays off: footsteps on the other side reach my ears. Somebody's running down the stairs. I swallow hard. The door opens before me and Dorian stands in the doorframe. I can't control a sudden trembling.

"Hi," I greet him hoarsely, blinking rapidly. "I came to grab my bicycle, remember? I hope I'm not bothering you."

"Zara—" He hesitates momentarily. "I'm sorry, but can we put it off until tomorrow?"

What did he just say?!

"Tomorrow… Umm… Sure… Tomorrow. Tomorrow works fine," I stutter. "No—it won't work, actually, because we're going to the movies with my friend." I try to collect my thoughts, standing no further than three feet from him, which effectively influences my ability to think logically. "But didn't you say that…" I don't finish. I don't want to finish. I can't acknowledge that he *forgot*.

An awkward silence fills the air.

"Dorian? Who is that?" A female voice comes to my ears; it doesn't belong to Rita.

It hits me all at once. There's a girl upstairs waiting for him. I've interrupted his romantic tryst with a new girlfriend. A pang of mortification pierces me.

He forgot all about me. I've been impatiently waiting for this moment all day, but Dorian was so busy taking care of his 'new intense adventure' that it slipped his mind that I was supposed to drop by.

I drop my gaze down to hide my disappointment. "I'll come over another time," I mumble. I don't want to see his face. I need to leave *now*.

I wheel around, ready to descend the stairs, but before I take the first step, Dorian grabs my wrist and makes me face him.

"I'm sorry." There's almost an imperceptible note of regret in his eyes.

I don't respond. I don't buy that he's sorry even for a second. Why would he be? I'm nobody to him.

I free my hand of his grip and trail down the path. Even though I have my back to him, I know his eyes are on me all the way to the gate. I look over my shoulder and see him disappear inside. The door closes. He's with her again.

For a second I stand still; my eyes narrow. All the excitement that gathered in me throughout the day has drained within moments. I don't know what to think, what to feel, or what to do.

The thought of going home is out of the question. It's too close to them. I break into a run. I simply run straight ahead, aimlessly, as far as my legs can carry me. I don't care about the distance, time, or weather. Everything that's going on around me has lost its meaning. I wish I could pass out from exhaustion, be unable to catch my breath, maybe even suffocate. I feel defeated and humiliated. How could I have been so naïve as to think he cared about me at all?

Clear your mind, Zara. That's what you need.

I reach the woods, where I finally jerk to a halt. Facing a wall of trees, I break into uncontrollable tears. I've never been anything special to anyone, and I never will be. I'm so ordinary, worthless and incapable. I don't even want to stop weeping; these tears have a cleansing power. I need to purge these pent-up emotions.

When I eventually run out of tears and regain my willingness to care about what's going on around me, I realize that the sun has sunk behind the horizon. Though it's still light overhead, the sky will soon darken. The woods aren't the safest place at night. Thirty minutes ago, I was eager to stop feeling anything, but now I don't exactly feel like being stabbed by someone. I scope the area out, and it dawns on me that I've never made it this far on foot before. I need to turn back right now.

With every passing minute my speed increases. I'd like to make it home before it gets pitch black. My feet hurt from the brisk pace, and my forehead becomes beaded with sweat, but I don't slow down. The silence around me, along with the empty streets, is more than enough encouragement to keep going.

All of a sudden, I clearly sense someone's presence behind. At first, I think it's just my brain playing tricks on me, but after a while I'm almost certain that someone's looking at me. Adrenaline begins flooding my system. I dare to peek over my shoulder, and I see a figure around fifty feet back. How long has he been walking behind me? Icy fear twists around my heart. *Am I in danger?*

I make a left and turn into the street that is parallel to the one that leads to my home. To my surprise and displeasure, the stranger behind me does the same thing. My feet scream at me to slow down, but my brain is in full survival mode; it doesn't even consider stopping.

I make another left, praying that my tail will finally leave me alone, but I couldn't be more wrong: the person keeps a steady pace behind me anyway. A shiver of panic runs through me. I keep glancing behind me. It's already dark, but as far as I can see, the stranger is a big, strapping man, limping on one leg. I start imagining the worst. I have to lose him.

I start running again; I don't need to look back to realize that the man has picked up his pace, too. I hear his footsteps moving faster. I have no doubt now that he's following me, not merely taking the same route by coincidence.

My only hope for rescue is to scream for help, but there's nobody in sight who might hear me and come to my aid. Everyone is hidden in their houses, probably watching TV shows too loud to hear someone's voice coming from outside. Never in my life have I thought I'd be so thrilled about reaching the street where I live. I take a quick glance over my shoulder one more time, but the man has vanished without a trace. I gradually slow down, eventually getting back to marching. My heart is still throbbing in my chest. I'm gasping for air. I'm done with running for this month for sure. I spot movement two houses away; someone is trotting down the street toward me. A flicker of apprehension courses through me.

No, not again! I groan to myself, getting ready to break into a run again. *But wait—there's something familiar about this guy.* I recognize his way of walking; he's trudging with no grace at all, taking familiar heavy and firm steps. It's Charlie. His presence makes me feel safe, though my initial desire to throw myself at him for a hug is restrained by the memory of the last incident; after all, we haven't exchanged a word since.

"Zara?" He also recognizes me from afar.

"Hi, Charlie."

"Please, forgive me," Charlie gabbles as soon as we stand only a couple of feet from each other. "You have no idea how stupid I feel right now. What I did is beyond any justification. I've wanted to visit you at least a hundred times, but I never made it to your house. I always gave up halfway there. I acted like a complete idiot... I was totally loaded... I hope that one day..."

I see a scarlet flush creeping into his face. Under usual circumstances, I wouldn't let it go this quickly, but at the moment I'm so relieved by the fact that the stranger didn't get me and instead vanished as if by magic that I pocket my pride and say a brief, "It's okay, we're good."

I even invite him in for a cup of tea, which is a big deal given that the last time he came over was during high school. At least I'm not torturing myself with thinking about Dorian. However, it gets to me anyway right before going to bed. There are two questions rolling around in my mind: *Who's the mysterious man who was following me? Is he connected to my neighbors somehow?*

I can't know for certain, but my gut is telling me that

there might be a link between them.

CHAPTER TWELVE

SATURDAY HAS FLOWN BY. It might help that I woke up only at two in the afternoon after having some sleep aid. In no time, the wall kitchen clock indicates five p.m., which means that in about an hour and a half Matt is coming to pick me up for a movie in Salem.

Shortly after five-thirty, when I'm getting out of the steamy shower wrapped in a towel, somebody knocks on my door.

"Come in."

"Hi, Zara." It's Cynthia—the first time I've seen her today. "Do you have a second?"

"I'm leaving in fifty minutes or so, but sure, what's up?"

"It won't take too long." She closes the door and sits on the edge of the bed. "We haven't been talking lately. I just wanted to make sure that you're doing okay."

"Yeah… Same old, same old. Why?" I unwrap the towel that covers my wet hair and brush it out.

"I just feel like you've been a bit withdrawn lately. You you're absent-minded all the time. Is something bothering you? Is there something you'd like to talk about? You know that you can trust me, right?"

"I'm fine, Auntie." I'm such a pathetic liar. "I mean…" I take a deep breath. "I want to apologize for my behavior that night when you and Maddie came back from Portland. I was such a jerk, not to mention that I didn't tell you the truth when you asked me about the reason behind it." I decide to be smart about it. I want to clear up the heavy atmosphere that's been in the air for a while by now. I'm reluctant to reveal the real reasons for my withdrawal, though. "I didn't want to tell you the truth so as not to bother you, but you're right. You've been taking care of me in place of my parents and I should've included you from the very beginning." I want to give her something—anything—that will draw her attention away from Dorian. "Well, that evening I met up with Charlie, and he was acting weird. I mean, everything seemed normal at first; we went for a walk, chit-chatted a bit, laughed and so on, but on the way home he started to be… aggressive."

"What do you mean, aggressive?" She frowns.

"He told me how he's felt about me for a long time and…" I bite my lips. "He tried to kiss me."

Her jaw almost drops to the floor. "I beg your pardon?!"

"You heard me." I flop onto the bed next to her.

Her features contort with anger. "He can't get away with that! I'll call his mother and tell her—"

"Cynthia, seriously?" I don't let her finish. "I'm not ten years old; you don't have to call the parents of the person I have issues with. I'm an adult, and I can handle the situation."

My aunt blinks fast a couple of times, bewildered. "It's not just issues! He tried to harass you!"

"I wouldn't go so far as to call an attempt to kiss me harassment."

"That's exactly what it is!" she cries out in fury. "That kid has crossed all possible boundaries!"

"I knew you'd react like this! This is exactly why I didn't tell you!"

I feel slightly guilty for using Charlie as my scapegoat, but it's not exactly like it's a lie; it did happen, just not when I've told her.

"Zara, honey, I apologize for my reaction, but I'm truly disgusted. But... hold on." She raises her index finger. "Didn't I see him yesterday in the house? I could swear that you brought him here, didn't you?" A confused expression is etched on her face.

"Yeah... I met him on the way home. He wanted to apologize, and he even told me that he wasn't a hundred percent sober when it happened. We're good again. I won't hold a grudge against the person who's been my friend for so many years."

Now my aunt grasps her head with both hands. "Say *what?* Not a hundred percent sober?!" She's lost her cool again. "You mean he met you while *under the influence of alcohol?* That's insane!" Her face blazes with resentment. "I would've never suspected that Charlie would allow himself to behave in such an ill-mannered fashion. He always seemed to be a man of such good manners. Zara," she looks me deep in the eye, "you should reconsider being friends with him."

"Don't exaggerate. You can't cut somebody off because they did something wrong once, which they regret later." I push myself off the bed; this conversation has gone on for too long. I need to finish getting ready. "I've known Charlie for years, and this is the first time something like this has happened. So, I'm begging you, let's keep this a secret, just between you and me. I don't want that one-time thing to color your opinion about Charlie. I'm over it now." I walk across the room. "He got carried away by his emotions a bit, that's all."

"Honey…" She gets up from the bed and comes over to me to give me a big hug. Her warm embrace feels nice. I've been craving someone's closeness, a comforting touch, for quite a while. "Now I understand why you've been so quiet recently; you must've been very upset." She strokes my hair like she used to do when I was a child. "I'm not going to lie and say that I'm not disappointed, but if everything's been clarified and we're on good terms with Charlie again, you're right; there's no reason for you to stop liking him."

Cynthia pulls away, and I notice her eyes glistening with tears. It's so easy to move her to tears; she's very sensitive. "Just… next time don't hide anything like that from me. I'm here to take care of you instead of your mom. I'll never replace her, I know, but I would like to give you the support that she would if she was alive. You should come to me every time you have an issue with anything. You know you can confide in me, don't you?"

"I'm know, but as I said, I wouldn't want that little incident to influence your opinion of Charlie."

"I'll try to treat him as usual. I have a request, though: please, don't bring him here for at least a couple of weeks. Is that okay?"

"Sure, don't worry about it." I'm willing to agree on any terms, so happy am I that I've managed to get away with everything. She won't touch on this subject again. She won't find out the truth.

* * *

Matt appears at six-thirty on the dot and hands me a gorgeous rose as the promise of a lovely evening. Even though it's a nice gesture and I thank him for the thoughtful surprise, my smile is erased from my face when we drive past the Hatches' driveway. I feel an icy ball drop in my stomach. I turn my head the other way, focusing solely on Matt; unlike Dorian, he deserves my attention.

To Rach's disappointment, by vote we choose a comedy with Kumail Nanjiani in the leading role. She stubbornly tries to convince us that the horror movie is a better option. I suspect that she wants to cuddle up to Brandon during intense scary scenes, or even bury her face in his shoulder, but unluckily for her nobody else is keen to watch that one. We spend the next two hours watching how a couple in love unintentionally embroiled in a murder mystery is trying to clear their names and survive the night.

The movie itself is hilarious, but I have to force my laughter quite a few times. I can't seem to relax and just let go of my nagging thoughts, even for a short moment. I peek at Matt every now and then. He seems to be having a really good time. How come I'm not? Isn't going on a date with him what I've wanted since I saw him for the first time? Apparently, Dorian has totally filled my thoughts and overshadowed all other feelings I had before I met him. He's absorbed all of my being. It's no longer simple infatuation.

When the show is over, we go for a drink, which is Rach's favorite part of the evening. I only drink alcohol occasionally, so when I do, I always choose light mixed drinks that won't go straight to my head. With that in mind, I plan to get a piña colada, which consists of more milk than alcohol. However, my choice doesn't meet Rach's approval; she announces that I should forget about it and orders a round of vodka for all of us. I'm not a fan of vodka—it's so bitter that it makes my face twitch—but as a one-time thing, I can stand its taste.

Unfortunately, as it turns out, I underestimated Rach's hunger for vodka shots; it goes up to four rounds. In no time, I'm spaced out. It's precisely the moment I need to pass on the next couple of rounds if I don't want to pull a stunt like Charlie's the other night.

I think Rach's intention was to help me chill out, but the alcohol I've consumed does the opposite, intensifying my misery. Now I'm not only a little bit upset, but really bitter.

Matt has a fantastic sense of humor. The other two are hysterical when he spins his hilarious stories. He mentions an incident that happened to him in middle school, a fight with his teammate on the soccer field, and a disastrous family reunion after years apart. He has the gift of amusing people, yet as during the film, I find that I have to force myself to burst out laughing. My thoughts filter back to Dorian no matter how hard I try to fight them. On top of that, Matt's cologne repels me; not because it's overpowering or obnoxious, but because it's not *the* scent. The one that I'm probably meant to be haunted by for the rest of my life. Matt's voice doesn't resemble the one that I adore so much. I don't want to seem like a terrible date, but I simply can't enjoy myself.

Rach must have noticed that something is wrong, as she asks me to go with her to the bathroom.

"Are you having fun?" she asks, standing in front of a long mirror, rummaging through her purse.

"Yeah, why?"

"Then why the long face?" She pulls out a red lipstick and deftly applies it to her lips with firm strokes.

"I'm tired, that's all." I glance at my wristwatch. "It's almost midnight."

"Zara, Zara…" Rach tilts her head back and peers at me. "You don't want to be here anymore, do you?"

"I don't mind staying."

"What happened to you?" She swivels quickly to face me. "Haven't you been carrying a torch for Matt and dreaming of a date with him for months?" She pushes herself off the sink and approaches me. "You have what you wished for, so what's the problem?"

"I don't know. I'm confused myself," I admit. "Maybe you're right; we should leave."

Rach seems puzzled by my mood. "You looked fine at the movies, but if you feel like it's too much for you, then so be it. I'll call a cab."

My heart sinks. Because of me, a perfect double date has just come to an end. Maybe I should sacrifice myself for a bit longer for the sake of my friend, but I can't bear the thought of staying here for another hour. Sitting beside Matt and yearning for Dorian is torture. It's also unfair. I should've never agreed to go out with Matt in the first place. It was an impulse. A need to prove something to myself.

An Uber comes to pick up Rach and Brandon. Matt didn't drink again, so he takes me home. When we arrive at my house, he doesn't let me go in by myself and walks me to the front door. The fresh air hits me, catalyzing the alcohol in my bloodstream, strengthening the effects of drinking. I do my best not to totter too much. I don't know if Matt ushers me because he has good manners, or because he doesn't want me to trip over my own legs.

"Thank you for a great time," he says when we reach the steps of my porch.

"No, thank you. It was a very nice evening."

"I would love to do it again." He comes one step closer to me, which automatically makes me back up after my unfortunate experience with Charlie. "But next time only you and me."

"Sure! We should definitely hang out one day again." Something cautions me to sign off as soon as possible.

Silence follows my words. Neither of us adds anything else. Matt must be used to having girls throwing themselves at him with kisses after every date, or at least with romantic hugs. I, however, stand motionless, favoring him only with my somewhat forced smile. I want him to go away already and leave me in peace; I need to think.

"Drive safely, and I'll see you soon," I say to break the silence.

"You're not going inside?"

"I will, but only after you drive off. I want to wave goodbye to you." It's a lie; in truth, a hellish plan has just been born in my head, probably triggered by the amount of vodka I poured into myself. If I was sober, I would never allow myself to do what I'm about to.

"That's nice of you." Matt gives me a kiss on the cheek and walks away to his car. A minute later I watch him pull out of the driveway and vanish around the corner.

Let's run the show, I think to myself. Not caring about the late hour, I sneak up to the house on the other side of the fence.

CHAPTER THIRTEEN

I KNOCK ON THE FRONT DOOR. It takes a good while before Dorian opens it, completely dressed even though it's after midnight. A bunch of butterflies takes flight in my stomach as his eyes roam over me.

I greet him wryly. "I thought you'd never open the door. I was sure you were playing your favorite 'intense relationship' game with one of your new, um… friends?" I have no fucks left to give right now.

"Nice to see you too," he replies, his face stony. "Why exactly are you here so late?"

"I came to pick up my property. Where is it?"

"Your property?"

"Where is my bicycle?" I clarify.

"You're coming for your bicycle at midnight?" He surveys the area behind me as though he wants to make sure nobody's watching us. "So what's the real reason you're here?"

I snort. "You want to know the truth? Oh, well, who would expect that? Welcome to my world, Mr. Hatch," I say, and lean against the door frame. "Perhaps His Mysterious Majesty will finally tell me what this is all about, huh?"

"I don't understand."

"Yes, you do. You only pretend you have no idea, but you know all too well what I mean! I've had enough of all these secrets!"

"Have you been drinking?" he asks, his voice sharp.

"Who cares?!" I say it way louder than I intended to.

Dorian grabs me by the elbow and pulls me inside with one firm motion, closing the door behind me. "Don't bother to answer; you already have."

"We're not talking about me right now." I'm trying to jerk away, but he's clutching me too tightly. "Maybe your cousin will join this conversation? I'm sure she has a lot to say, too."

"Rita's gone for the weekend. But it doesn't matter. What matters is that you'll regret this ridiculous behavior tomorrow, so I believe it'll be better for the both of us if you politely let me walk you home instead of yelling at the top of your lungs." Dorian pierces me with his stern eyes.

"No! Let go! Get off of me!" I manage to wrench myself free and pull away a few steps. "No! No! No! I'm not leaving this place until you tell me what secrets you're hiding!"

"Zara, we're leaving," he says, his voice full of finality, and takes a step toward me; I immediately jolt backward again. It's like playing cat and mouse. Dorian grows impatient. He looks sexy when he's angry.

"I said no!" I'm implacable.

The next thing I know, Dorian is pinning me to the wall behind me. A jolt of arousal shots through me. Our chests are touching, and I can feel his torso moving quickly up and down with his breathing. He gazes at me as if he wants to read something from my eyes.

"Do you think you have any power over me?" Dorian asks. His lips are only about an inch from my ear. His warm breath causes a shiver to run down my spine. "You can't tell me what to do and what to tell you, nor how to treat you." His face is tense, and he looks utterly intimidating, but I'm not scared.

More than by fear, I'm paralyzed and sobered by his closeness. I'm trapped in his muscular arms. I rest my trembling hands on Dorian's chest, gorging myself on the warmth he's emanating, but a second later he grabs my wrist, thwarting me.

"Stop that!"

"Why?"

We freeze, locked in a mutual gaze. My throat feels parched, and my knees tremble, but I don't break our eye contact. His eyes hide a secret; I want to discover it. I need to discover it.

"Who are you, Zara?" This time he whispers, leaning his forehead against mine. All his anger seems to evaporate like magic, giving way to frustration, as if he can't solve a simple puzzle.

"You know who I am," I respond, closing my eyes. My breath speeds up.

"You don't understand." Slowly, he traces his fingertip from my lips, which I part slightly at his touch, down to my neck. An unfulfilled need grows in me. "But how is it possible that you don't know anything…?"

"I want to understand; you can tell me," I assure him, wrapping my arms around his neck and inhaling his scent deep into my lungs.

"I can't."

"Yes, you can."

"No…" He grabs my hand, but doesn't pull it away from his neck; rather, he squeezes it gently. He seems to be battling with himself. "You're different. You can't be one of them. I don't want you to be."

"To be who?" The blood is pulsating in my ears. When Dorian brushes his lips against mine, I'm shrouded in a mist of desire.

"No."

Maybe if I were a bit more persistent, he would finally break and reveal the truth. However, I'm too drained to keep pushing. The only thing I want right now is for Dorian to stop teasing me and actually kiss me. I want to savor his taste and cross this intimate boundary that's keeping us apart.

Dorian perfectly deciphers my silent request, but instead of crushing his lips against mine, he teases me, gently biting my lower lip. It stokes a slowly growing fire in me, and a sigh escapes me. Our eyes meet again. His pupils dilate; he wants it as much as I do.

Finally, his lips land tenderly on mine in a soft kiss. Excitement wells up in me as I inhale his scent, which I know so well. Now I get to learn his taste as well, and my instincts take over. My fingers run up his neck and though his soft hair. My heart races in my chest; my breathing quickens, and I begin kissing him more fiercely, hungry for him. I push my hips into him, angling my neck so that I can deepen the kiss further, and as I do so, he breaks our kiss and pulls away.

"We need to stop. You don't know what you're doing," he pants.

"I know exactly what I'm doing." I take a step toward him.

"How strong is your will?"

He catches me off-guard with the question; it takes a moment for my brain to register what he just asked me.

"Why are you asking?"

"Answer," he demands.

"Infinite," I say with no hesitation, "but I still don't under—"

"Are you sure?" he cuts in.

"Yes."

There's a brief moment of charged silence, and then everything speeds up. Dorian slams his tongue into my mouth this time, kissing me frenziedly. I don't resist; on the contrary, I let myself go with the flow of passion and respond enthusiastically. This kiss sends new spirals of ecstasy through me. My fingers are clenched in his hair. He slides his hands down my body and grasps my hips, and lifts me up. I wrap my legs around his waist. I'm burning, driven by desire. I clutch his neck, and without breaking our intoxicating embrace, Dorian carries me all the way through the living room and then past the kitchen.

I know where we're headed; every step he takes assures me I'm right. My heart thumps in my chest. I'm right—the bedroom downstairs is our destination. As we walk through the door, he pulls away a bit.

"Zara, you can still say no."

"Not in a million years," I say, and attack his lips again. He doesn't let me indulge in his sweet taste for too long, pushing me onto the bed. Irresistible, uncontrollable desire makes me feel like I'm losing my mind.

Dorian snatches my wrists and pins them to the bed. "Don't move," he instructs me as he strips off my clothes, leaving only my underwear on.

I feel an incredible urge to touch him, pull him closer to me, feel the warmth of his skin, but I obey him, holding as still as I can. He places hundreds of kisses on my body, starting from my neck and finishing right above my underwear. The spots that he kisses and bites sear pleasantly. I tremble; thrill after thrill rolls through my body, increasing the tension to breaking point. I'm drugged with him, his touch, his scent, his taste, overwhelmed with lust.

Dorian is a master of reading the signals of my body; he doesn't need me to guide him. He pleases me exactly the way I want, touches where I like it the most, neither too hard nor too soft—just right. Our eyes lock; the desire between us is excruciating. I can't take this anymore.

At last, he presses his body to mine. I rip off his shirt and throw it aside, then dig my nails into his back and rake them down along his spine. He groans quietly.

"I want you," he whispers, burying his face in my neck, inhaling my scent. "You're so irresistible." His hands wander across my body. I can't keep up with the sensations bombarding me.

"Then take me," I encourage him, and wrap my legs around his hips.

He thrusts his tongue into my mouth. It's rough and I like it. He seems desperate, out of control. I've never seen him with his guard down like this. The only things separating us are the remaining clothes, which Dorian hastily gets rid of. He pushes my legs apart. I twine my legs around him to lock us together, inviting him to finally slide inside me, but he lingers, keeping me in painful anticipation.

"You're so different," he gasps. "I don't want to hurt you."

"You won't hurt me." I close his lips with a passionate kiss.

There's no more fighting, no more doubt. He gives me sweet relief, slowly, inch by inch. My body welcomes him with pleasure. I can hear him whispering how good I feel into my ear, which sets me on fire. I shudder beneath him, crying for more. He stimulates parts of me I didn't even know existed. Our souls seem to meld together while we're so close.

When he finally brings me to the edge and over, I clutch his arms, unable to hold back my screams at the pleasure that explodes through me. I melt into him; there's no Zara and Dorian, there is only us, fused by our bodies, minds and souls. A piece of me will forever stay with him.

When we're done, his chest heaves; I lie on top of it. My face is nestled in the crook of his neck, devouring his smell. I'm happy in his embrace. After a dreamy silence, I lift my head and fix my eyes on his face; Dorian seems far away, present only with his body, not his mind.

"Penny for your thoughts," I say, cuddled up against his chest.

"How are you feeling?"

"Perfectly fine," I reply through my grin. How could I feel any different while a whole flood of endorphins is filling me up to the brim?

"It's hard to believe," he says.

"What is?"

"That for the past ten minutes you haven't stopped smiling."

The bedroom is enveloped in darkness; how does he know? "How do you—"

"A wild guess."

"Bravo," I say, and place a kiss on his smooth cheek. "Is that what these intense relationships look like?"

"Roughly speaking." He runs his fingers through my long hair.

"Are we in one now?"

"Wil you ever stop asking me questions?"

"I will when you start answering them." I stroke his chest.

"We can't continue this."

His bluntness feels like a slap in the face. The upturned edges of my mouth go down.

How can he be so callous? He should at least pretend that he cares as long as we're in the same bed.

A wave of humiliation rushes over me. I feel used and deceived, even though deep inside I'm conscious that I have no right to feel this way; Dorian never promised me anything before I decided to end up in bed with him.

"Why?" I sit up, breaking our embrace.

"Because."

"That's not an answer. Don't I deserve a couple more words from you?"

"Please, don't make this harder."

Something breaks inside me. I'm like a little child who's been given the most delicious candy in the world, and after having it, have been told I'll never get it again. I want to cry, yell, maybe even throw a glass against the wall. Over the last ten minutes I've been hoping that everything will change from now on between Dorian and me, and even that maybe he'll eventually open up to me. He, however, remains unmoved. It never even crossed his mind to let me into his little world of secrets. The fact that I just gave myself away to him means nothing.

I swallow hard and bite back tears. "You're a jerk, Dorian!" I pull away from him, collect my clothes, strewn over the floor, and try to put them on as quickly as I can with trembling hands. He throws on a silky robe and walks up to me as I'm about to leave the room.

"Wait." He grabs my hand, preventing me from opening the door. "It will be better for you this way."

"Sure—I let a guy bang me who doesn't even pretend that he cares." I jerk my hand free from his grasp. "Do you say that to every girl? Is that your standard excuse?"

"You don't understand anything," he says, a note of pleading in his voice, but I'm not listening to him anymore. I'm so fed up with all his secrets that I leave the bedroom without looking back. I slam the front door closed and burst out crying uncontrollably.

CHAPTER FOURTEEN

I SCAN THE AREA WITH MY eyes wide open. I know where I am. I recognize this misshapen thicket, the odor of decomposing woods and the stuffy air. Paralyzing fright takes away my ability to concentrate. A familiar presence lurks in the darkness. My chest is tight; my skin crawls with the need to escape. But where am I supposed to run? Nowhere is safe. He's aware of all my hideouts; he knows everything about me; he can read my thoughts and foresees all my actions.

I need to do something before it's too late.

But I want him to catch me!

No, not yet! I'm not allowed yet!

I take a careful step forward. The sole of my shoe is submerged in slushy muck. As I'm about to break into a run, sudden darkness rolls in. I can see nothing, as if someone has covered my eyes with a blindfold. Even though there's only blackness before me, I can sense his presence closer than ever.

He's found me.

There's no point in fleeing anymore. He has me close at hand, watching my every move. I fear him, but I have a simultaneous desire to touch him. I stretch out my hand in an attempt to find him somewhere in front of me.

I WILL TEAR IT TO PIECES.

I jerk back as a voice whispers right in my ear. I'm not sure if it's just in my head or if someone has actually spoken to me. I wish I could see his face and discover what he looks like. I need to know.

Who are you? I ask in my mind, but instead of receiving an answer, it feels like heat begins to radiate from my heart in all directions. At first it's a pleasant, calming sensation, but as its intensity increases in waves, it becomes unbearably hot. It seems like living fire is moving through my veins, burning me from the inside out. The flames engulf me completely, and I start to scream. I can't breathe; I'm suffocating, burning fiercely like a torch. A bursting pain pierces my skull. Never before have I been exposed to such torture. Only death will bring me peace.

I WILL RIP IT APART.

I wake up, trembling all over. A cold sweat covers my back; my heart is pounding. It was just another nightmare, but a headache that started while I was dreaming has remained. It's splitting my skull. My electric clock displays six a.m., which is about two hours after I finally fell asleep. I need to make it to the bathroom and take some of the Advil that I keep in my mirrored cabinet.

I sit upright, but I don't have enough energy to get to my

feet. I also feel like I'm on a carousel that's spinning around in circles so quickly that it makes me feel sick. My stomach clenches unpleasantly. I can't hold it in any longer.

Hand to my stomach, I lean over the bed and puke on the floor. A bitter taste spreading inside my mouth, along with the acidic smell coming from the colorful stain inches from my nose, makes me even sicker. I throw up again. The carousel doesn't stop spinning. My room whirls. I have lost all sense of space, and I have no idea whether I'm up or down, on the floor or the ceiling. Everything goes completely black again.

* * *

It takes several slow blinks before I'm able to fully open my eyes. I didn't close the drapes, so the sun dives into my room and stabs my eyes. I squint and moan unhappily. My eye-sockets hurt, my mouth is dry and full of thick saliva, my forehead is moist with sweat. I wince, smelling an obnoxious odor.

Yuck. It's the dinner that chose freedom.

Next to the bed, I find a disgusting stain on the carpet, which would win any contest for the most hideous gastric contents in the world. The memory of puking is fuzzy, but I get down to removing the vomit without delay. I don't want Cynthia to find out about my little accident.

Around two I go to the kitchen to get something to eat. Cynthia and Maddie are sitting at the table, looking like two hamsters indulging themselves with Chinese food, at the sight of which I feel my stomach twisting.

"Good afternoon, Zara, are you feeling okay?" Cynthia asks as soon she sees me, biting a piece of sweet chicken off her fork. "You're awfully pale."

"I'm fine," I mumble, and lumber to the water dispenser to pour a glass for myself.

"What time did you come back last night?"

"I don't remember… around one?"

"I don't think so," Maddie disagrees, biting on a small shrimp.

"What do you mean?" I frown.

"I mean that you didn't come back at one." She shrugs and continues offhandedly. "I woke up around that time and came down here to grab a glass of water. When I walked past your room, it was empty."

Why is she trying to turn me in? We're supposed to cover each other's asses. Is this her revenge for when I reprimanded her in front of her new friend?

"Well, as I said, I don't remember exactly; maybe it was one-thirty. Something like that."

My aunt finishes chewing the chicken she's been munching on for a good thirty seconds. "It's none of my business how you spend your time—you're an adult—but you're aware of the house rules."

"I'm aware of them. By midnight Maddie and I are supposed to be home. No later than that." I guzzle the glass of water.

"Exactly." Cynthia rummages with the fork through a white take-out box full of rice as if she's looking for a surprise inside. Once she pulls out the fork, I notice with horror that there's something moving on the end of it. I stare at it, unable to believe my own eyes, and blink several times to make sure it's really happening. Cynthia's about to eat a *worm*—a slimy, wriggling worm. I feel like I'm going to vomit again.

"What the hell is that?!" I scream. "Kill it!"

"Kill what?" My aunt apparently doesn't realize what is stuck to her fork.

"That worm!" I point to her fork. "It's so nasty! Do something!" I'm yelling like I'm possessed, but the view of the clammy worm that is inches from Cynthia's mouth triggers absolute disgust in me.

"Zara, I have no idea what you're talking about," she says, and brings the fork to her mouth.

"No! Stop! Don't eat that!" I knock the fork out of her hand at the last second. It lands on the floor next to our feet.

"Zara!" Cynthia hollers. "What are you doing? Are you crazy?!"

My gaze flicks to the floor, where the silver fork lies with a piece of chicken speared on the tines. The worm is gone.

"I swear you took a worm out of the box! Didn't you see it? Big, brown, slimy worm!"

"Are you nuts? There's no worm!" my aunt scolds me.

"I didn't see anything, either," Maddie says. I transfer my stare to her; she raises a glass filled with some red liquid to her mouth. When she takes a sip, the fluid smears all over her mouth. "Maybe you're hung over, huh?" As she's saying that, I notice that the drink has settled on her teeth as well.

I blink a couple of times to make sure I'm not just seeing things.

Holy crap, it's blood!

"Maddie, don't drink that!" I bellow in horror. I'm about to knock the glass away as well, but my aunt prevents me from doing that by grabbing my elbow.

"Look at me, Zahara!" I drag my gaze from Maddie's glass to Cynthia; her eyes drill into me. "Did you take any drugs yesterday?"

"Excuse me?!"

She bristles. "I am asking whether you TOOK ANY DRUGS YESTERDAY."

"No, I didn't. I have three witnesses who can confirm my words. Where did that even come from?"

"Do you really have no clue?" She looks at the fork on the floor out of the corner of her eye.

I don't respond. After all, there's no trace of the worm, and water seems to have taken the place of the red liquid in Maddie's glass. I waver, trying to comprehend what just happened.

"I guess… maybe I didn't get enough sleep."

"I hope that the lack of sleep is the main reason for you being as white as a sheet, not to mention acting like a maniac. You'd better go for a walk and get some fresh air, young lady. Maddie will go with you."

"No, I need to go on my own," I state firmly. "I need to think over a couple of things."

"That's a fantastic idea." Maddie pours more water into her glass. "I would like to avoid Zara pushing me into an upcoming car because she thinks it's a pony from Ponyland."

"Maddie, please refrain from such stupid comments. Zara, bring your cell, and call me in case you need anything."

"Sure." I'm not hungry, so I only grab an apple from a fruit dish standing in the middle of the table and head to the living room.

"Also," Cynthia stops me before I reach the stairs, "you have a curfew for the rest of the month. I don't want to see you come back home later than ten."

I spin around, exasperated. "*What?* I'm twenty-two—I can take care of myself."

"As long as you live here, you have to obey the rules. If you break them, you have to face the music," she says matter-of-factly. "That's life."

"I see." I keep my cool, even though a flash of anger shoots through me. "It's interesting that those rules don't apply to everyone." My gaze travels to Maddie, who fixes her amber eyes on the table.

We all know what I'm driving at. The other night she brought her male friend home close to midnight, which is against the house rules, yet my aunt didn't seem to punish her for that. I've always been under Cynthia's scrutiny, whereas Maddie can get away with murder.

"See you later," I say before anyone can reply, and leave

them alone.

* * *

I've been driving around so much that I've forgotten how enjoyable strolling can be. The sun shines warm against my face and a gentle breeze caresses my skin. I don't go too far from home for my walk, but I choose a path away from the main street. I need to calm my mind and be away from any hustle and bustle. I dawdle along at a snail's pace; I'm anything but in a hurry. It's good for me to spend as much time outside as possible, and especially away from my neighbors. The thought that I could bump into Dorian makes my stomach swirl.

I hate to realize that there are two Zaras waging an inner struggle within me. Reasonable Zara, who hates Dorian and would be the happiest person in the world if she could get away with choking him with her bare hands, and wistful Zara, who languishes without him and would love to throw herself into his arms.

I wish he would vanish from the surface of the earth, but at the same time that he would take me with him.

How is it even possible to have such contradictory feelings for another person? Can you love and detest the same man?

Have I lost my mind?

There's not a single minute that I don't think about his touch, his kisses, and the caresses that ignited my body not so long ago. I remember everything so vividly—every moment from the very first kiss until the last one. A memory of his gaze when we stood in the foyer right before we decided to take it to the next level sneaks into my mind. He was confused. He wanted to make love to me, but there was something holding him back.

I still don't get why he asked me about my willpower. Why does it even matter?

My thoughts are interrupted by an odd cawing sound. I keep a sharp lookout.

CAW!

It's a bird.

CAW!

Where is it?

I glance to the left and the right, fruitlessly. The only things I see are two big homes with perfectly mowed lawns. I pick up my pace to move away from the sound. I've had enough inexplicable events for one day. No sooner do I think that I'm free from the bird than its call reaches my ears again—this time an inch from my ear.

It scares the life out of me. I spin around and search frantically for the bird, which a second ago cawed right in my ear and now is gone like magic. *What the hell?*

I start walking again, but after taking several steps but I feel something ruffling my hair, and it's not the gentle spring breeze. Before I know it, the back of my head gets smacked by something. I duck and look up, and realize that it's a big black raven.

The bird loops around and, like a boomerang, returns to me. I dodge it at the last second before it divebombs into me.

Why is this raven attacking me?!

My astonishment reaches its peak when, way off in the distance, I spot three black points in the sky that seem to be approaching me at full tilt, taking on a clearer shape with every fraction of a second. *More ravens?* My gut tells me that their intentions aren't good.

For what feels like the millionth time this week, I race down the street.

I don't turn around, but I can hear their ominous caws. I yell for help at the top of my lungs, but no one who could tame those flying beasts comes out. I run like crazy, my heart drumming—I'm terrified.

I have no clue how long I sprint like this—it could've been seconds or hours—but suddenly silence falls. Total stillness. The birds have vanished. I stop and gasp for air. I've covered a tremendous distance; I feel like I'm spitting out my lungs. I lean against a tree. The street in front of me and behind me is clear. I can collect my breath in peace.

Holy shit! What was that? Where did those birds come from?!

I don't have long to wonder about the peculiar phenomenon, because my attention is suddenly stolen by an odd sensation. I feel warmth washing over the hand that rests on the tree trunk. I goggle at the sight of my hand *on fire.* It's a living flame that spreads over my skin.

I'm burning!

Across the street, I notice a sprinkler in someone's yard. I couldn't care less that someone might see me; I simply run to it and place my hand under the stream of water. A soothing coolness wafts over my skin. I sigh. Something very strange has been going on with me since this morning.

"What are you doing here?!"

My blissfulness is interrupted by a man's rough voice. Some guy is standing over me and, like the ravens, doesn't seem to be friendly. I'm pretty sure he's about to tell me off for bending over the water sprinkler in a private garden, perhaps even his own.

He's tall, clad all in black. What immediately attracts my attention is the item he clutches in his hand. It somewhat resembles the handle of a golden knife, all covered in dozens of sparkling, colorful jewels. It's a real masterpiece.

"I'm so sorry; I didn't mean to sneak up on your property. I only…" *I only what? Wanted to put out the fire on my hand?* "I simply… My hand…" I shift my eyes to it, but there's no damage; the fire didn't affect it at all. I examine my hand on both sides, but apart from being wet from the sprinkler, there's no evidence that it was burning like a torch three minutes ago.

"You look very suspicious," he says, and squeezes the mysterious thing that he's holding. Shiny eight-inch blades pop out on both sides of the sheath with a click. They look sharp enough to break skin on the slightest contact. Terror washes through me.

My heart jumps in my chest as I get up. I slowly look

from his hand to his face, and my heart stops. There are scars all over it—some deep, some shallow, but all of them equally appalling. I choke back a scream at the sight of his left eye, missing both an iris and a pupil. His long, snow-white hair spread across the collar of his black coat, along with unnaturally pale complexion, make him look like an albino.

I feel deep in my bones that it's the same man who was following me the other day.

"I need to ask you a couple of questions." His nostrils flare. "In private," he adds, making an attempt to grab my shoulder. I manage to jump away just in time.

I assess my situation. I have no getaway plan in my head; my only chance of escaping is if I kick him between the legs, punch him in the face or use any other act of violence that would weaken him and make him unable to chase me. But his horrifying appearance takes away all my will to even try. Panic riots within me. I have no clue where he intends to take me, but I don't think he's got an amusement park in mind.

He's planning to drag me to the woods, where he'll bury me alive, my vivid imagination whispers.

Just when I lose all hope of salvation, I hear a car at the end of the street. It's approaching us at a crazy speed. Seconds later, it screeches to a halt in front of us, and the front window rolls down. To my astonishment, it's Rita in the passenger seat, yelling, "Zara, get in, now!"

The creepy man studies the Bentley thoroughly and clicks the weird item in his hand again, making both blades pull back inside. I barrel past him, still trembling. The only thing I need right now is to drive off, far away from that freak, who keeps staring at me with his dreadful eyes. Thank God Dorian's in the car too. With him I'm safe.

CHAPTER FIFTEEN

I SIT STIFFLY IN THE BACK seat and fold my hands like I'm going to pray. I remain motionless all the way. I don't ask any questions. I don't demand any explanation. I refrain from speaking at all, and even catch myself unconsciously holding my breath.

"Zara, don't leave your house again today," Dorian says, breaking the silence that has settled over the car interior, looking at me in the rear-view mirror. His eyes are fierce and peremptory.

Still reeling from the shock, I don't dare to object. I only nod my head in response.

"Is everything alright?"

I'm about to nod again, but then my eyes fill with tears; I'm not okay at all. Since the crack of dawn, inexplicable and odd phenomena have been tormenting me. It seems to me that I'm ready for the nuthouse. First my nausea that morning, followed by the hallucinations in the kitchen, the crows attacking, my burning hand, and then finally the man in the garden. *What else is going to happen to me today?*

"Nothing's okay," I say quietly.

"What's the matter?" Dorian asks, making a left onto the street where we live. "Tell me. Now," he insists.

I hesitate, but I'm unable to resist the urge to vent. I have a feeling that Dorian will understand, that he knows where all this is coming from—the cause and the cure.

"Everything today has been so weird. I don't understand anything." I bury my head in my hands.

"What's weird?"

"Like I said, everything. I don't know how to explain it." I'm reluctant to tell them the truth. I don't want them to think I'm crazy, but I need to get it out of my system anyway. "I can't tell what's real from what's not," I say, and lift my head. "Was that man real?"

"Damn real," Rita confirms.

What is she even doing here? Wasn't she going to be gone all week? Is she real?

"How come you drove by?"

"Don't ask. Just be grateful," she says.

"Do you know him?"

"I would say yes, we do," Dorian says, pulling into their driveway.

"Perhaps we should take her in with us until we make sure that the area is clear," Rita suggests. "What do you think?"

Dorian turns around and, after scanning me from head to toe, says, "You're totally right."

He gets out of the car and makes it all the way around the

vehicle to the passenger door. He opens it for me.

"Can you make it to the door by yourself?"

"Yes," I say with no hesitation, but no sooner do I touch the ground with my feet than my legs rebel. Dorian catches me at the last moment, before I hit the hard concrete with my head. He takes me into his arms and carries me to the house.

"I'm sorry," I whisper.

"No, I'm sorry."

"For what?"

Dorian doesn't answer. Most likely he meant last night, but I don't want to dig into it. He lays me down on the couch and drops next to me. The shock that has been wearing off has an intensely dizzying effect on me. My system needs to get some rest and cool down.

"Dorian," I say, grabbing his shoulder as urgently as if my life depends on it, "promise me you won't go anywhere, okay?" I give him a look full of supplication. I feel like a terrified child who just woke up after having a nightmare.

"I won't move, I promise." He puts his hand on mine and gently brushes his thumb along the side of my wrist as if he wants to comfort me.

I'm confident that nothing bad will happen to me as long as he's near. I'm safe.

Fixing my eyes on Dorian's concerned profile, it dawns on me that I could never hate him. Once I'm lying so close to him, I realize it's not aversion that I feel for him. The only hatred I have in my heart is for myself, for not being capable of walking away from this man more mysterious than any other person I've met in my life. But maybe that's what attracts me to him so much?

That evening when I decided to sit with him on the porch was a trap, my bane; nothing was going to be the same anymore. But how was I supposed to predict that things would pan out the way they have?

"I'm going to check out the area." I recognize Rita's voice from behind the couch. "I'll be back soon."

"Be careful," Dorian warns her. "You know how cunning they can be."

"She doesn't look too good." Rita must mean me.

"Just go."

As soon as the door closes behind her, he turns to me. "Zara, can you clarify what you meant when you said you couldn't tell what was real from what wasn't?"

If there's one person to whom I can confide everything that's been bothering me without worrying about accusations of being a freak, it's Dorian. I let myself go and let out all the tension that's gathered in me from the moment I came back home last night up until now. I familiarize Dorian with even the smallest details. With every sentence, his features tighten. He doesn't cut in, but listens carefully to my story. Most importantly, there's no hint of suspicion or doubt in his eyes as to the truthfulness of my words.

Dorian must know something, at least, that would explain his unshaken reaction to the crazy things I say. No other person would take me seriously; they'd probably question eighty percent of my story or try to find some logical explanation for it. Not Dorian, though. He only says, "All the things you told me about were hallucinations. The only real thing was the man."

"But where are those hallucinations coming from? I've never had them before. Maybe," I say, and bite my lip, "someone added something to my drink."

"To your drink?" He shoots me a perplexed look.

"Yes… I went out for a drink before I came here." My cheeks start to burn.

"I suspected that. Otherwise you wouldn't have had the courage to come here after midnight."

"I was only a bit tipsy." I avert my eyes from him.

"Who did you hang out with?" He grasps my chin and turns my head back to face him.

"Does it matter?"

"Very much."

"With my girlfriend."

"Only your *girlfriend?*" A pinch of discontent in his voice.

"No, not only."

"Did you go out with the same guy who tried to make out with you in your driveway?"

"No; the one I was with is a gentleman who'd *never* take advantage of me." My double-edged remark is followed by silence.

I have no idea what Matt's intentions really were, and I don't know why I said that. Maybe to make Dorian feel bad about what he said to me last night. But why would he?

After all, he gave me multiple chances to withdraw, but I stubbornly insisted on going beyond the point of no return. I willingly let him possess me; he didn't make me do it. My stupid hopes that it would change something between us are on me. He didn't promise me anything.

I'm hurt anyway.

"Then why did you come here if your date was so perfect?" His eyes sweep over my face with such intimidating power that it's hard for me to stand my ground, but I don't look away.

"I don't know, Dorian." My thoughts and emotions are an absolute mess. "The more I try to block you out, the more I need you."

"Do you regret last night?"

The silence is even heavier than before.

"No," I say fiercely, even though only a couple hours earlier I would've responded differently. His closeness has a disorientating effect on me. I have this irresistible desire to touch him again, feel his texture of his skin under my fingertips, devour his lips. "I only regret how it ended. You?"

I give him one more opportunity to make things right, even though I already suspect what he's about to say.

He drags a breath deep into his lungs and lets it out. "I do regret it."

At least he's honest, but it doesn't alleviate my bitter disappointment.

Dorian places his index and middle finger on my lips and slides them down slowly along my chin and neck, stopping on my chest, near my heart. He carefully watches my reaction to his subtle caress. "I loved every minute of last night with you, but it wasn't the right thing for us to do." My pulse hammers. I feel alive under his touch again. "There's so much life in you." He places his hand on my heart. "You beam with vitality."

"Is that a bad thing?"

"You shouldn't depend on anyone's mercy. You should be free."

"Why mercy?" I knit my brows.

He doesn't respond, and I don't wait for him to do so; instead I pull myself up to a sitting position. Our faces are close. His eyes are on mine.

"If you regret it, why are you teasing me again?" My eyes drop to his lips. Lips I've already tasted, and for which I'm hungry again.

"Because that's what we do, and I can't help it."

"We?"

"No questions." His voice is soft and seductive. I detect a flicker in his intense eyes. I know that he's not indifferent to my closeness either. He just won't admit it.

A shiver slips down my spine as his fingers twist into my hair. We stare at each other, lips almost touching. I'm scorched by the warmth of his breath. His eyes gleam with lust, but it's not just carnal; there's a hidden need for something more profound.

"Are you looking into my soul?" I ask, pressed by his piercing gaze.

"Maybe."

"And what do you see?"

"Hope."

He catches my head in his hands and brushes his lips against mine. The temptation is too much to resist. His lips are so tantalizing. I close my eyes and gasp, feeling a flicker of desire somewhere around my navel. It quickly ignites, bursting into flames that rage out of control. I can't take this anymore, and crush my lips against his. Our tongues meet, entwining. I savor his taste. His hands slide down my back; he pulls me close, and I climb onto his lap. The heat of his body draws me like a magnetic force and deprives me of my sanity.

"Wait," he gasps, breaking our furious kiss.

"I can't wait," I object, but he grabs a handful of my hair and gently pulls my head away.

We freeze for a moment. His face expresses a blend of contradictory feelings. He wants to keep going, but something's preventing him. He's waging the same inner fight as he did last night. The intense desire hanging in the air is excruciating.

"I need you," I whisper. To swing the balance in my favor, I bite his lower lip and roll my tongue over it. As I thought it would, my little trick rids him of any leftover resistance. Wasting no time, Dorian slides his tongue into my mouth. He's wild and possessive. My body reacts immediately with an explosion of lust. I press against him, receiving more and more voracious kisses. There's some kind of animal magnetism in him that I can't resist. He starts kissing my neck; I arch back so that he has easier access to it. His soft, warm breath on my skin makes me tremble. His hands roam up and down my back. I want to be a part of him, and I want him to be a part of me.

"Let's go," he says, breaking away from me for just a fraction of a second.

We get up, glued to one another; blindly bouncing off everything on our way, we head upstairs. I've never been in Dorian's bedroom before, which triggers an extra pang of excitement in my abdomen. We clear the door; everything here smells like him. The view of the king-sized bed with silk sheets on it perched by one of the walls sets my insides on fire. Even though it's still light outside, the drawn curtains immerse the room in semi-darkness.

He closes the door and pins me against it. I strip the shirt off him, anxious to finally melt under the warmth of his skin, and bite my lip at the sight of his naked torso. I slide my fingers down his abs, stopping at his leather belt.

"You're perfect," I say, impressed.

I'm about to get rid of the necklace as well, but he doesn't let me touch it, snatching both my wrists and pulling me toward the bed. We strip off our remaining clothes on the way. Every passing second seems like forever. I finally lie down on the bed, feeling the pleasantly cool silk fabric on my skin. I need to melt, become one with Dorian right now.

He grabs a soft length of material that sits on the nightstand as if it's been waiting there for a moment like this, ties my wrists with it, and hitches it to the headboard. I can't go anywhere; it's too late. I'm subdued, defenseless.

"Did you like it last night?" he whispers into my ear, triggering a million shivers throughout my body.

I nod.

"You've seen nothing yet," he murmurs, and bites my earlobe with a lascivious smirk, filling my body with pure desire.

Dorian reaches into the top drawer, from which he pulls out a black blindfold.

"Is that necessary?" I'm not quite certain if I want to try this.

"Yes, it is," Dorian replies, blindfolding me.

"Why?"

"You'll understand," he says, and strokes my cheek.

I trust him, in spite of the basement incident. For some reason I just know he won't hurt me physically again. There's some incomprehensible connection between us that puts me at ease.

The moment his hands start to wander over my body, warm shivers run through me again, reaching every particle. In darkness, every touch, every kiss, and every caress seem to be more intense. I'm lost in a world of passion, completely surrendered to Dorian.

When we finally unite, everything loses its meaning. It's only me and him. Time and space don't exist anymore. Our souls have merged, our hearts beat in sync; our breaths are combined, our bodies following one passionate rhythm. It's something much more than just a physical activity. It's an escape of my soul into a different reality.

CHAPTER SIXTEEN

I LIE ON MY BACK, DRAINED. The blindfold, along with the strip of material that Dorian used to tie me to the bed, is discarded on the nightstand. Dorian leans on his elbow, caressing my stomach, his fingers traveling down toward my belly button and up again to the hollow between my collarbones. He's focused, contemplating my body inch by inch.

"You must've had a lot of women."

"Why?" He doesn't raise his eyes to me, still watching the reaction of my skin to his touch.

"Because you read me so well. You know exactly what a woman wants."

"Perhaps we're just perfectly suited for each other." He drags his finger around my navel in circles.

"You know it's not the case."

"I do," he openly admits.

"You also know where those hallucinations were coming from."

"I do." As he says this, gloom creeps over his face. "How

are you feeling now?"

"You asked me the same question yesterday."

"Just answer," he orders.

"I'm fine," I say, and lay my hand on his chest. "Do you regret it again?"

"I don't know." He looks at me. "There's something about you that confuses me. I've never been perplexed like this by anybody before. Whenever I say no, I mean it, but not with you."

In a strange way, it makes me feel special for at least this short while. If I'm the only woman that has the power of confusing him and influencing his decisions, maybe I'll manage to change his mind with regards to revealing his secrets as well? It's worth taking a shot.

"Dorian, I know that there's something you don't want to tell me about. Don't deny it," I add, realizing that he's about to chime in. "Have you told that secret to anyone?"

"No."

"Rita's the only one who knows, then?"

"Yes. She's my family."

"I guess you'll never tell me, then?"

Dorian stops caressing me.

"I can't. I'm sorry."

I sigh. "How long do your intense relationships last?"

"We're not in one," he asserts.

"It doesn't matter. Just answer."

"It depends."

"On what?"

"On how strong your will is."

His response intrigues me. Last night he asked me about the exact same thing. Only when I said my will was *infinite* did Dorian stop resisting and let himself indulge in our passionate embrace.

"I don't get it. Don't relationships end when both partners can't stand each other anymore? What would a strong will even matter when it comes to people's decision to go separate ways?" I ask, holding my eyes on him.

"In my case, it has a lot to do with it. More than you think."

"That I'm aware of. But can you be a bit more specific?"

"What I can tell you is that I'm the one who decides when it's over."

There's a beat of silence before I respond to his words. Instead of clarifying things, he's just lost me even more. "You? But haven't you just said that the length of the relationship is up to her strong will?"

"That's exactly what I said." His face crinkles into a smile; he seems to be enjoying confusing me like this.

"I don't get anything now," I say, resigned.

"It's better for you that you don't understand." He goes back to tracing his fingers all over my stomach. "And you're cute when you mull over something."

"Am I?" I send him a little smile.

"You have a little wrinkle between your eyebrows that shows up when you're deep in thought." He touches the spot. "Right here." He draws two fingers down to my lips.

I kiss his fingertips, which he then drags even further down, and say, "I want to know who you are, Dorian."

"And I wish I knew who *you* are." As he gently presses my breastbone, I quietly hiss; it feels like a light stab. "Does it hurt?"

"A tad. I'm not fond of this spot. It's been bothering me lately. I've gone to two different doctors before, and both of them told me that it wasn't anything serious. It's just a weird birthmark."

"Interesting." He draws a couple of small circles around my strange little lump. "Have you always had it?"

"Yes."

"There are some things that traditional medicine can't explain."

Dorian seems to be silently putting together some thoughts in his head. What would I give to be capable of sinking into his mind for at least several seconds and scanning it to finally really work out who Dorian Hatch is.

"Will you tell me how many women you've been with before me?" I can't refrain from asking it.

"No," he says tersely.

"Please. It doesn't make any difference to me."

"Then why do you ask?"

"Out of curiosity."

"I won't answer."

"Okay. I won't insist." I change the question to a different one. "How long was your longest intense relationship?"

"Umm… Good question." He frowns. "About a month."

Only a month?! I holler on the inside. I was expecting something more like half a year or at least several months. Thirty days sounds like a second on the clock of life.

"Wouldn't you like to beat the record?"

"We need to establish a daily limit of questions you can ask if I am to consider seeing you more often, because I know where you're going with this."

I grin at that comment. I realize how annoying it must be when almost every sentence coming out of my mouth is a question. I can't resist, though. I'm hoping that my persistence will eventually pay off and Dorian will start answering properly, simply for the sake of his peace of mind.

"Can you at least promise that you'll consider *us*?" I look at him with sheep's eyes, hoping he won't be able to resist.

He rolls on top of me and answers with a kiss. I'm not sure whether that means yes or if he does it to finally shut me up, but I don't care, and devour the softness of his lips. My hands travel from his strong back to his muscular shoulders. The tension is growing again deep within me.

"Dorian!"

It's Rita crying out downstairs. Our lips break apart. The tone of her voice leaves no doubt that this is something urgent.

"Fuck." Dorian sighs. "I'll be right back." He climbs out of bed, quickly pulls on his clothes, then adds, "Rita's panicking again." His face is stern. He doesn't like that he needs to go down to calm his cousin down.

I wouldn't be myself if I didn't take advantage of such an

opportunity. Seconds after Dorian leaves the room, I sneak up to the door on my tippy-toes and open it a crack. Even though both of them are in the living room, Rita's voice is clearly audible even from the second floor. She's fuming.

"Are you out of your mind?! You told me that she was out of the question and the moment I leave to look for Rafael, you bang her! She lives next door, for God's sake! Do you want her to find out *everything?!* You're wasting your time; they'll be here next week! Show it to me." I have no clue what she wants him to show her, but a second later, she goes on, "Only two? ONLY two?! Dorian, that girl will ruin everything. Either you take her into consideration, or stop seeing her at all. You know far too well that it's pointless otherwise."

"First of all, calm down, and don't tell me what to do," Dorian says. His voice remains unshaken, regardless of Rita's screaming. He speaks slowly and clearly in a way typical of him. "Second of all, I don't do anything without a reason. She has one of them."

That sentence echoes in my head. *She has one of them. What do I have?*

"I beg your pardon?!" Rita's as stunned as I am. "Oh my God! How do you know?"

"I need to make sure."

"But how do you know? You told me that she was a hu—"

"Shh!" he shushes her. "No, she's definitely not. I was wrong. But she's not ordinary either. Do you remember how fast she healed after her bicycle accident? Doesn't it sound familiar?"

"Of course it does. But how does she have one? It's impossible." There's a moment of silence. "You're going to take it away from her, right?"

"It's not as easy as you think."

I don't have the first clue what they might be talking about or thing I own that they desire so much. But now at least I know that Dorian has a purpose in maintaining our contact. *Is that the only reason he's been interested in me at all?*

"Dorian, is everything okay? You haven't been yourself lately." Rita's voice changes entirely; instead of anger I can hear concern in her tone. "Is it because of her?"

"No, I'm fine. Don't worry." He doesn't sound too convincing.

"It's her. It's that Zara messing with your head."

My heart sinks. I stick my head out the door to hear them even better.

"I'm not sure, myself."

"Dorian… you can't do it," she whimpers. "It's not the way it works. We can't have feelings for anyone."

"There's something about her," he says harshly. "Something different—inexplicable."

My heart starts palpitating; his words prove that he sees something in me that he didn't in all other women he's been with. *Is that possible that I affect him somewhat the way he affects me? Is it mutual?*

"Don't make that face, Rita. There's no reason to worry; I know what must be done. You don't have to remind me."

"Does it mean that you're counting her as well?"

"No." His voice is stark. "I'll learn who she is and where the gem is—that's that."

The gem?

"You can't just leave her now," Rita splutters. "It's too late. That's against the rules!" She's livid. I can hear her heavy steps; she must be pacing up and down the living room.

"If you say the word rules again, I swear, I'll leave."

"Dorian"—she halts and sighs—"you have to obey the code. Do you want the Guild to find out?"

A tense silence fills the house.

"Just trust me."

"You'll get us into trouble," she says with conviction.

"Did you find Rafael?" Dorian changes the subject.

"No, he's vanished. I suspect he's holed up somewhere in the woods and waiting until the girl is by herself again. You need to keep an eye on her."

"That's my plan."

"Fair enough. Go upstairs. She'll start wondering where you are."

Dorian doesn't say a word more. When I can hear his footsteps at the bottom of the stairs, Rita says, discontented, "I still think it's crazy, what you're doing."

"I have my reasons."

Heavy steps on the stairs; he's coming. I swiftly get back

inside the bedroom and slide under the sheets. I need to keep my face straight so that Dorian doesn't suspect I heard their conversation.

I grab my cellphone to make it look like I've been browsing the internet all along. When I glimpse the screen, I freeze as I notice twelve missed calls from Cynthia and four unread messages, each of them asking where the hell I am. I lost touch with the world for over four hours since leaving the house to go for a walk.

Dorian comes in and shuts the door.

"I think I'm in trouble," I announce to him.

CHAPTER SEVENTEEN

WHEN I CROSS THE THRESHOLD of my house, Cynthia is already waiting for me in the kitchen, sitting at the table. A stern, rigid expression is engraved into her face. I have no idea how long she's been waiting for me like that, but her frowning eyebrows and tightened lips tell me that it's been long enough. A knot forms in my stomach. I'd do anything to avoid confronting her right now. Cynthia can be frightening when she looks at someone with that piercing, dreadful stare. She seems to be a different person then—no longer all sweetness and light, but a vicious creature.

"Where have you been for so long?" she asks when I clear the kitchen door.

"I met Charlie. He treated me to the movies in the city. That's why you didn't hear from me; I had my cellphone on silent, and later I forgot to turn it on again," I say with a shrug. "It's only seven; I came back way before ten. Wasn't that the deal?"

"You met Charlie…" She gives me a flat look. "And

went to the movie theater with him?"

I nod, trying to avoid further questions and even more lies. I'm aware that Cynthia doesn't believe me, but I endure her deadly look without admitting to dishonesty. I'm grateful I can't read my aunt's mind—I'm certain that there's nothing positive going on in there right now. She clearly wants to dig into the subject further, but at the same time, she knows me well enough to realize that unless I spill the beans of my own volition, she won't pull the truth out of me no matter how hard she tries.

Having nothing else to add, I simply turn around and head upstairs. My rumbling belly is urgently crying for food, but I'd rather starve than feel that suspicious look on me. At the top of the stairs I notice Maddie. She isn't lounging there accidentally; she's been waiting for me on purpose.

"Why did you lie to her?" Maddie doesn't beat around the bush.

"How can you be so sure I lied?"

She gives me a self-satisfied smirk. "Leaving the Hatches' house through their back door, looping around and using the path leading to Charlie's house so that it looked like you were just coming back from his place was very clever. Unfortunately, visible from my room."

If she decides to snitch on me, I won't have a curfew anymore. I'll be kicked out of the house.

"Maddie, I'm begging you, don't tell on me." I peek over my shoulder to ensure that Cynthia hasn't shown up at the bottom of the stairs, listening to our conversation.

"Will you tell me the truth then?" She narrows her eyes.

If that's all it takes to make Maddie keep her mouth shut, then why not? Obviously, skipping some key elements will be unavoidable.

"Our neighbors aren't a couple. They're siblings," I begin, aware that Maddie will draw the correct conclusions and instantly decode the message I hid in that one short statement.

"You… Are you dating him?" She opens her eyes wide with disbelief: she's impressed.

"Sort of."

"Oh, shut up!" The bewilderment on her face grows bigger.

"No joke. I'm telling the truth, just like you asked."

"Since when?" She's hungry for details. Telling the truth will undeniably lead to a torrent of further questions, but I'm ready to answer them to satisfy my cousin's curiosity.

"Since the weekend when you and your mom went to Portland."

"The weekend when you came back home late hysterical?"

I'd love to erase that evening from my memory.

"Yes."

"Why haven't you been telling her the truth? She's concerned about you," Maddie says. "Plus, what was that scene supposed to be this morning? *Did* you take anything yesterday?"

"Would you have told her if you were dating someone

who lives literally on the other side of that wall?" I point to the wall across from us. Silence falls. "Exactly. As for the morning, I… think I might still have been a bit drunk after yesterday."

My cousin blinks, baffled. "Wait a minute, didn't you go on a double date with Matt last night?"

"Yes, but I did it more for Rach than myself."

That's not a total lie. I mostly agreed to go out with them for the sake of my own self-confidence, but Rach contributed to my decision to some extent as well. She's been asking me for years to go on a double date with her, but as luck would have it, we never dated guys at the same time.

"I'm guessing she also doesn't know about… What's his name, anyway?"

"Dorian." When I say his name my stomach twists again. I can't believe I'm talking about him with Maddie. "And yes, you're the only one who knows." I say it to please her even more. Hopefully this will encourage her to keep it a secret between us.

"Dorian…" she repeats slowly and gets to her feet, standing at my eye level. "Have you and him already… you know… did you sleep with him?" She whispers it so quietly that I can barely hear her, even though she's inches from me.

"Maddie! Who do you think I am?!"

"Okay, okay! I'm sorry," she says, making a sweeping, apologetic gesture with her hand. "But promise me that you'll tell me when you—"

"You wish," I snort, but wink at the same time. I've

played it well; I have Maddie on my side. The moment of truth has come. "Can this stay between us?"

"Are you kidding? Of course I'll keep my mouth zipped!"

Mission accomplished.

* * *

Although it's Sunday, I don't join Cynthia and Maddie for a movie night. Over the past several weeks I've been avoiding them both as if I'm scared that they'll be able to see into my mind and learn everything I've been hiding from them. Even though I've told Maddie some of the truth, I won't tell her everything. She would never understand the peculiar pull I have toward Dorian. I don't understand it myself.

Wiped out after the eventful day, I jump into a hot, soothing shower. I close my eyes and let the warm stream of water caress my skin. Leaning my head against the cool tiles, I picture Dorian's face: soft lips, sexy pronounced jaw, slightly snub nose. Last time I saw him was no more than three hours ago, but it feels like long weeks have passed since I left his place.

I step out of the tub and wrap a fluffy towel around myself. My muscles are relaxed, my mind calm. I come up to the sink to finish my evening beauty routine. The mirror is steamed up and I can't see my reflection, so I wipe it with my hand, forming a small circle in the middle. My eyes are bloodshot. I need a good sleep. I rub my neck and bend down to wash my face.

When I straighten up and look back into the mirror, my heart almost jumps out of my chest. I see the terrifying face of the man with the knife. He's standing right behind me, staring at me with blood-lust.

I twist around in a flash, but there's nobody there. I'm all by myself. Panting with terror, I transfer my gaze back to the glass surface. The man's gone.

Am I crazy?

I finish in haste and jump into bed, covering myself up to the neck with the blanket. Motionless, I stare at the ceiling for a good fifteen minutes, unable to erase the ferocious face from my mind. The hostile look on his face when our gazes met will be haunting me for the next few days.

Where did he want to take me? And why me in the first place? How come he even knows who I am?

This question triggers another thought. What if he's after the same thing as Dorian? What do I possess so precious that two men desire it? My life has always been peaceful. I've never stuck out of the crowd. Nobody has ever considered me special.

I let out a long sigh and turn my head to the side. My eyes land on two framed photos of my parents hanging on the wall. Their smiling faces forever captured in those two photographs are all I have to remind me of them. I have no recollection of either my mom or my dad. Would they know what this is all about? Does it have something to do with their past?

The fact is that I'm not even sure where I come from. I barely ever touch the subject of my family history with Cynthia. Her excuse to avoid the topic is that she doesn't want to upset me with the harsh truth. After all, when my parents died, no family members wanted to take care of me; only Cynthia took me under her wing.

There are so many unknowns. Things that remain secret and mysterious.

I strive to push away the nagging thoughts about my family, but the second I manage to suppress them, they're immediately replaced by the memory of Dorian and Rita's conversation, which only raises more questions with no answers. Their words were complete Greek to me. I have no idea what the gem he mentioned is, and what's the 'right thing' he has to do so badly? How I am even involved in it?

Amongst the chaos consuming my brain, I can single out one sound; it's a man's voice which I've heard before only in my dreams. I recognize its depth and slight roughness.

I WILL TAKE IT AWAY FROM YOU.

Fear curls in my gut. Even though I search the room thoroughly, I know that it's in vain. I won't find anyone hiding in the walls, because that voice came from inside my head.

I squeeze my eyes closed. Adrenaline rushes through me. Never in my life have I seen or heard things, but today all those past years have apparently caught up to me with full force. I cover my head with a pillow like it's going to drown out my thoughts. I'll go crazy if those hallucinations and voices don't stop haunting me tomorrow.

* * *

Is it morning yet? Maybe it's still the middle of the night.

I can't tell with my eyes closed. Even though I've been desperately trying to open them over the last minute, I can't. My exhausted body sends the clear message to my brain that it must be four a.m. at the latest. Unfortunately, my alarm disagrees as it goes off; it's actually already six a.m. I need to drag myself out of bed if I don't want to be late for my morning shift at Walgreens.

Paralytic grogginess often greets me in the mornings, but never to such a degree. Today it's reached a critical level. My whole being seems to yell at me, commanding me to lie under the warm comforter for the rest of the day and not, God forbid, go out anywhere.

Eventually, I pull myself out of the bed. It's so difficult to walk, as if weights are attached to my feet. I switch on the light in the bathroom; it stabs my eyes, and I squint. Everything's blurry and vague. The lavender scent that I usually adore is now seems sickly. I step on the fluffy mat and lean against the sink, panting as though I just ran three miles. I rinse my face with cold water. After drying it with my pink towel, I glance at my tired reflection in the mirror. Dark circles under my eyes only highlight the milky-white color of my skin, making me look deathly pale.

I brush my teeth at a snail's pace. Even if I wanted to, I

couldn't move faster. As I spit, the sink suddenly begins to spin. I shake my head, but it doesn't help. The world swirls viciously around me.

Oh no...

I know exactly how this is going to end. Thousands of sparkling, colorful points appear before my eyes. I drop down and feel the cold of the floor tiles, followed by total darkness.

* * *

I open my eyes and see the white bathroom ceiling. Something's not right with me. I can't gather my thoughts. Did I fall asleep? Did I pass out? I move my head to the side and notice my blue toothbrush on the floor. I try to reach out for it, but my limbs feel unnaturally heavy; I can't lift my arm even an inch. I feel so groggy... it's a challenge not to close my eyes again.

I fight with my weighty eyelids, trying to keep them open, but I lose the battle and drift off once more.

* * *

"Zara!" I hear someone's voice. "Zara! Wake up!" It's not just in my head; someone's calling my name from afar.

I slowly regain consciousness. When I open my eyes, a blurry image of Cynthia is leaning above me. I blink to sharpen my vision. My eyes feel like sandpaper and my head is exploding with excruciating pain, whereas my chest is burning like it's on fire. It's been a couple of days since it bothered me last.

"What on earth are you doing on the floor?!" My aunt's eyes drill into me as she kneels down. "What are you doing here?"

I look around, breathing heavily. I'm lying on the cold bathroom floor, still wrapped in my fuzzy bath towel. Heaven only knows how long I've been here like this. I can't recollect what happened.

She grasps my arm and helps me sit up. "Tracy, your manager, called the house to ask why you didn't show up at work, so excuse me that I let myself into your bathroom without knocking." She slides me a leery look. "I come in here and what do I see? You, lying on the floor, blacked out. Did you sleep here all night?!"

It takes a while for me to marshal all the facts and work out how I ended up on the floor. Cold brushes against my exposed legs; it spreads from my toes to my thighs. Shaking, I wrap my arms around myself and make an attempt to look at Cynthia's face, but instead of one Cynthia, I see three.

"No. I only…" My aunt takes my head between her hands; her face is so close to mine that the tips of our noses almost touch. No sooner does she try to look me deep in the eye than my stomach contracts. I push her hands away, and at the speed of light I transport myself on all fours to the toilet. I embrace it as if it's my best friend and with a dramatic splash, empty my stomach. This can't work in my favor in

Cynthia's eyes.

My throat burns, and my mouth tastes of puke. A disgusting reek of acid invades my nostrils. My stomach is still clenched, but not because of the nausea—now I have to face Cynthia.

Gradually, I turn around. I lift my head; our gazes meet. Luckily, only one pair of fuming eyes is glaring at me now.

"Zara, what's going on with you?"

"I must have eaten something bad last night."

"Don't try to fool me! Have you *seen* your eyes? Bloodshot, with dilated pupils!" I'm taken aback; I couldn't have anticipated that my eyes would look abnormal. My blurry mind isn't capable of coming up with a good cover story. "I don't know what you're taking, but it needs to stop! This is my last warning! There never have been and never will be any drugs in this house! If you're not going to respect this rule, then you should leave!" She wags her finger at me. "What's going on with you recently? I don't recognize you." She tosses me one more frosty look, then, without waiting for my reaction, exits my bathroom.

I feel so sick, as if I really did take some drugs last night. Cynthia's expression when she was reprimanding me was filled with exasperation, but also disappointment, which hurts me the most. She knows that I've been deceiving her— but how could I have told her the truth if I myself don't know what's been going on with me?

I massage my chest. The pain is slowly going away; so are the rest of the odd symptoms. I peek inside the toilet and wince at the view of the colorful vomit. I flush it, praying for the image to be erased from my memory soon.

* * *

When I finally get to work, I manage to placate my manager by using the excuse of sudden gastritis, which was severe enough to impair my ability to even hold a cell phone in my hand and drop her a line about my condition. All my listening to Tracy's endless complaints about her loser husband eventually has paid off. As the only employee she can vent to, I've gained a lot of brownie points that now can be translated into avoiding punishment.

I feel perfectly fine for the rest of the day. No health abnormalities. The only thing that's impaired now is my capability of thinking about anything other than Dorian Hatch. It's like I'm tangled up in a web of thoughts. The more I struggle to break free, the more I entangle myself.

I'm jonesing for him. My whole body suffers when he's gone; every single minute without Dorian causes me actual pain. I don't just want to see him, I desperately need his presence. Flashes of those moments when we were closer than ever keep looping continuously in my head. I can't control them. Everywhere smells like him. I'm addicted to his voice, touch, body. Dorian is my fix, and if I don't see him soon, I'll go insane.

Sneaking out is out of the question, since Cynthia has been keeping an eye on me since I came back from Walgreens two hours ago. Taking a trip to Dorian's certainly wouldn't escape her notice, no matter which way I might choose to go. Besides, I want to prove to her I've taken her words to heart and am not going to do anything 'bad'. I have to somehow suck up the lack of Dorian and try to function normally so I won't get into trouble for at least a few days.

But no matter how hard I endeavor to keep my mind occupied, my thoughts, like a boomerang, relentlessly come back to Dorian. I try reading, studying, even leveling up in Candy Crush, but nothing helps. I can't focus on anything. My body starts to ache. Heady despair intoxicates me. I have to do something, anything.

I rush down to sit on the porch. The Bentley is gone, but that doesn't discourage me from falling into the swing chair. I pull my knees to my chest and wait until he comes back. The cool wind tousles my hair; the afternoon air is refreshing. I'm willing to stay here for hours just to be able to see Dorian for a fleeting moment. One look into those blue eyes will do for a short while.

My eyes, fixed unblinkingly on my neighbors' front yard, prickle. In my head, I've been constructing different scenarios of the moment when the car shows up and Dorian gets out of it. Unfortunately, none of them come true. Long hours pass, yet the driveway remains empty.

The only time I look away is to check out my buzzing phone. Someone has sent me several messages. It's Matt, asking me out to a concert that is taking place in a couple of days.

The thought of Matt makes me chuckle internally. I can hardly believe that I used to perceive him as an embodiment of perfection. My standards have changed dramatically. He doesn't hold a candle to Dorian. As a matter of fact, I doubt if any man with the capacity of having such an intense influence on me as Dorian does has ever been born.

I don't respond right away. I don't want to waste my time looking at the phone screen. Matt can wait.

* * *

Dinner time has come, which means a family meal. I'd prefer to skip it, but I'm smart enough to realize that if I don't screw anything up and don't suddenly start throwing plates against the walls or something, it may work to my advantage.

We sit down to eat lasagna, which is Cynthia's signature dish. Initially, the atmosphere is rather thick. However, Maddie, who usually dominates in conversations, doesn't let me down this time either. She saves the dinner with random small talk: "I'm wondering what color shoes I should purchase that won't clash with the dress for my prom. I saw one pair today that I kinda liked, but in the end, I thought they were a bit too shiny. I don't know what would work."

"Silver matches pink," Cynthia says.

"I personally like the pink and black combo, to be honest," I say, cutting out the first piece of lasagna, which is always the hardest to pull out from the casserole dish.

"But black is the color of sadness."

"If you were dressed all in black then, yeah, you'd look like you were going to a funeral. Aren't we talking about only the shoes, though?" I drop the piece on my plate with a splat.

"Perhaps you could come with me one day to a shopping mall and help me choose something. How does that sound?" Maddie asks.

Her question, for unknown reason, fills me with some inexplicable anxiety. Am I being paranoid about leaving the house after the incident with the man with the knife?

"With pleasure, but remember that I have school and Walgreens, which means only late evenings or the weekends are doable for me." I take a sip of water. "Correct me if I'm wrong, but knowing you, I'm guessing that by the end of this week you'd like to have everything all set."

"Yeah, that's a good guess," Maddie says with a discontented voice. "No worries, I'll take Lara or Maria with me. Isabel, in the worst-case scenario." She rolls her eyes at that thought. Maddie doesn't get along with Isabel; she only pretends to like her because Isabel is one of the most popular girls at the high school.

"Why do you even need anybody to assist you?" My quiet aunt reminds us of her existence. "Don't feed me the line that you need advice. We all know that you'll make a choice regardless of any advice. As usual."

It's so true. Maddie doesn't listen to anybody when it comes to clothes. Even when she asks someone about their opinion, she only does it as a courtesy to make her companion feel wanted and needed. In the end, she picks out the pieces that her taste dictates her to take, not the people around her.

"I hate roaming around alone, especially after the series of break-ins that you mentioned, Mom. Those thieves might as well be rapists," Maddie says, skewering a tiny piece of lasagna with her fork and examining it thoroughly from all directions. "What kind of cheese did you use?"

"Fat-free," Cynthia says to calm her down, but her words make me gulp and wonder what I'm actually eating. *What's left in the cheese when you take away all the fat from it?*

"So, what was I saying? Yeah, um… Break-ins, of course. This afternoon, as an example, I popped out to buy some yogurt, because someone forgot to buy it"—a digression that is entirely a dig at Cynthia—"and I had a feeling that on my way back some guy was following me."

Some guy was following me bounces around in my head. My body stiffens, and I feel my face go pale as I stare at my cousin.

"What did he look like?" My voice is agitated, and Maddie and Cynthia both look at me. They must notice that the mention of the man has shaken me a bit.

"I don't know." Maddie shrugs. "He was tall and had a hood on, so it was hard to tell. Besides, he was behind me, not the other way around."

"Weren't you scared of him at all?" My jaw almost drops at her indifference toward the matter.

"It was at three. I was among plenty of people. What was

he supposed to do? Stab me?" She finally puts the small bite of lasagna in her mouth.

Maddie's arrogance bothers me somehow. How can she be so sure that he wasn't going to hurt her even in the middle of the day? She has no idea what he is capable of, but it's probably not the best time to point that out to her.

"How do you know you were being followed? Maybe he was going to the same destination?" Cynthia tries to find a logical explanation and avoid spreading the panic.

"That's possible," Maddie says, still nonchalantly. "But I could've sworn that he caught up with me whenever I sped up, and slowed down when I did. Obviously, it might've been just me." She wipes a drip of tomato sauce from her lips with a napkin. "Anyway, no worries; he was limping, so if I had broken into a run, there's no chance he would've gotten me." She giggles.

Now I'm confident it wasn't just any man. It *was* the man with the knife, and it can't be an accident that he chose Maddie as his victim. He must want something from me. From us. If not, then how come he's already followed me twice and stayed on Maddie's heels today?

Shivers go down my spine at the thought that he might harm my family. But didn't Rita conclude that I'm the one he wants, and I'm the one Dorian should keep an eye on? Maddie has nothing to do with that.

"At the end you went separate ways, right?" I hold my breath.

"Duh," she says, like it's obvious. "I made a turn into our

driveway. Of course he didn't walk into the house with me."

Now he knows where we live. Wonderful. I give myself an imaginary facepalm.

"Maybe he paid a visit to the Hatches?" It's like pulling teeth to get Maddie to tell me as much as possible.

"I don't think so. He stared at our house for a minute and then walked away."

"Why didn't you tell me about any of this?" My aunt frowns.

"Oh boy, I'm telling you right now," Maddie says, irritated. "It was today in the afternoon, not a week ago."

"Maddie, you're not careful enough, and you're way too cocky," Cynthia rebukes her. "Are you even aware that Liz Lawson's daughter has been missing for a couple of weeks now?"

"Gina?!" Maddie drops her fork and covers her mouth with her hand.

My eyes bulge at the news as well. Gina was Maddie's best friend at elementary school. Even though it's been years since we last saw her, the thought that she might have been kidnapped is disturbing.

"Yes, Gina." A swift silence descends. "I was sure that you knew about it. Aren't you interested in current events in the neighborhood at all?" A flicker of disappointment briefly passes over her face. "She's not the only one who left home and never came back. Danielle Leigh went out to visit her friend on Thursday and has been missing ever since, too. Her family has had no contact with her. She's vanished without a trace."

"How do you know about these things?" I ask, fidgeting in the chair.

"Are you kidding?" She tosses me a pitying look. "I read newspapers and chat with people. That's all it takes to stay informed in this city."

The name Danielle Leigh doesn't ring a bell, but for some reason, I immediately connect her and Gina's disappearance with the shady creep. I have the strong feeling that he might've had a hand in both cases. I can't control the trembling within me because, though I hope I'm wrong, all the signs indicate that the next target is either Maddie or me.

Dorian and Rita must know who that man is. I don't care what Cynthia's going to think; I need to speak with them. Dorian will understand that it's a matter of life and possibly death, so he'll have to tell me who the man is.

"The police have taken care of it already," Cynthia continues. "They've opened up an investigation. It surprises me how little you know about current matters. You should be more interested in local breaking news."

Me and Maddie cross 'oh no, she's starting with this again' glances. Maddie decides to justify our ignorance by saying: "But nothing like this has ever taken place in Keizer. It's a small town where everybody knows each other. You can't fart without other people knowing."

My aunt grimaces at Maddie's digression, but then her face softens. The news about her former friend Gina must've taken away Maddie's appetite; she's pushing the plate away with an almost untouched piece of lasagna.

"Honey." Cynthia covers her daughter's hand with hers. "Nothing is absolute and unchangeable. You have to recognize that. Today we have peace, but tomorrow we may have to face a war. Right now we're safe; in a week, we might be in danger. That's why I must insist that the both of you do not wander around alone after dark." She moves her eyes to me. "At least, not until we make sure that the area is safe."

"Definitely," Maddie agrees. I obediently nod, even though deep inside I'm already planning to skip out unnoticed later tonight.

CHAPTER EIGHTEEN

I WAIT PATIENTLY UNTIL Cynthia and Maddie go to bed, lock themselves in their cozy bedrooms and, ideally, fall asleep. My plan is simple: use the back door, and from there sneak to the Hatches' house unseen, as my aunt's bedroom faces the other side of the neighborhood. The worst that could happen would be Maddie catching me red-handed, but since she agreed not to say anything, it shouldn't be a problem. I'm sure that regardless of the late hour, Dorian and Rita are still awake.

I was right. Rita, who opens the front door, is still fully dressed and has makeup on. In fact, I'd say that she's getting ready to leave, not to turn in.

"Zara?" Her eyes pop. "What are you doing here?"

"Hi, Rita. I know it's late, but it's urgent. It's about that man I met yesterday."

Rita seems to have anticipated that sooner or later this subject would push me their way and I'd end up at their house asking questions. She glances at me, distracted, and then moves to the side, giving me enough space to walk through the door. "Come in."

When I deftly step inside, Rita scours the vicinity to ensure nobody followed me and then slides the door shut. "Dorian's still out, but he should be back soon."

It's just the two of us, then, for the first time since I met them. It's a bit awkward; after all, I showed up to speak to Dorian and her if need be, not the other way around. Nevertheless, my crafty brain prompts me to take advantage of the situation.

"Would you like something to drink?" she asks as I sit in the corner of their leather couch.

"No, thank you." It's not that I suspect she's up to something, but I kind of have some trauma related to inexplicably dropping off on their couch a while back.

"How can I help you?" She sits on the opposite side, keeping the distance.

"I have a couple of questions, which I hope you'll be able to answer."

Rita gently smiles. If I didn't know how she really feels about me, I wouldn't suspect she's uncomfortable right now at all. "Of course."

"That man, yesterday. Who is he?" I peer deep into her eyes.

The corners of Rita's mouth slightly uncurl; her little smile has changed into a tight, thin line. She takes a deep breath and swallows hard. Without Dorian standing by her side, she must be uneasy.

She clears her throat and says, "Yes, I know him," then

pauses for a second. "He's dangerous, and you'd better stay away from him." She doesn't say anything I didn't already know, but I didn't expect her to let the cat out of the bag right away.

"I'm all for evading him, but there's one problem. Apparently, he doesn't want to stay away from *me,* because I've come across him twice so far. I'm positive that wasn't by accident."

A heavy silence settles over us. Rita purses her lips and starts bouncing her legs as if she wants to hide her nervousness. "Just don't walk alone. Always have someone with you."

Is that really her fabulous advice?

"Are you telling me that I should live like that for the next, what, six months? A year?" I furrow my eyebrows. "What kind of life is that—being constantly scared to go out by myself? Plus, I won't have someone with me at all times. It's not doable."

"He'll leave eventually; you can trust me on that."

I don't trust her even an inch. They both have an agenda, and as much as Dorian's made me feel that he cares about my well-being along the way, she hasn't. I'm only a stranger to her, who is messing with her cousin and unconsciously thwarting their plans. She'd like me to be out of the picture so that they can peacefully finish what they have started, without me disrupting.

"But who *is* he, and why the hell did he pick me to follow?" I demand. She looks away without responding.

"What if I run into him again? How am I supposed to defend myself?"

"You won't run into him if you don't walk by yourself. It's that easy." Rita glances back at me.

A surge of irritation sweeps through me. Her resistance toward telling me the truth is unbelievable. "Do you think that will calm me down?" I glare at her. "That guy held a *knife*, or at least something resembling one, and was ready to use it on me!"

Rita jerks to her feet and turns her back on me like she can't stand my eyes on her anymore.

"Rita, I'm begging you, tell me what's going on." I get up from the couch as well and come over to her, continuing in a desperate voice. "Not too long ago my cousin's friend went missing. There's another girl who's magically vanished, too. Do those cases have anything to do with that man?" I take one more baby step. "Was that all his doing? I need to know this, Rita." I'm standing one step away from her. The mass of her wavy black hair is right in front of my eyes. "He followed my cousin today all the way home. I don't want anything bad to happen to her!"

"Zara, simply ask her not to go out—"

"—By herself. I've heard that already," I cut her off, even more irritated. "It's not a solution to the problem. I don't want to live in perpetual fear. What if he's lucky and manages to get my family or me? What then? How should we defend ourselves?!" My voice grows louder. Her advice is ridiculous, and she's obviously aware of that, since she refrains from trying to convince me otherwise. I can't hold back my resentment anymore. "Tell me!"

"It will end soon." Rita swirls around to face me, remaining rigid. Her alabaster skin is paler than ever. Her emerald-green eyes are shadowed by secrets, just like Dorian's are.

"You know who he is. You went looking for him right after you dropped me off here." I won't let her stall me; I need to know the truth. "Is he responsible for what happened to those two girls?" Heat fills my chest.

After my questions, silence surrounds us. It tells me more than a hundred of Rita's words would. Even though she's impossible to read, I have my answer.

"Please," I say, grasping her arms on both sides. Maybe she'll finally budge and help me understand everything.

"Stop asking me; it's Dorian who decides everything," Rita says, trying to pull away from me.

"Is he the one who forbade you to speak?"

Strange, because it's always her who seems to be the guardian of their secrets, and whenever Dorian is about to say too much, she freaks out...

"Those are the rules. You have to live with that."

The word *rules* makes me see red; I can't keep my fury in check anymore, and I lash out. "I can't believe that you don't give a damn that some maniac is out there, walking the streets of Keizer right now, free to do whatever he feels like! You know very well that he wants to hurt me, don't you?!" How can she be so indifferent to my life possibly being in danger?

"If you don't want to get hurt, then stay away from us!" she finally snaps back. Her chest heaves. Apparently, I'm not the only one whose triggers have been pulled.

Under the influence of emotions, she's spilled out something that she'd probably never have said out loud under normal circumstances. There's something hidden in her advice. A message. *Are they the ones who want to hurt me, then?*

"Why is that?"

The roar of an upcoming car is Rita's rescue; the headlights break through the curtains. She runs up to the window and peeks out at the approaching vehicle. The engine fades. A car door slams. It's him.

"Dorian's back," Rita exclaims in relief.

She rushes at breakneck speed to the front door and opens it for Dorian before he even makes it to the porch steps. She's in haste to have him finally relieve her of my cross-examination and face it himself. It doesn't bother me; quite the opposite—a sense of satisfaction rises in me.

"Dorian, we have a guest," Rita announces first thing when he steps in the foyer.

"Zara?" he guesses.

With a hunger of an addict, I zip to the foyer to get my fix — him.

Dorian's dressed in a tracksuit, looking like he's just returned from an evening jog. He takes off his hood, exposing his chiseled face. I can't help but dart past Rita and jump into his arms. I breathe his scent deep into my lungs; he smells fresh, like the night's crisp air. I'm safe now. Nothing else matters. I don't care about Rita's frown: she doesn't exist to me now. I need *him,* his embrace and warmth, his protection.

"Is everything all right here?" Dorian asks, not reciprocating my hug.

"No, nothing's alright," I say, squeezing out every last drop of air separating us. "I'm scared."

"Of what?"

"Everything around me. I had hallucinations again. I saw that man standing behind me in the bathroom mirror." I tilt my head and look into his clear blue eyes. "What's going on with me? You must know, but you don't want to tell me."

Dorian, who's been standing stiffly, now strokes my head. He gently runs his fingers through my hair to comfort me. "Everything will be fine."

I trust him. I love the feel of his body against mine. I could stay like this forever.

"Who is that man, Dorian?"

"His name is Rafael."

"Dorian!" An admonishing growl escapes Rita's mouth.

"I've known him for a long time," Dorian continues, regardless. "Rafael belongs to the kind of people who believe in certain ideas to the bone and are ready to sacrifice everything for those beliefs." He tucks a loose strand of my hair behind my ear. "He belonged to an affiliation that supported and shared his views, which was like a family to him. United under the same set of rules and customs." With every sentence he utters, Rita's face goes whiter and whiter. "Unfortunately, recently he got kicked out of that group. Now he won't cease until he's proved to the members who excluded him that they made a mistake and should let him come back. He's overzealous and unpredictable in his actions, so determined is he to make his point."

My heart thunders in my chest. "What are you trying to tell me?"

"Rita are I are in the process of explaining things to him so that he won't be a bother soon."

He's a tad better at explaining things to me than Rita was, but I'm still not satisfied with his elucidation. It's not specific enough. He's giving me only specks of truth.

"Do you and Rita belong to that group too?"

At my question, they lock their eyes. A brief uncertainty flashes in Dorian's gaze, while Rita nervously flattens her cashmere sweater.

"No, but it doesn't matter." He peels my arms from his sides and frees himself of my clasp. The time for tenderness is over.

"The police should track him down. He's dangerous," I say to Dorian, who's now taking off his hoodie. I can see his strong muscles through the fabric of his shirt. My palms itch with the longing to touch his skin.

"Dorian, it's pointless, she doesn't understand," Rita says, pushing her hands through her hair in frustration.

"The police…" Dorian says unenthusiastically. "You

could report Rafael, but what are you going to say?" He sends me a questioning look.

"That a suspicious and shady man who has lately shown up in our neighborhood carries a knife on him and therefore is a grave threat to our society."

"Perfect! Sounds like a reasonable report," Rita interjects. "Now, it'd be better if you went back to your place. You'll be much safer there."

Rita is very passive-aggressive. Even though she's doing it in a nice way, she's still throwing me out. It's no secret to me that she wants to be left alone with Dorian. She probably doesn't want to have any witnesses while telling him off and asking what he was thinking by revealing Rafael's identity to me. It makes me wonder again: who *actually* decides things in this duo?

"What is that thing he had, anyway?" I turn to Dorian. That question has been bothering me since I saw it for the first time, inches from my head.

"It's a dagger."

Rita shudders at the word.

"It looked like one taken from the royal treasury," I say, unfazed by Rita's freak-out; I'm pretending she's invisible.

"Those are gems."

"Dorian! That's enough!" Rita can't take it anymore. Any resistance she's been holding back now breaks free. "I don't know what the hell you think you're doing, but you're breaking all the rules, one by one!"

Dorian's gaze roves over Rita's face. He's sizing the

situation up, deliberating whether he may tell me a bit more or if it's better that he stops. "That's all as for Rafael." He remains calm in spite of Rita's blow-up.

"I still don't get why he's been following me. Today he stuck to my cousin and walked behind her all the way to our house."

"Let's say that he think's you're someone else," Dorian says.

"Who?"

Before Dorian can open his mouth again, Rita grabs a vase standing on a small square table in the hallway and slams it against the wall. With a loud smash, the vase shatters into dozens of pieces. It was a purposeful act to drown out whatever Dorian was about to say. We can't ignore her anymore. Not without further damages.

"Zara, you know more than you're supposed to," Dorian says, without even looking at the vase remnants; he gets Rita's message. "I don't want any casualties in this house, so let me walk you home."

He stalks over to the front door and motions me outside. Rita attempts to follow us, but he slants her a freezing look, giving her a clear sign that she's not allowed to.

Ice spreads through my stomach. He's just turned up, and yet in less than five minutes we'll be apart again. Every step we take fills me with panic. I don't want him to leave me. I need him. Without Dorian my inner peace is in disarray. I feel like there's a ruthless monster in my chest who tries to claw my heart out whenever he's away.

"Dorian," I say in a low voice, stopping on the last step at the bottom of their porch, "please, don't leave me alone." I wrap my arms around his waist, pulling him tight. I need his closeness like the air.

"I have to."

"I'm begging you," I cry, and coast my eyes over his face. Pure despair is speaking through me, inspired by some sort of inexplicable madness. "You don't even have to touch me. I just want you there."

Dorian cups my cheeks in his hands and locks his eyes on mine. Dry-mouthed, I wet my lips and gulp. His words say one thing, but his eyes suggest another. A lurch of excitement grows within me.

"We can get into the house from the back. Cynthia sleeps with ear plugs on; she won't hear anything. As for Maddie, even if we ran into—"

"Let's use the front door." He doesn't let me finish. I've convinced him.

"But…"

"Do you trust me?"

At first I want to object, but it dawns on me that there must be something about Dorian's request that I don't understand, as is always the case. I follow him. Adrenaline rushes through me while we're tiptoeing through the dark house. I'm breaking one of the primary rules set by Cynthia, and it gives me some sort of a guilty pleasure. No remorse or regrets; my inner rebellious child is set free. I even feel like giggling as we sneak along the hallway.

Several steps away from my bedroom, Dorian grabs my hand and pulls me to a halt. "What does it feel like?"

"What?"

"Breaking rules. Exciting?" His lips curve in a smirk.

"Very much indeed," I say slyly.

When I close the door behind me and stretch out my arm to turn on the light, Dorian stops me. "Are you afraid of the dark?"

"Not with you." I leave the room shrouded in darkness.

We comfortably settle down on the bed, both on our sides, facing each other. Dorian rests his head on his hand. There's almost no space between us. I soak up his luscious scent, my body trembling. He examines me thoroughly with his eyes. We stay quiet, but it's not an awkward silence; we both need it to organize our thoughts.

"You told me a lot, regardless of Rita's objections. Why? She'll make a fuss about it," I whisper, breaking the silence.

"Well, you're not the only one who likes breaking the rules." A shadow of a mischievous smile creeps across his lips.

"Is there anything else you'd like to tell me, without Rita flipping out and throwing plates against the walls?"

"I'd like to tell you everything, and that's the problem." He brushes his fingers against my cheek, and his touch triggers goosebumps on my neck. "Because if I do, I won't be able to take it back." His lips look so soft and inviting; I wish we could sink into a passionate kiss right now, but I hold my impulse.

"So what?"

"Sometimes it's better not to know. Believe in what you see. That way is easier."

"I don't want to take the easy way out."

Dorian sighs heavily. "What do you feel when I'm close to you?"

"I feel peace." I put my hand on his chest and drink in the heat of his body. "Your presence makes me believe that there's no time and space—just you and me. Nothing else matters." I run my palm up and down. "However, when you're gone, then I feel like part of me is slowly dying."

"Interesting." He sweeps one loose hair off my face.

"And you?" I flick my gaze to him. His eyes seem to glow in the darkness.

"I…" Dorian takes my hand off his chest and tangles his fingers with mine; never before has he allowed himself to make such an intimate gesture expressing emotional connection. "I feel that everything will fall into place thanks to you." He kisses each one of my knuckles. "Like you have something that I need to make it happen."

It's a perfect moment to touch upon this subject. I take a deep breath. There's no reason to fudge the truth.

"I have a confession to make," I say, and clench my fingers tighter on his hand, as if what he's about to hear will cause him to run away. "Remember when you left me in your bedroom yesterday and went downstairs to speak with Rita?" Dorian nods. "I heard your conversation."

"Did you eavesdrop?"

"I'm sorry." I look down in shame.

"What did you hear?" He pulls my chin up until I look back at him. My cheeks are burning. Hopefully he can't notice their crimson shade in the dark.

"You mentioned that you needed something that I had. What is that? I'll give it to you."

A dark shadow fills Dorian's eyes. His features harden. Some kind of strange feeling radiates from him that I can clearly sense, yet not decipher. Multiple times, I've noticed that he's imposed on himself some inner commandment which he relentlessly obeys and that prevents him from being transparent with me. Even when Rita isn't around.

I penetrate him with my gaze, trying to read anything from his face, in vain. His expression is inscrutable. I'd love to gain his trust, assure him that no matter what his secret is, it won't affect my opinion of him. Even if it was something dark, unforgivable, my heart wouldn't let me judge him or hate him.

"It seems to me that you're involved in something that you don't like," I ponder aloud. "But for some reason you won't give it a rest. Same with regards to me. You want to have me close, but you keep a distance at the same time."

I usually suck at drawing correct conclusions, but judging from Dorian's serious face, this time I've hit home.

Dorian doesn't say a single word; he just looks at me with that intense gaze. His eyes wander around my face, as if he's trying to learn it by heart, to store every single feature in his mind. He slides his fingers into my hair. Holding my head close to his, he plunders my mouth. It's a possessive kiss of pent-up desire. He's drowning in need for me. I kiss him back, running my eager tongue along his, savoring his taste. It's addicting.

Excitement sparks through me as he pushes me onto my back and gets on top of me. His body presses me into the soft bed. I place my hands on his strong back, his hot skin burning through the thin fabric of his shirt. The ache of a mad desire throbs between my thighs. I wrap my legs around him tightly and cling to him as though I want us to melt into one body. Every piece of me needs him. Craves him. I'd do anything to make him mine forever.

"I'll give you whatever you want," I say, without breaking our passionate kiss. "Just tell me what it is."

Then I open my eyes. Dorian's gone. I'm in my bed by myself, and the digital clock displays 6:27 a.m.

I rub my eyes. A second ago I was making out with Dorian, and now there's nobody else with me. My heart is still beating fast, and my desire is still burning within me. *What happened?*

I get up and open the curtains of the closest window. My mind spins in bewilderment when I realize that it's a bright and sunny morning on the other side, and that my clock isn't acting up.

How is this possible?

CHAPTER NINETEEN

I URGENTLY NEED TO SPEAK with Dorian, but the black Bentley is gone from the driveway, plus my morning class apparently starts in an hour. It will need to wait.

At school, I recall that today I have a quiz in Sociology, which totally slipped my mind. I didn't even look through my notes from Yvonne, one of my groupmates who always jots down thoroughly everything that is said in the lectures. On my lunch break, I swing by the cafeteria to have a bite to eat. I won't skip dessert today; I need a pick-me-up after miserable failing the quiz. It's there—standing in a long line with a plastic tray in my hand and looking at the menu board, trying to make up my mind about what I feel like having— that I hear a familiar voice behind me.

"Did you happen to lose your cellphone?"

It's Matt, whose intention seems to be to pull out from me why I didn't respond to his text. It's not the best timing, as my hunger takes away my ability to think, but I'll have to face him at some point sooner or later anyway.

"Hi, Matt. I'm so sorry, but the weekend was so crazy that I totally forgot! I sat down a couple of times to answer, but every time I did, I got distracted by something else. Besides, lately I've been fighting with my aunt a lot, and…" I shoot words at Matt like they are bullets and he is my target. I'm sure he's gotten lost after my second sentence, but I hope that if I pound him with even more words, eventually he'll forget why he wanted to speak to me.

"So, would you like to go to the concert with me?" He doesn't let me fool him.

"Most likely I'll be in Portland this upcoming weekend. I promised Rach that we would finally have our girls' getaway with a sleepover." I wave to Rach, who's sitting at the table by the window on the other side of the cafeteria, keeping it for us. It's not a regular wave, though. I use our secret code that only we both understand. To third parties it doesn't mean anything, but when I move my hand to and fro in a wider motion than usual to Rach, it's a sign that I need her help. She stands up and pushes her way through the crowd to help her friend in need. Before I can even say *speak of the devil*, she shows up by my side.

"Rach, which weekend did you ask me to go with you to Portland? It was this upcoming one, right?"

The 'right' at the end of the question is an element of our code as well.

"That's right. I asked for this weekend." She energetically nods, which looks a bit fake. "Hi, Matt, by the way." She grins at him. "How are you doing?"

Our conversation doesn't last too long. Rach obviously detects that something's eating me up inside, so she uses several other of our tricks to get rid of Matt.

We cut through the cafeteria, passing students grouped into cliques, and make it to the table, which luckily hasn't been taken by anyone else yet, where we plop onto the plastic chairs. "You won't go to the concert with Matt, who used to be your biggest crush," Rach says while pouring Caesar dressing onto her salad, "and when he talks to you, you look elsewhere." She slants me a meaningful look. "Long story short, you have the name Dorian written on your forehead. If you claim one more time that you don't feel anything for him, I swear, I'm going to choke you, woman."

This time I don't mind filling Rach in on the situation. Maddie knows, so why can't my best friend? I only reveal as many facts as necessary to deliver the gist. I skip any inexplicable and supernatural phenomena that may cause weird reactions from her.

"You're such a sucky friend!" escapes her lips after listening to my story. "You're only telling me about all this *now?"* Resentment drips from her words.

"Sorry, but you know me; I only speak openly about things I'm certain of."

"Yeah, but your tendencies don't mean that this is how being friends works." She brandishes the plastic fork she's holding. If I didn't know that she always makes wild gestures while speaking, I'd think she wanted to stab me with it as a punishment. "Promise me you'll keep me in the loop from now on." It sounds more like a command than a request.

"Of course, Mom," I say to lighten up the atmosphere, but Rach clearly doesn't feel like laughing or even cracking a smile.

Her lack of any form of contact with me throughout the rest of the day indicates that she's still not happy with me: if Rach doesn't flood me with dozens of texts, it's a clear sign that she must have an issue with something I either did or said. The good news is that unless I massively screw up, it never takes more than one day for her to start talking to me again. She always surrenders as soon as she misses a companion she can ramble for hours to.

Today she breaks faster than usual. She reaches out to me again in less than six hours from the moment when she decided to give me the silent treatment, which is very soon by Rach's standards. I'm even a bit concerned when I see her number pop up on my cell phone in the evening.

Rach: Hey Zara, you won't believe it, but I bumped into your prince with some brunette at Whole Foods. She just gave him an obnoxious smooch in the veggie isle. I'm so sorry…

I read the message twice more. At first, a weight forms in my chest; I can't believe that Rach has really just made this up to punish me for keeping my life news from her. However, when the revelation sinks in, my blood starts to boil. I know that she would never do something like this to me. I keep myself in check, though, because it might be one big misunderstanding.

Me: Are you positive it's him?

Rach: Are you kidding? Do you think I could mistake him for someone else?!

Nope, I say to myself.

My blood boils. When I picture some strange woman kissing the lips that are *mine*, I tense up; jealousy explodes in my chest and fills me to the brim. It's so strong that it hurts. I want to scream, throw things against the wall, maybe even punch something. I can't handle the rage that grows in me with every second.

I jump to my feet and stomp up and my room, trying to collect myself. Nagging thoughts race through my mind.

Didn't he admit last night that there was something special about me that other women didn't have? Besides, it would make sense to tell me if he had changed his object of desire so that I didn't have any expectations and hopes. Or maybe he's never considered me as one—it was just my stupid brain thinking that I mattered. The truth is that I never did. He can kiss and make out with whoever he wants, and I was just naïve enough to believe that there could be something between us.

Over the next hour, I grow more and more agitated. Tears

tremble on my eyelids, but I don't let even one of them run down my cheek. My head is bombarded with self-loathing thoughts.

Unable to stand the chaos going on in my mind, I simply leave the house to wander aimlessly around the neighborhood. I ignore Dorian's warnings not to be alone on the streets and risk coming across the unpredictable Rafael. In fact, that's exactly what I want—a one-on-one encounter with him.

Maybe I do it to make myself terrified and let another feeling overshadow the pain that spreads though me, or perhaps I just need to make sure that Dorian really doesn't care and won't come to save me. Or will he? Maybe I just want him to see me suffering and feel remorse. Feel *anything*… But for me, not another woman.

There's not a single hint of a vehicle on the road, nor anyone walking. A soothing breeze caresses my face while I stroll down the street. My brisk walk has calmed me down a tad and brought peace to my thoughts. My anger still swells within me, but it doesn't affect my logical thinking anymore.

I should go back home as soon as possible. No man is worth me risking my life for him.

I stall in the middle of the street. If Rafael's genuinely after me, sooner or later he'll turn up. I scan the surroundings, my heart steadily speeding up. In the distance, I spot a fuzzy point that resembles a human silhouette more and more with every step it takes in my direction. A chill goes down my spine. The closer the person gets, the more my courage diminishes. I want to curl up into a ball and wait for someone to rescue me.

Is it him?

Several more seconds go by, and I still can't move. Suddenly it gets unusually dark for this hour; an icy wind arises and whips my face. I'm frozen to the marrow of my bones. My legs refuse to take even a half a step. Perhaps it's fear that keeps me rooted to the ground. The figure is approaching me at a dangerously fast pace. An ominous raven's caw echoes somewhere behind me. Anxiety spurs through me, my pulse erratic.

It's not happening. It's just another hallucination.

The houses vanish. So do the trees, sidewalk, sky, and ground. I feel like I'm standing in a dark tunnel where I and the figure are the only things that remain. I'm pierced by a cold chill when I notice that the man walking toward me is clutching a shiny item in his hand. A knife.

Cover your eyes. It's my own voice coming from the back of my head. I do as I'm instructed, and squeeze my eyes closed. All of a sudden, the ground beneath me starts to sway back and forth. It's difficult to stand on it anymore.

What's happening? Where am I? Am I still on the street?

I strive to open my eyes again, but I'm unable to do so. My eyelids are too heavy. Panic spirals in me with every passing second.

A strong shove hits me somewhere around my chest. It can't be human hands; it feels more like a sudden gust of wind that's just pushed me in full force. It's so powerful that it sweeps me off my feet. I fall to the ground. It's not a painful crash, but hard enough to take my breath away. I cough in an attempt to get some air. Adrenaline surges through me. I know that he's coming. I can sense his presence.

I need to get out of here. Wherever *here* is.

CHAPTER TWENTY

I'M LYING DOWN COMFORTABLY on something soft. It must be a bed. My breath is calm and measured; I'm not panting anymore. I open my eyes.

It must've been a nightmare.

As soon as I regain visual acuity, I get my bearings. What is before my eyes is the last thing I expected to see. I've been here only once, but I remember every detail of this minimalistic bedroom. Dorian's sitting by the bed, surveying me from head to toe. Something sinister washes over his face. He looks like a volcano that is about to erupt. I pull myself up on the pillows and slowly regain the ability to think clearly.

I'm in big trouble.

"You're reckless and irresponsible," Dorian says, giving me a withering look. If looks could kill, I'd definitely be dead. "I don't think you realize the gravity of the situation."

"What am I even doing here?" I ask weakly.

"You went for a fucking stroll by yourself," he snarls. "You completely ignored all my warnings." I must have really pissed him off. "What the fuck came over you?!" His eyes are narrowed in anger.

I look down, unable to hold his eyes. "What happened? Why am I lying here? Were you there all along?"

"Not all along, but long enough." Dorian runs his fingers through his hair, his voice still aggravated. "I brought you here."

"Was all that real?"

"Yes—to you, not to me or anyone else."

I look back up and meet his glare again.

"Wasn't it only a hallucination then?"

"Yes and no."

His responses are so lame that they only contribute to an even bigger mess in my head.

"A voice," I recall. "It ordered me to cover my eyes." I can't recollect the rest that happened after I obeyed the voice. "How come he left me alone?"

"You're welcome," Dorian says, and places his cold palm on my forehead as if he wants to check whether I have a fever. He's still tense, but his features gradually relax as he speaks. "He put you under hypnosis. Whatever you saw was real solely in your head." He grabs my wrist and holds it to measure my pulse. "He manipulated your mind to lure you to him. Let's say that I got to you before it was too late."

"How come if, you didn't see what I saw?"

"I knew what he was doing to you. You looked like you were sleepwalking, unconsciously approaching the lion's maw of your own will." He pauses to count the number of my heartbeats, then continues, "You walked here with me, but you can't remember that because you were still under."

"I came here on foot?" My jaw drops open. "That's impossible, I don't—"

"Remember, I know," he finishes for me. "That's how powerful his hypnosis skills are. I'm surprised that you've already woken up."

"What time is it?" I ask, nervously looking around.

"It's almost nine."

"How did you know where I was?"

"It doesn't matter."

"It does matter. Everything matters, and you know that." I take a few deep breaths, frustrated. "For example, why can't I remember what happened after we kissed last night?" My voice grows firmer.

"You fell asleep. No big deal." He shrugs.

I feel like rolling my eyes, but refrain. "You know it's not true. People don't just fall asleep like that." I fall back onto the pillows and sigh heavily. "I've started to mingle dreams with reality, and it bothers me."

"Okay, let's say that I helped you just a bit."

I stiffen immediately, tossing him a perplexed gaze. "Who are you? You don't seem to be a normal person, Dorian. Everything that's been taking place since I met you… I don't know… It's just weird."

"I'm nothing that you'd want in your life." He lets go of my hand.

"Can I decide about that?"

I see a small vein throbbing in his temple. "Why can't you just let it go?"

"Because I need to know why I've been going crazy ever since I met you!" I jolt upright; frustration has finally taken over. "Why can't I stop thinking about you? Why do I suffer every minute when you're away from me? Why do I need you so badly?"

Dorian lurches to his feet and paces the room. His jaw is tight. He's fighting an inner battle on whether or not he should let me in. He wants to tell me, he downright *needs* to, but he can't.

"I'm your worst nightmare."

"What do you mean? Should I be scared of you or something?"

"Yes, you should." Dorian's face is taut, his voice serious.

We stare at each other across a sudden ringing silence.

"Do you want to hurt me?"

"No."

"What's the matter then?"

"If you're close with me, I'll have to." I spot concern in his eyes. Those are the eyes of a man who's tormented by something.

"Why do you *have* to?"

"Because it's in my nature. I can't change it."

I place my feet on the fuzzy carpet, and slowly get up from the bed. I desperately want to get closer to him and take away some of his troubles; help him win the inner battle of thoughts that confuses him so much. The muscles of his arms are tensed as he leans on the windowsill. Driven by the urge to soothe him, I clamp my hand on his shoulder. He's even more knotted than I thought.

"Who are you?" I eye him like he's some kind of an endangered species. "Or *what* are you, rather?"

"You'll learn soon, I promise."

"I'm not scared of you," I say with confidence, looking at the side of his face. "I never have been, and I never will. When you're around I feel something entirely different than fear."

"It's desire." He slowly swivels to face me. "You lust after me. You're hungry to be with me, want to have me only for yourself. You can't function without me near you." His voice is distant, his eyes unfathomable.

"How do you know all that?"

"Because that's what the process looks like."

"The *process*?"

"Yes, process—you heard me right."

Another moment of silence stretches between us.

"What's its purpose?"

"I can't tell you that."

Of course; what did I expect?

"I know that you're dating another woman." A living fire of jealousy consumes me from the inside when I bring her up. "Does she feel the same as I do?"

"Zara, don't do this." He shakes his head, unwilling to talk about her.

"Does she?"

Dorian knows I'm not going to drop the subject, so he finally responds. "Yes."

If there was a flicker of hope left in me, it's been doused. I'm just next on the list. There's nothing unique about me. I want to burst into tears, but I hold them back. Ultimately, Dorian never promised me anything, and I know that far too well. He's been honest from day one and made it clear from the very beginning that he didn't do relationships. I can't deny that. I'm the one who didn't take his words seriously and blindly believed that sooner or later I'd be able to change his mind. I need to face the facts and pull myself together.

"Did she ask you about these things too? Why she has hallucinations and why she feels the way she does?"

"None of them ever ask me any questions. They know the rules. Even if any of them tried to, they never got an answer."

Thinking about the brunette makes me heartsick, but trying to grasp the idea of even more women involved with Dorian is excruciating. I can't stand the thought of him driving them all crazy in the same way he does with me. The bitterness rises like bile into my mouth. My face, neck, and chest burn. I still hold my tears in check, but I'm not certain how long I'll be able to do so, so I take a few steps away from him. With my back facing Dorian, I'm less vulnerable; less weak. I don't want him to see me like this. It's not who I am.

"Then why do you answer me?"

"Because with you, it's different. I've already told you

that you affect me in an inexplicable way. I'm not indifferent toward you, as I have been with the others."

He's lying to me. Not only is he shameless, but he also thinks that I'm naïve. Which I guess in a way I am. I want to trust him. I want to believe that we have a special bond.

"If that's true, then why the hell do you keep insisting that you can't be with me and date some brunette who, I'm sure, you've already slept with?" I blurt out. My exasperation goes through the roof.

He sneaks up to me almost soundlessly. I shriek as he suddenly spins me around to face him. His fingers curl around my shoulders.

"I can't be any different." Despair spreads over his face. Time is suspended for that brief moment as we stand, staring at each other.

"Why? Because that's your nature? Is that your excuse?" I ask, my voice filled with anguish. I swallow hard and bite back my tears yet again. "Do those women also have something that you want to take away from them? That's why you deal with them—I mean us—because we have something that you desire?"

"Yes."

"Great. Don't count on me." I try to shy away from him, but he holds me too tight.

"It's not up to you anymore."

"Who is it up to, then?" I snarl.

Tense silence fills the room once more. A hot wave of resentment and chagrin sweeps over me, but it can't drown out my other feelings. Something chemical attracts me to Dorian. It was just a tiny spark when I first met him, but over time it's burst into flames, raging out of control. He's a drug that I *need* to function. I know that I'll never be able to erase him from my life of my own free will.

"It depends on you," I answer myself. "You're the one who decides when it's over." I recall his words after the second time we slept together, finally coming to realize that they make more sense than I thought. None of us would be able to finish a relationship with Dorian willingly. Each of us lusts after him more and more every day.

Dorian nods. His grip goes slack, but I don't pull away this time.

"What do you want from me?" My voice trembles. "Take it right now and leave me alone!"

"You're giving up so easily. You told me you had an infinite amount of willpower. I'm disappointed in you." He sounds genuinely frustrated.

"I hope you realize that you're not the only one in this room who's let down," I sputter. "The worst is that I'm most disappointed in myself."

"Why is that?"

"Because I still want to be yours!" I say, overpowered by a welter of emotions. "I want you to possess me and sink into my soul. And it drives me crazy!"

I drop my head into my hands. If it was up to me, I would extract all those desires from my mind and my heart, but as Dorian mentioned, I can't control them anymore. I finally know the kind of desire Dorian described to me that rainy evening when we met on his porch — a constantly unsatisfied, never-ending thirst for him.

"What do you feel for us?" I raise my eyes, which collide with his.

"I feel nothing for *them*. No attachment, no caring, no sympathy, no love."

His words cut through me like a knife. I strive to keep composed, but hot tears sting my eyes again, this time with double force.

He wipes a stray tear from my cheek and brushes his fingers across my skin. "Don't be upset. You're not like them. I just don't know what you are to me yet."

I sigh. "It's hard to believe that you're not deceiving me right now."

"I know. I don't blame you. I don't understand what's been going on either. What I do know, though, is that I want to protect you. Not harm you." He studies my face in silence. "But it's not how the process works."

"Who cares about some stupid process? What the hell does that even mean? Why do you need to have all these secrets?" I say with a moan of distress. "I guess you also can't explain to me what it is in you that has such a profound effect on me? Why does it mess with my brain to such a degree?"

"That's another question that I can't answer."

I slightly shake my head, disturbed by the amount of secrets that can't be revealed. "Then tell me at least whether

Rafael has been after all of us or just me."

"He's only been interested in you."

Fantastic; someone apparently thinks I'm unique. But why does it have to be some freak who always carries a knife?

"Why me?"

"I told you, he thinks you're someone else."

I'm smart enough to put all the dots together after all I've been told. It doesn't take a genius to figure out who Rafael thinks I am.

"He thinks I'm someone like you are. Whatever you are. But why? Why does he think that I'm… umm… that?" It's hard to verbalize my question.

"That's a good question. I don't have an answer, though. I've been trying to figure it out myself."

"Let him get me. Let him do whatever he wants."

"Are you deaf?" His expression darkens, and his voice rises with determination. "Haven't you heard me say multiple times that you somehow matter?"

"No! Actions speak louder than words, and all you've been doing is—"

He doesn't let me finish. Without any warning, he yanks me up close and crushes my mouth with his lips. My mind shuts down; all I can do right now is give myself over to the delightful feel of his voracious kiss. I'm desperate for it. I wrap my arms around his neck and cling on to him tightly. He devours my body with his hands, arousing me to the point of dizzying torment. I've been caught in his trap and I don't want to be released. He backs us up and pins me to the wall, causing a flame of lust to erupt somewhere in my abdomen. We both shrug out of our shirts and toss them to the floor, unable to wait any longer for our burning hot bodies to connect again.

The cool metal of his pendant touches the skin on my chest. The moment I grab it with the intention of taking it off him, Dorian pulls away and tears it out from my hand.

"Don't ever do that," he orders.

I instantly go rigid. I completely forgot he never takes it off. I feel like I just violated some sacred object by touching it. When I examine the pendant, it seems to me that the engraved number on it has changed. I'm sure it used to be 2001, but now it definitely says 2002.

"How many pendants do you have, Dorian?" I ask, still panting from our passionate kiss.

"Only one. Why?"

"You're lying. Last time it showed a different number."

He doesn't respond right away. Instead, he grabs the shirt that a minute ago he threw on the floor in a rush and puts it back on, hiding the pendant beneath the fabric. I'm about to protest when the door opens with a slam. Rita storms inside without knocking. Her face is stark white with terror. Seeing me without my shirt on only in a red bra makes her falter, but she doesn't withdraw or apologize, simply getting to the point: "Dorian, they're downstairs."

"*Today?!* They were supposed to come next week!" Dorian's eyes open wide; he's alert. "Did you let them in?"

"No, they're waiting outside."

"Who did they send this time?" His gaze sparkles with indignation.

"Damien, Raven, and..." She gulps. "Blair."

"Fuck!" He doesn't hide his fury. Rita stares at him mutely, as if she's waiting for his decision.

Dorian transfers his eyes to me. There's something in his face that I've never seen before. Could he be nervous?

"We need to hide Zara; we gotta be quick." He tosses me my shirt. "They can't find her here."

CHAPTER TWENTY-ONE

HIDE?! I sincerely hope I have misheard this. "Why do you have to hide me?" The Hatches' reactions imply that the situation is serious, but I can't figure out why it would be.

Dorian isn't eager to straighten it out for me. Instead, he grasps my wrist and pulls me firmly toward him. He cups my cheeks, drawing my face closer to make sure he has my undivided attention. "There's no time for explanations. You have to go with me now without asking any questions, understood?"

I nod, and obediently let him pull me through the room.

"Where are you thinking of hiding her? They'll sniff her out anywhere, especially Blair." Rita's voice raises, matching her escalating fear. "We better tell them up front that she's here."

Dorian stops abruptly and, without letting go of my hand, pivots to face Rita. His eyes are bright with rage. "Over my dead body." Then he clutches my wrist so hard that I flinch, and commands, "Don't you dare mention anything about her."

Rita's hands shake. Fear rises behind her eyes. "Are you out of your mind? We'll be in trouble because of her!" she whispers frantically.

"We will indeed, if you don't stop freaking out. Dread is written all over your face; even the dumbest idiot would figure out that something's wrong, looking at you." I haven't seen this rude version of Dorian before, but it's somehow satisfying to witness him finally speaking up and challenging her panicky behavior.

They continue this discussion, ignoring the fact that I'm standing right next to them and listening to their heated exchange, completely in the dark about what's going on. *Who are the people waiting to be let inside, and why do Dorian and Rita have to hide me from them? Are they dangerous?*

"Can anybody tell me what's happening?" I butt in indignantly.

"Dorian, I'm begging you." Rita disregards my request. "Be reasonable. It's just another girl, for God's sake…"

Dorian bites his lips, obviously furiously thinking about something.

"I have an idea." He sprints to the closet and rummages through it, scattering his clothes over the floor. "Put these on," he says, and slings me two pieces of his clothing.

"Why?" I regard the clothes, baffled.

"Now!" he orders; his voice is menacing. "If you want to make it through this alive, be a good girl and put those on immediately!"

Stunned, I don't ask any further questions. I don't even care that they're both staring at me while I'm changing. I quickly throw on the sweatshirt he was wearing when I met him, along with gray sweatpants. Dorian takes my clothes and hands them to Rita.

"Take these down to the basement. Don't forget to close the door behind you."

"Okay, this is cunning," Rita says. "Even if they sniff her out, we can direct them to the basement and say that these belong to one of them. Maybe it will work out." She seems to have calmed down, which doesn't make any sense to me.

I open my mouth to ask again what the whole masquerade is about, but bite my tongue because I can anticipate their reaction. They'll both respond that there's no time for explanations.

"Let them in only when you're back from the basement, not before you go down. Tell them you were in the shower when they appeared. I'll be there soon. Copy?" says Dorian. Rita nods. "We're going to the attic."

We split in the corridor. Rita scampers down, whereas we trot upstairs. Dorian holds me tight as we climb the steps, imposing such a fast pace that I can barely keep up. I almost stumble twice as we take two steps at a time. When we reach the attic, and he pushes me through the door, I'm panting to catch my breath. The stale air doesn't help me breathe.

"Zara," he says as he grabs my face in his hands again and pulls it close to his, preventing me from looking anywhere other than into his eyes, "under no circumstances should you go out of this room or take off my clothes. Stay quiet."

"Can I at least breathe?"

Dorian scolds me with a stern look. "Those guys downstairs are something far worse than a nightmare."

"What will happen if they find me?"

"They won't!" he says, loud and clear, as if he is trying not so much to convince me as himself.

"Are you afraid?"

Dorian takes a breath to answer, but he restrains himself at the last second. He only runs his thumb along my lips and then assures me that everything will be okay. He closes the door behind him.

I'm left by myself in the dark. Sitting in the corner on the cold floor, I bring my knees up to my chest. I can hear the wind beating against the house. This spooky attic frightens me way more than those strangers, who must be inside the house by now. The hum of human voices reaches my ears from below. I can't understand what is being said because two floors separate us, but I can tell that several people have indeed paid the Hatches a visit.

Dorian's reaction to their arrival makes me assume that they must be really sinister. I should be scared to death, but I'm not. Perhaps that's because I have no idea what they are capable of, as nobody has explained anything to me. The only thing I got was Dorian telling me that if I wanted to live through the night then I should stay quiet.

Are they murderers? I shiver at the thought, but I'm also oddly intrigued. I want to know what's happening downstairs, but at the same time I don't want to push my luck.

Sitting against the wall, I tilt my head back and breathe out. Dorian's clothes emanate his scent to the extent that when I close my eyes, I could swear that he's sitting next to me. My mind is congested with questions.

The time drags frustratingly. Waiting always makes every single minute pass at least twice as long as normally, and I have nothing to keep me occupied. I glance at the old, rickety couch across the attic, some dusty picture frames, and an old vacuum. *Did they belong to Mrs. McConelly?* I begin to wonder whether that poor old lady actually died a natural death or whether she somehow got tangled up in whatever is going on with the Hatches. I'm still haunted by the question of what their secret plan is and whether I have been included in it all along.

Whoever the uninvited guests are, they must be associated with the secret, somehow. Most likely they're discussing its details right now. It even crosses my mind that maybe *they're* the ones who want something from me, and Dorian's only their minion whose mission is to obtain it from me. Unfortunately, I have upset their applecart as Dorian unexpectedly developed some peculiar feelings for me, and now he wants to protect me from them.

Perhaps they know my name, who I am, and what I do. That's why I've been put here in the attic. If they found me, they'd deprive me of whatever they desire so badly. But wait… I practically live in the same house as the Hutches, so it wouldn't have been a problem to knock on my door this evening and handle things with me directly.

I'm so done with living in a state of constant confusion, experiencing more and more strange anomalies taking place around me, that I decide to take my chances and sneak downstairs. I'm encouraged by the fact that I've already managed twice to go unnoticed while eavesdropping on Dorian's conversation with Rita. There's much more at stake this time, but the risk is worth taking. I'm willing to do anything to find out what's been happening right under my nose. I might not have such a golden opportunity ever again.

Since Dorian doesn't want to let me into his world of secrets, I'll have to invite myself.

I creep soundlessly out of the attic. My heart speeds up as I tiptoe down the first set of stairs. When I reach the second floor, I glance over my shoulder and swallow hard. *I can still go back.* The awareness that Dorian told me not to leave the attic under *any* circumstances makes my stomach churn. I have a second to make my final decision, but the voices coming from downstairs encourage me to keep going.

I plaster myself to the wall and stalk barefoot down the hall, shrouded in darkness. I feel like I'm walking towards a monster's cave. Fighting a shudder, I slowly approach the next staircase, which leads to the first floor. I stall at the top of it. The voices haven't eased off, which assures me that none of the strangers have discovered my sudden presence.

Standing here, so close to them, a surge of adrenaline hits

my bloodstream. It's the fear of the unknown. I realize I'm trembling, and my heart is pounding so loud that I can almost hear it. I have no idea what would happen if any of them found out that I'm shamelessly listening to the course of their conversation. Even Dorian's warnings haven't prevented me from coming all the way here. My hunger for the truth has won over common sense.

I clutch the polished banister with my shaking hands and lean forward, trying to find out what they look like, but I'm too far away to see anything. I have to be satisfied with just eavesdropping, so I strain to listen.

"We have exactly a half," a female voice says. "Aidan and Shahla found onyx last week. They told me that Michelle Elliot whimpered like a dog when she was reconciling her fate." The speaker howls with monstrous laughter that gives me chills.

"Without this little jewel she wasn't that brave anymore." This time it's a man's voice, equally entertained by the topic. "Aidan told me everything with details. I wish it had been me who ripped her apart."

His blood-chilling statement reminds me of the words that I've heard in my dreams many times: *I will tear it to pieces. I will rip it apart.*

Does the voice that I hear belong to this man? But that's insane. I'd never seen or heard him before I began dreaming of the creepy man. What does all this even mean? Is it some slang between them that I don't understand?

"How about you? Any tracks?" the woman asks.

"We thought so, but it was a red herring." That's Dorian's voice. He's unshaken.

"Rovenna won't be pleased," the man says. "She counts on you, Dorian."

"You don't have to remind me. I know that very well."

"We gotta hurry; those hunters think they're smart enough to play games with us," the woman says angrily.

Deafening silence spreads through the room. My skin instantly prickles with goosebumps. *They've realized I'm here!* I take a panicked step back, but then a new voice speaks up.

"Dorian, the moment I met you, I knew right away you would be the greatest of them all." The deep, velvety voice belongs to a woman. Her accent would suggest that she's either British or Australian. "I was the one who noticed potential in you, regardless of the fact that you were not one of us back in the day. You seemed to be predestined for this role." She goes silent for a few seconds, and I hear footsteps across the room. She must be moving, but the echo of her steps suggests that she's going the opposite direction from the stairs; I'm safe. "I simply do not understand why this"—she must've pointed to whatever she means, as she pauses for a short moment again—"shows that you have been losing your grip, honey. Two thousand and two—only two more than the last time? What has been going on with you? Are you hiding something from us?"

She must mean the pendant on Dorian's neck. The urge to take a peek at what's going on down there is hard to resist.

Listening isn't enough anymore; I want to know what the owners of all those voices look like. Are they as stunning as Dorian and Rita? Or are they a bunch of monsters?

My curiosity draws me forward. I crouch, but in vain. They are out of my sight. There's no other way; to be able to catch a glimpse of them, I have to descend at least a few steps. My pulse pounds in my ears, but I do it anyway. As quiet as a mouse, I perch on the third top step. I put my hand over my mouth to subdue the sound of my breathing. I don't have the best view, but at least I can see some part of the scene taking place below me.

On the couch, I spot Rita, who hasn't spoken up even once so far. Her knees are pressed tightly together, her palms down on her knees. She looks like she has swallowed a stick and now is sitting unnaturally straight. I can tell she isn't enjoying this visit whatsoever. Beside her, I spot a woman. Her dark complexion, high cheekbones, and almond-shaped eyes make me guess that she has some Native American ancestry. Over them stands a blonde-haired man, not too much taller than Dorian, with a strong, square jaw and wide forehead.

I transfer my eyes to the window, where I see Dorian who, unlike Rita, seems very confident. He's leaning against the windowsill with his legs and arms crossed. His face doesn't express any emotion at all. My throat tightens at the sight of him.

My attention is drawn to the last person in the room. She's very different from the other woman, far more sensual and feminine. Her body's slender, her hips slim. Rich, bright burgundy curls cap her head. Even from afar, I'm able to see her necklace; it's different from the ones Dorian and Rita wear. It's a silver snake, coiled around something that looks like an eye.

There's something about each of these people that makes them feel like a strange work of art. They look like human beings, but there's one feature that they all share, which makes adrenaline flood my system — their eyes, completely black. From my perspective, I'm unable to tell the pupil from the iris apart. No normal person has such unnaturally dark eyes.

The woman with the characteristic accent is standing barely a foot from Dorian, holding his pendant in her small hand. Their proximity makes my cheeks flush. I clench my hands into fists and press my lips flat.

"I'm not hiding anything; I'm just focused on a different task," Dorian says to her. "As you remember, I have something to find here."

"Dorian, Dorian, Dorian." She smirks, shaking her head and yanking him closer by the pendant. Their faces are maybe three inches apart. "You are lucky that you are mine. Otherwise, I would not accept such an excuse." She leans in even closer, rubbing her cheek against his. She lowers her voice, but everyone can hear her anyway. "You must try harder, my love. Next time I pay you a visit, I hope you will have better news for me." She pulls away abruptly and releases him from her grip. "Today, I am genuinely disappointed. *She* is not the best at this game," the woman says, motioning to Rita, who twitches with fear, "and she never has been, but you?"

Reaching into her dress pocket, the woman takes out something resembling a black stone. She floats to the table in front of the couch and places it there. "I am leaving this with you until my next visit. They warm up when another one is nearby. Bear that in mind."

She ambles through the living room back and forth. Everyone's waiting for what she's going to say next. She suddenly comes to a halt and slowly inhales the air deep into her lungs.

"Now. Whose scent is that?" My heart sinks. "Karla Whitaker? Vanessa Prynn? Leslie Dean?"

"What's the difference, Blair?" Dorian asks, remaining calm.

"No difference; just curiosity." She shrugs. "Is she in this house? Does she know what awaits her yet? Or does she still live in blissful unawareness of what is yet to come?" She laughs like a maniac. Her high-pitched voice echoes through the whole house, seeming to make the walls vibrate.

I'm petrified when the woman turns around and briskly marches toward the stairs where I'm perched. My whole body stiffens, but I manage to take two steps back. My heart races with adrenaline. I'm so stupid; I never considered having a plan B that would answer what I would do if they decided to come upstairs.

A sudden burning sensation sears through my chest. I

double up, unable to stand straight. It increases with every step Blair takes toward me. It radiates to my limbs. My blood is on fire! Right before she makes it to the bottom of the stairs, I manage to duck into the corridor. My legs feel wobbly; I hit the wall with my back.

"Ha-ha," she cackles, "is anybody up there? I see you! You cannot hide!"

I shake, her voice chilling me to the bone. I'm unable to keep backpedaling; the only thing I can do right now is writhe. It's over. She's noticed me and will drag me down there to hurt, maybe kill. I hope Dorian's frosty look will murder me first.

"I am joking; stop looking at me like that, Ethan. I do not like this house. Too many stairs. I hope that you two will move out soon. This neighborhood is so dull."

She was kidding. Sudden relief washes over me. I seem to have made it.

She didn't amuse me whatsoever. She's as bad at telling jokes as she is at using contractions. Her footsteps edge away from my hideout, but I'm unable to take a sigh of relief; I struggle to breathe, my lungs contracting. My birthmark throbs with pain. I quietly fall to my knees and then to all fours. I take a couple of deep breaths, trying to collect myself. Soothing coolness gradually fills my veins. My heart calms down slightly.

"It's a waste of time, Blair," the blonde man says. "They have nothing for us."

"Because they are slacking!" Blair cries out. She acts

like she's insane. First she snickers, and a minute later her monster laugh is replaced by a shriek at full tilt. Not to mention that she keeps prowling the living room like she's obsessed with searching for something. "We have no time! Rovenna wants to have twelve gems before the next new moon. If she does not have them, she will be very *angry*." She emphasizes the last word to get her point across.

"I can't speed up anything," Dorian says flatly. "You know that it's not exactly child's play."

"Sweetheart, anyone can say that but you." Blair's voice is stable again. "You are a master of deception, and you always take whatever you want. You are my masterpiece; do not forget it."

Although I'm much better, and the debilitating sensation that randomly came over me is almost gone, my limbs still tremble. My body feels tremendously heavy. It's hard for me to hold my weight up, so I drop weakly to the carpet. I couldn't return to the attic even if I wanted to.

Lying flat, I don't see as much as I did before, but I can still see Rita and the other woman. The rest of them are out of my sight.

"Enough; we're leaving," the brunette says. "I'm so done with listening to this bullshit and sitting beside this mute idiot."

"Rita," Blair says, her attention diverted from Dorian, "frankly speaking, I have not even noticed your presence here today. Is everything okay? You are even more quiet than usual." She comes up to Rita from behind and slowly runs her fingers through Rita's black, shiny hair. She grasps a thick bunch and pulls it firmly so that Rita's head violently arches back. Blair leans forward. She comes so close to Rita's face that it seems as if she's going to kiss her. "Do you want to quit? Leave our ranks? You know what the consequences are, right?"

"Leave her alone." Dorian's stern voice.

"Well, well, well. What do we have here?" Blair lets go of Rita. Her smirk has been wiped off her face. She veers right and scutters toward him, disappearing from my view. My heart rate triples. "Be careful; I might get jealous." Blair pauses. "You prefer me to take care of you, then? And leave your little cousin, as you call her, alone?" Silence rolls in. "Apparently, those pathetic few hundred pieces that you have left are still too many. I can take away half of them right now."

"NO!" Rita finally, and spectacularly, reminds them all of her existence. She even gets up from the couch, so determined is she to protest. "Take mine!"

"Lovely."

I'm not certain what has just happened, but the moment Blair snaps her fingers, Rita goes limp and collapses to the floor as though someone has deprived her of the use of her muscles. Her face, naturally pale, now has the color of a china doll. She doesn't move.

"You're sick," Dorian says, but he doesn't move.

"I never claimed otherwise. Very well," Blair says, clapping her hands several times, "our gorgeous Rita will remain unconscious for a while, so I guess the party is over. Let's go, my dear companions."

"Finally." The other woman lets out a sigh of relief.

"I expect that next time you will have more to show me," Blair says. "I will see you soon, baby. I miss you already." The sound of an obnoxious smack comes to my ears.

Did she just kiss him? A stab of jealousy pierces my chest. That bitch has some nerve. After everything she's done, she has the audacity to kiss Dorian goodbye. Why would she even do that?

She says one last thing.

"Remember, you will always be mine. I will never share."

When the door slams closed behind them, it takes a good while before what I have just witnessed sinks in. I'm relieved that those lunatics have left the house, but simultaneously my head spins in confusion. I close my eyes, trying to collect my thoughts. The majority of what was said doesn't make any sense to me.

What 'pieces' did she mean? Why would that blonde man want to rip someone apart? What is Dorian supposed to find?

Those and dozens of other questions roll around my mind. It was naïve of me to believe that eavesdropping would give me any answers. My mind races, searching for the answers so intently that I don't even realize when a pair of legs appears a few inches from my face. It's Dorian, who just made it to the top of the stairs. An unpleasant tingling swings across my neck. I've just been caught red-handed.

"I guess I'm in troub—"

Before I finish pronouncing the last word, he pulls me up by the sweatshirt I'm wearing and stands me at his eye level in one swift movement. He's panting in fury. All of his muscles are tensed, and the blue color of his irises is all gone; they're entirely black, like the eyes of the strangers. He's ready to attack his prey — me.

I hold my breath. For the first time, I'm scared of Dorian. My whole being is whispering to me that I'm in danger, especially the small spot on my chest, which starts pulsating.

"Is that who you really are? What you really are?" I ask, my mouth dry.

Dorian jerks me forcefully by the arm. The discomfort ripples through my shoulder socket, but I don't make even a single sound. I let him drag me down and walk me through the living room. We go past Rita, who's now deadly stiff, lying on the couch. A stony expression is engraved on her face. She seems not to breathe.

"Is she… dead?" I whisper.

"Stand here," Dorian orders me, letting go of my hand. He seizes the black stone that is sitting on the coffee table, and then grabs it with one swift motion. "It's hot," he announces, squeezing it in his palm. "Now, go to the kitchen." I follow his instructions and edge to the kitchen, even though I have no idea what he's doing. "It's warm now. Move upstairs, but stand exactly where you were located while watching us."

Without a word of objection, I stride upstairs. I stop on

the step where I spent the most time.

"Lukewarm," he says to himself, just loudly enough for me to hear. "She must've felt the same when she was holding it. That's how she knew that another gem was close. I bet she thought we were deliberately lying to her," he says to himself.

I slowly descend the steps, still a bit shaken by his sudden outburst, and stand a few feet away from him. "Dorian, can you explain to me what's going on?"

Dorian inhales deeply. His eyes regain the blue shade. He's himself again. "By your stupidity you've jeopardized our safety and put us in incredible danger. Blair could feel you. She was aware that we were hiding someone in this house."

"Didn't you just say she thought it was another gem that you were hiding, not a person?"

"It doesn't matter now. A lie is a lie."

"But they left you alone, regardless. The danger has passed, hasn't it?"

"No. I'm afraid that the real danger has only just begun."

He lifts Rita up in his arms, tramps past me, and carries her upstairs without looking at me even once.

I screwed up big-time.

CHAPTER TWENTY-TWO

IT'S NEARLY MIDNIGHT. I bounce my knees, waiting for Dorian, who still hasn't come back down. Although millions of thoughts rush through my head, I don't dare go upstairs and demand explanations. It's the last thing I'm eager to do. I can't even take a step toward the stairs. The second floor is a forbidden zone for me right now.

Cynthia has sent me about ten messages asking where I am. It's way past my curfew. I decide not to lie, but not to tell the truth either, so I only respond that I'll be home soon. Nonetheless, when the longer hand of my watch reaches twelve, I can't wait any longer and choose to return home. The desire to sneak upstairs is overwhelming, but I need to suppress it. Instead, I leave a note written on a piece of napkin:

Dorian, I'm begging you, don't let me live in ignorance any longer. It only makes things more complicated. I need to know the truth, even the worst. I'm ready. Zara

* * *

The light in my aunt's room is turned off, but the kitchen lamp is still on. I didn't expect Cynthia to go to bed while I was out. I won't be able to avoid having a conversation with her no matter which door I use to enter the house, so, unwilling to play games, I use the front door and lumber into the kitchen.

"Good evening," she greets me, still browsing the newspaper she's holding in her hands. "What kept you so long this time, huh? Chatting with Rach? Movie theater with Charlie? And why are you wearing a man's clothes?" She looks at me from across the table.

The tumbling emotions caused by recent events have completely obscured my ability to think. I forgot that I was still wearing Dorian's clothes. There's no point in deceiving her anymore. The only way to make things right is to tell her what I should've done long ago.

I plod to the table as if I wanted to extend the moment of the confrontation. She's clicking her fingernails against the table, waiting for me to explain myself. I pull in a deep breath and spill the beans.

"These are Dorian Hatch's clothes. I've been… dating him. I was at his place all this time."

"Dorian Hatch?" Her eyes widen. "Do you mean our new neighbor next door?"

"Him, yes."

"Since when? And why on earth are you dressed in his

clothes?" She doesn't raise her voice, but she doesn't need to do so for me to know that she's not happy. She takes off her glasses to be able to see me better.

"Since about two weeks ago. And these clothes—mine were wet because… I had to wash them… I spilled juice all over me. Actually, I dropped a whole jar, and everything on me was sticky and dirty." I look down at my hands; they're shaking. I'm not certain if it's because of the tension wearing off after the incident with the strange guests or, quite the opposite, the pressure rising under my aunt's grilling.

"Is he the person who's been giving you drugs?"

I squint. "What? No! I never took any drugs. That part is on you."

"Or rather on your system's reaction to them. Your memory is short." She puts away the newspaper and places her glasses on it. "Tomorrow I'm going to talk with Hatch and will demand he leave you alone. I doubt you'll break up with him yourself."

I shake my head in frustration. I finally gathered enough courage to tell her the truth, and this is how she's treating me. She's so confident that what she's going to do is right she doesn't even take my feelings into account. She just throws her commands at me.

"Can you not stick your two cents where they don't belong?" I ask, irritated.

"No. Your mother would expect me to do this."

"How can you know what she'd like you to do?" I frown. "Maybe she wouldn't even care!"

"Well, unlike you, I did speak with her about you, and I know for a fact that she'd like to defend you at any cost—so please stop being ridiculous, young lady!" Cynthia's voice roughens and her jaw tightens.

"Defend me from what?"

"From everybody! You were the apple of her eye. She wouldn't let some drug addict load you with drugs."

"What are you talking about?" My blood starts to boil. The only ridiculous person in this room is her. "I regret telling you the truth. I should have kept it to myself. I'm going upstairs, and you mustn't even dare to get involved in this." I swiftly stand up, unable to continue this conversation.

"I have every intention of getting involved," she says before I clear the door.

"It won't help."

"You'll be surprised."

"Blah, blah, blah," I mutter. Ordinarily, this comment would earn me a huge reprimand. Now, however, Cynthia doesn't even tell me off. Perhaps she's just so tired of this situation that she'll let me get away with such disrespect.

I lock my bedroom door and throw myself on the bed. I need to collect my thoughts, which are disturbed by Maddie's constant chattering from the other side of the wall. She must be having a Skype conversation with one of her besties, since she bursts out laughing obnoxiously every couple of minutes.

I can't stop pondering over the surreal scene I witnessed. I had a hunch that something peculiar was going on right under my nose from the moment when my chest started bothering me for the first time, weeks ago. It usually acts up when Dorian's around.

I shiver at the memory of his face when he found me on the second floor. He looked so dreadful, strange and inhuman. After all, our eyes are said to be the windows of our souls, but I couldn't see anything in his then. Those black eyes were completely empty. Maybe I'm crazy to still interact with him out of my own free will after he told me that he had the intention of hurting me. I should run away from him, but he has me in the palm of his hand by having made me addicted to him. It's happening. I got hooked like a fish, and now it's up to Dorian when I'll be pulled out of the water, and whether I'll be set free again or left to suffocate.

* * *

I dash through the woods again. Surprisingly, I recognize these curved paths, wind-damaged trees leaning drunkenly against each other, and even the earthy smell of decomposing leaves. I've been here before. I swallow the sharp cold air while winding through the thicket. Something is different this time. I jerk to a halt. Sweat trails down my back. I hear the sounds of ravens approaching; an entire murder flies over my head, above the trees crowns, and forms a pitch-black cloud of wings.

Something flits behind me, like a wild animal. I

automatically wheel around, almost losing my balance. I hear it again, but this time on the other side. I shriek and look over my shoulder. I still can't see anything. Something slides against my calf. I spring back and look down. The thick mist has enveloped my ankles so that I can't see the ground. Whenever I think I know where the thing is, it moves somewhere else. Struggling to get away from it, I lose my balance and fall on the ground.

I crawl to the nearby tree, lean against the trunk and quickly get up, using it as back support. I can't lie down defenseless; I need to stay on my feet, scan the area regardless of the limited visibility.

YOU'RE MINE...

My ears are filled with a male voice. I glance left and right, but there's no one next to me. I see only the thick mist swirling around me.

I WILL TEAR IT TO PIECES. I WILL RIP IT APART.

My legs get wobbly; my hands sweat.

Who are you? I ask, but my voice doesn't come out of my throat. *Who are you*?

I finally notice him, far away, leaning against a tree.

ZARA...

Although he's standing at least fifty yards away from me, I can clearly hear his voice whispering to me. It sounds familiar; I've heard it before. All of a sudden, I feel something moving on my body, like an invisible snake coiling around me. It slowly goes up, tightly squirming around my ankles, calves, thighs, stomach, chest. I'm trapped. Cold hands are wrapping around my throat, squeezing gently. The grip becomes stronger.

YOU BELONG TO ME…

The invisible, freezing hands squeeze my neck even more tightly. The obscure man in the distance remains unfazed, with his eyes fixed on me.

Do you want me dead?! I cry in my head.

When I begin losing my breath, I hear a scream coming out of the darkness. It's a feminine voice, which rips through the air and echoes from the trees. She's alternately sobbing and screaming bloodcurdlingly. She must be suffering some excruciating torture. I want to help her, but in my situation, I need to be rescued myself.

Those hands are choking the life out of me. The grip is too tight.

Let me go!

I cough, kick, and try to yank away, but I'm tied to the tree. It's too late.

RUN AWAY IF YOU WANT TO SAVE YOUR LIFE, the man's voice tells me, and I'm suddenly freed from the deadly grip.

* * *

I wake up screaming bloody murder. My forehead is covered in cold sweat. I pant, rubbing my neck. My chest feels tight and uncomfortable. I raise myself up on my elbows.

"It was just a nightmare. Just a bad dream," I say out loud. *But it was so unbelievably realistic. I really felt the muddy ground under my soles and the cold air stabbing my lungs; I even remember pine needles scratching my arms. And the female voice... I really heard it. It wasn't just a dream. She was going through hell, and it was not my imagination.*

It's almost five-thirty in the morning. There's no point in trying to fall back asleep because I have to get up soon anyway. Apparently, I didn't wake anyone up with my scream because the hallway is barren. I tiptoe downstairs to make some coffee. The house is blissfully silent at this time. I know by heart the usual morning rituals of Maddie and Cynthia.

The former sets her alarm at six-thirty, then spends at least half an hour readying herself. When she feels that she can finally present herself decently, she comes down for breakfast, which I'd rather call a morning snack. My aunt is up at six-fifteen. She begins every day with a cup of energizing black coffee.

Since I woke up so early, I feel like life has slowed down a tad and I can actually enjoy it instead of rushing at a breakneck speed to leave the house. Sipping my delicious coffee, I rest my head on the back of the chair and sigh at the thought that here comes another day, over the course of which I'll be immersed in Dorian's world of questions, presumptions, and considerations. At the same time I'll be forced to live in my normal reality—dealing with professors at the university, clients at Walgreens, and probably Rach, who will try to make me explain to her who the mysterious brunette was. I feel like going back to bed when I realize all this.

I take another sip of coffee, which pours in a warm stream down my throat. That's exactly what I need—caffeine. On the table by me sits a folded newspaper, which I'm guessing is the same one that Cynthia was reading last night when I came home. The whole front page displays the face of a girl that looks familiar. Nevertheless, even though I force my brain cells to an intense effort, I can't recall who she is. I transfer my eyes to the headline. *BREAKING NEWS: Another woman reported missing.* It's continued below in smaller letters: *Local girl still missing after 5 days.*

Right away, I open the newspaper and look for the article to learn some more about the case. It's not hard to find it; four pages are devoted to the missing girl. The same face that was looking at me from the front page is inside the newspaper, surrounded by a few more pictures. These are all photos from a family album. In one of them the girl is clad in a black graduation gown, holding a diploma, grinning. In another one she stands among a bunch of girls with a colorful drink, making a silly face at the camera. I'm sure I've seen her somewhere before. Maybe at the university? Or at Walgreens? With every sentence of the article I read, my eyes widen.

"The state Police in Salem are investigating the disappearance of twenty-eight-year-old Leslie Dean. The

desperate mother of the girl, Alexandra Dean, reports that Leslie was last seen on Thursday evening, May 1st. 'It's totally unlike Leslie to go so long without any contact,' says Gregory Dean, the father of the missing girl. Leslie's family and friends are devastated. According to them, Leslie was not involved in any conflicts and did not belong to any group whose members might have had something to do with her disappearance. 'She's a responsible and lovely girl who's never been interested in any sort of suspicious substances, groupings and places,' adds Yvette Fisher, Leslie's sister. The family and friends have united in a search for the missing girl. Anyone with information regarding Leslie Dean's whereabouts is asked to call state police…"

I skip this part and continue reading two lines below.

"Due to the fact that the number of missing people has recently significantly increased in the Salem area, the state police advise to obey the basic safety rules, i.e., not leaving the place of residence alone after 10 p.m., not getting involved in a discussion with strangers who…"

I give up further reading. I'm familiar with the safety rules far too well from when they were all hammered into us at high school. Whoever wrote this article is right—more and more women are going missing in Salem. *I bet that poor Leslie was Rafael's victim. It must've been him who had a hand in this and all the previous disappearances.*

It suddenly occurs to me that Dorian's plan might be aimed at Rafael's elimination. *Maybe they moved here to catch him and get rid of him? It would make perfect sense.*

I push the newspaper aside. Hearing footsteps on the stairs, I grab my mug with both hands to give the impression that drinking it is all I've been doing. After the heated discussion with Cynthia about Dorian, I want to avoid getting involved in any sort of conversation with her again for a while. This is disturbing; not too long ago I loved gossiping with her, keeping her up to date with my current life, and exchanging the latest news. I'm aware that it's my fault that everything's changed. I destroyed our good relationship.

We walk past each other as I leave the kitchen, exchanging no more than "Good morning" and "Have a nice day" as an act of courtesy. I notice that my aunt's eyes almost pop out when she sees me up so early, but she restrains herself from asking any questions. It doesn't come without an effort, I'm sure, as she's the classic example of a person who always needs to know and understand everything. I don't blame her, though; I'm just the same.

* * *

At the liberal arts library I bump into Rach, who immediately bombards me with questions: "Why didn't you respond to my texts? Who was the brunette? Did you talk to Dorian? Did you pay him a visit? What did he tell you?"

To a third party I must look like a celebrity who's being harassed by a very nosy paparazzi, making it difficult for me to walk on. At one point I simply stop in the middle of the hallway and say very explicitly, to avoid the necessity of repeating myself, "Rach, leave me alone. I don't want to talk about what happened last night."

"Excuse me?" Stunned, she halts.

"You heard me."

"Why don't you just tell me to fuck off? That's clearly what you want to say to me," Rach says bluntly, obviously hurt.

I've done it again. I've pushed my innocent friend away, just because I want to avoid answering her questions.

"No, no, not at all! I'm just really late for Theory of Psychology, so sorry, I'll catch you later." I begin to stride away.

"Lately you've had no time for me," she remarks to slow me down. "I could vanish from your life, and it wouldn't make any difference to you."

"What are you talking about?" I stop again, my jaw clenched.

"You've been very distant recently. You don't need to confide in me anymore. You've been devoting all your time to that guy who's already interested in someone else anyway, instead of focusing on people who care about you."

The *who's already interested in someone else* comment is like a red rag to a bull.

"Do you mean other people, or just you? Just because we've spent a little bit less time together than we used to doesn't mean that I don't give a damn about you." My voice gets louder. "I'm perfectly aware that you're a person who demands non-stop attention and devotion, but don't let yourself get carried away, Rach. There are certain aspects of my life that I would rather keep to myself and won't share with other people, no matter who they are. It's my right!" My anger is about to explode.

"First of all, *a little bit less time*? Seriously?" She shakes her head in disbelief. "Secondly…" She hesitates for a fraction of a second. "Your aunt called me."

What?! That's all I need right now. Cynthia and Rach sticking their noses in my business.

"Why? What did she want from you?" I'd love to scream to let my rage out, but I need to control myself; we're in public, and surrounded by a bunch of other students.

"She thinks you haven't been yourself recently. She told me she felt like she was living with a stranger and couldn't figure out what was going on with you."

"What I'm hearing is that the both of you chitchatted as you always do when I'm not around," I say, and scowl at Rach. "Great—I hope you had a blast."

"What's wrong with you? We want to help you, can't you see that?"

"If you want to help, then leave me alone! Neither of you can help me!" I can't stand this discussion any longer. I turn around and trot away, fuming.

"Zara, wait!"

I don't even think of waiting. I want peace of mind. Neither Rach nor my aunt are capable of helping me. If I told them the truth with all the details, they would probably put me in the nuthouse.

Then again, when I think about it, Cynthia would probably send me to rehab instead and set the police on Dorian.

My life has become so frustrating that I can hardly take it anymore. Keeping secrets from the people who not too long ago were the ones I'd always confide makes me feel as if my soul is being pulled apart. Every single thing I decide to hide weighs heavier and heavier on my chest, leaving an uncomfortable imprint on me. Still, no matter how much I'm tempted to let them step into the world of my secrets, I immediately discard that idea, knowing how crazy I'd sound.

The really scary thing is, I'm afraid that me actually going insane is only a matter of time.

CHAPTER TWENTY-THREE

I HAVE TO STAY AT SCHOOL FOR a couple more hours to take some tests. The spring term is about to be over, so I need to catch up with everything that I've been putting off. The moment I eventually step outside the building and feel a gentle breeze wafting over my face, my stomach reminds me of its existence with a massive rumble.

Cynthia didn't have time to go grocery shopping yesterday, so to avoid coming across an unpleasant surprise in the form of the fridge full of air and nothing else, I swing by a small market a few blocks from my house. Starving, I could put literally everything on the shelves into the basket. I restrict myself to a box of Ritz, some Haribo, Twizzlers, and a small carton of chocolate soymilk. An extremely unhealthy mix, but the hunger pangs are in charge. I can't fight them.

I'm standing in the line served by a terribly slow cashier, who, to make the whole process even slower, gets into a discussion with one of the clients regarding the mouthwash that removes plaque most effectively. I'm boiling inside.

What's wrong with her? If the whole country shared her idea of work pace, we'd be a hundred years behind where we're now.

Frustrated, I roll my eyes, which by accident land on a small TV set hung above the cashier. Breaking news is being announced, reporting the latest facts in the case of the missing girl I read about this morning. The TV is muted, so I can't hear what's being said, but I see a video showing the girl. I squint to see better, staring at the blonde girl who's waving to the camera, dressed in a loose T-shirt and denim shorts.

A blinding flash comes over me, and I realize where I know that face from.

It's the girl I saw with Dorian several times!

When her name pulls up on the screen, Leslie Dean, I repeat it a dozen times in my thoughts.

Leslie Dean.

Leslie Dean.

Leslie Dean…

"Is that everything?" asks the cashier, who is finally done with the mouthwash client and is scanning my goods.

"Yes. That's all."

"Personally, I like the cheddar Ritz more," she says, making an attempt to engage me in a conversation like she did with her previous customer, but I'm not eager to fall for it. I only smile without responding to her comment and get back to repeating the name of the missing girl in my mind. There's something else I'm missing, something I've forgotten…

"Oh my God!" I cry aloud. Time seems to slow down as suddenly everything falls into place. *Why didn't I realize this before?*

Leslie Dean was one of the names enumerated by Blair the other evening. She *was* the same girl that Dorian was seeing.

A heavy feeling settles in my stomach.

"What's wrong?" the cashier asks, confused by my reaction.

"Umm… those Haribo aren't on sale?" I say the first thing that comes to my mind.

"No, sweetie, they never have been."

A minute later, I stumble out of the market. My revelation makes my stomach twist. Even my hunger and thirst have gone away, I'm so upset. With shaking hands, I pull my cell phone out from my purse to look up the registry of missing people. I suspect I'll find the names of the other two girls mentioned by Blair as well.

I am concentrating so hard on the small screen of my iPhone that I don't even notice the man standing in my way as I go to the car. I smash into him with a thud and drop my bag of groceries.

"I'm so sorry, I didn't see you, sir," I apologize to the stooped, middle-aged man in a checkered shirt who's peering at me. In spite of the fact that I just bounced off him, he's not moving. He neither helps me pick up my groceries nor replies to my apologies. He doesn't even blink for a while.

He just stares at me. That's it. "Is everything okay? Did I hurt you?" He stands, petrified. "Okay… if you're all right, then, I guess, I'll just walk away."

What a weirdo, I think to myself, and walk past him. No sooner do I look at my phone screen again than he suddenly grabs me by the elbow, startling me, and pulls me back to him. Giving his face a quick once-over, I see a wide scar extending along his eyebrow right above his eye, which makes me shiver. I also spot a tiny tattoo on his neck that resembles some kind of symbol.

"I said I was sorry. I really didn't mean to bump into you. It was an accident."

The man takes on a sinister look and speaks in a low voice. "Stay away from the Hatches!"

No, not again. Another stranger connected with the Hatches!

"I beg your pardon?!" I jerk my elbow from his grip.

"You had better be careful. It's already begun."

It sounds like a line from a horror movie. I have no idea how the guy knows I've been dealing with the Hatches.

"What has started?"

"The process…"

"What process?"

"*Horribile dictu.*"

"I don't understand. What does that mean?" I demand frantically.

"You're next!" he warns me, and stretches out his arm, pointing at something far behind me. I look around in the indicated direction, but I don't spot anything unusual besides two Afro-American women loading their trunk with dozens of shopping bags, making the car sag under the tremendous weight of the groceries.

"I can't see any—" I turn back to him but don't finish my sentence, for the man's gone. He simply vanished. I blink twice, as if it will bring him back.

Was it another hallucination? A man couldn't just evaporate like that.

Leslie Dean and the strange man who appeared out of nowhere are the final straw. I've been patient far too long. Being a crucial part of something that I don't understand, and surrounded by a bunch of people who are involved in it but unwilling to talk, is draining me. It doesn't let me live a normal life. It's my right to know what's going on with me. Whatever it is, I want it to be over already, even though the man told me that something has just *begun*.

Horribile dictu… what does it even mean?

What process?

What does Dorian have to do with Leslie Dean?

I'm at my limit. I desperately need to know the truth. No more excuses. I'm done with this bullshit.

While driving, I keep one eye on the road ahead and the other on my phone, where the list of missing people is still on the screen. I scroll down it. *Bryan, Cooper, Evans, Monroe…* and here we go—*Prynn, Vanessa,* and three people below, *Whitaker, Karla.* Both of them have been missing for no longer than a month.

It tumbles into my head that maybe Rafael *isn't* to blame for the mysterious disappearances. Could the Hatches be behind them? A massive weight falls somewhere to the bottom of my stomach. Maybe the villains of this whole story are Dorian and Rita, after all…

That conjecture makes me press the gas pedal to the floor. I feel in my bones that this is it: the evening of truth. I won't let Dorian or even Rita delude me again. I need to dispel all the doubts that have been tormenting me.

I make the turn onto my street. The blinding glare of ambulance and police-car lights is clearly noticeable from a distance. My heart lodges in my throat. Every second not only brings me closer to the house, but also confirms that my apprehension is right. Those vehicles are parked in *my* driveway.

I stop the car with a screech, feeling the blood drain from my face. Despite the late hour, my house is surrounded by a crowd of gaping onlookers, whispering to each other, on the phone, or standing with their jaws dropped. I see a yellow *Police Line: Do Not Cross* tape cutting off my part of the house. The last time I saw a similar scene was in a documentary where the whole family was murdered by a serial killer.

The front door is wide open; something terrible must've happened while I was out. My chest tightens. My knees feel wobbly. I need to pull myself together and find out what happened.

I thread my way through the dense crowd. I'm about to

bend and go under the yellow tape, but I'm stopped by someone's hand grabbing my arm. It's a police officer.

"Can't you see no one is allowed in?" he roars.

"I live here!" I scream right into his face, aggravated, like the fact that it's my house is written on my forehead and the officer is too lazy to bother reading it.

"Zahara Logan?"

"Yes, it's me! What happened? I want to get inside! Who called you in?!"

"Calm down, Miss Logan. A break-in occurred about an hour ago."

"A break-in?!" His words panic me even more.

"We were called by Madeline Montgomery. One person was seriously injured," the officer says, his voice unfazed. He must have dealt with worse crime scenes, so this one doesn't make any impression on him—whereas I'm totally shattered. "Unfortunately, we got here too late and didn't catch the bastard. We have a description of the criminal, though. Do you recognize this man?" He brandishes the sketch of a man's face several inches from my nose. Even though it's not an exact match, I recognize the man.

Rafael.

"Who's hurt?"

"Cynthia Montgomery; the paramedics are already taking care of her. She will be transferred to the hospital shortly. Do you know this man, Miss?"

"No, I have no idea who he is," I lie. "I want to get into my house."

"I'm afraid it's impossible at the moment," he says, barring my way. His bulky physique makes me assume he would be able to knock me down in a second, so I don't even try wrestling with him. "No one is allowed to cross the tape. I would appreciate it if you would stay where you are."

"But she's my aunt! I want to see her! That's my right!" I protest. "Where's Maddie?"

"If you mean Miss Madeline Montgomery, then she has already been taken to the hospital."

"Why? You said that only one person was hurt!"

"There was a minor scuffle between her and the burglar. Miss Montgomery was in shock when we got here. She did not require immediate medical assistance, like Mrs. Montgomery, to stabilize her, but it was necessary to take her to the hospital."

"I need to see my aunt and make sure she's fine." I make an attempt to walk past him, but in vain; the officer prevents me from taking even one step further. I feel warm tears running down my cheeks. It's my fault. Rafael was looking for me, not them.

"No one is allowed to enter the crime scene. I understand your frustration, Miss Logan, but I'm not authorized to let anybody pass this zone. The most I can do for you is to take you to the hospital."

"What did he do to her?"

"Mrs. Montgomery was stabbed a few times with a knife."

A knife. That knife.

I'm paralyzed.

But why? What did she do to make him stab her? Why did he even break into my house? Didn't Dorian assure me that we weren't in danger as long as we stayed safely at home?

"Will she make it?"

"Her condition is grave."

A pain jolts through my heart. It radiates through my bloodstream, my bones, my muscles. My whole body shakes. I don't even want to imagine what I have put Cynthia and Maddie through. The thought of what they must have felt when that spooky man showed up at the house and attacked them makes me sick.

I'm wondering how they managed to come through it alive. How did Maddie call the police while Rafael was still inside? I obviously can't get in, so the only thing I can do at the moment is let the officer drive me to the hospital and talk to my cousin about the incident. But before I can ask him, I feel the very well-known touch of a hand on my arm. I know this scent; I know the feeling of his hands on my body.

"Zara, come with me."

It's his voice. I recognize it as well as I recognized Rafael's face on the sketch. I should jump away from him, keep myself no closer than the distance of an outstretched arm. Maybe I should even identify him as a suspect in the case of missing Leslie Dean. Actually, it's *not* me who's responsible for what happened—it's him. His actions have contributed to the situation I'm in right now. All those secrets have led to this.

I wish I could hate him. I wish I could shout in his face that I want him to go to hell, but I can't. He's stolen my heart along with the will to rebel. I belong to him; he's a piece of me. If he wasn't in my life, I wouldn't want to *be* alive.

"Dorian…" I'm not certain what I want to say. Without caring about the police officer standing in front of me, or the people who are around me, I throw myself into his arms and burst into uncontrollable tears. I need him, his closeness. I don't ever want to break this embrace. When he's here, I can be brave. "Do you know what happened here?"

"I do."

"Will you tell me? I'm begging you. I need to know the truth. It's been way too long."

"I will. But not here. I'm taking her to the hospital," Dorian announces to the police officer. Holding my hand, he pulls me through the sensation-seeking crowd.

"I want to know what really happened," I demand first thing after getting into his Bentley.

"We're not going to the hospital," Dorian says, pressing the engine start button.

"Where then?"

"Somewhere where we'll be able to speak freely, with no witnesses."

"About Rafael?"

"About everything."

"What do you mean?"

"I mean we'll go over everything that I've been hiding from you so far."

I think I've misheard for a second.

"What has changed that out of blue you want to enlighten me?"

"You're in great danger. That's what's changed."

"Wasn't it you who wanted to hurt me?"

"Not here. Keep your questions for later."

Still weeping quietly, I fix my eyes on the windshield before me and let him drive me away.

CHAPTER TWENTY-FOUR

THE DISTANCE THAT WE'RE traveling seems to be endless. I sit, bleary-eyed, staring through the windshield. I'm lost in my thoughts, recalling the street in front of my house full of lights, people, the police and the ambulance. The weight on my chest doesn't go away. I press my palm to it and try to suppress my sorrow, but it doesn't help. My temples pulsate as if they're about to explode. I want to yell, cry, lash out, or simply disappear. I'm willing to do anything just to numb the guilt that consumes my entire being.

Tears slip down my cheeks. I can't get rid of the nagging feeling that all this really is my fault. After all, I was the one who willfully intruded in Dorian's life, disregarding his multiple warnings not to get too close to him. My persistence drew the attention of that bloody Rafael, who for some reason chose me as his target, as well as my whole family. But it still doesn't make any sense to me why the man crossed the threshold of my house. Especially without me inside.

"Can you explain to me how Rafael broke into my house?" The question that's been bothering me cuts through the silence.

"He forced the back door."

"That's not what I meant, and you know it!" I shift my eyes from the windshield to Dorian, focused on the road. His hands are tight on the steering wheel. "Why did he even do that? Both you and Rita agreed that he was after me. You even assured me that as long as I didn't leave the house by myself, I wasn't in danger."

"To be perfectly honest with you, I don't understand it myself. He had no right to do that. It was against the rules."

"What rules?"

"We'll reach our destination soon; I'll explain everything there."

I don't pursue the subject. I've managed to live with no answers for so long that a few more minutes won't kill me. For the remaining miles, Dorian's face is impassive. He doesn't make a single sound—doesn't cough, sigh, yawn. I have the impression that he's even stopped breathing. He's simply staring ahead at the road.

We've left civilization behind. There hasn't been a single house in over thirty minutes. We come off the main road, make a turn and come to an almost invisible, narrow side-road hidden by a thicket of trees and bushes. If I were driving, there's no way that I would have even noticed that turn, it's camouflaged so perfectly by this green maze. I'm curious how Dorian even knows about its existence.

He stops the car in front of a mid-sized, rustic, one-story wooden cabin. The first thing I take in are blades of grass reaching the windows and a short, half-rotten flight of stairs leading to a warped doorframe. This place is obviously neglected. The outside lights are on, but no lights come from within.

"Whose cabin is this?" I ask, getting out of the car.

"Don't ask any questions, but follow me," he commands, and makes his way toward the cabin.

"You've dragged me here to the middle of the woods, so I guess I have the right to ask about my whereabouts. Besides, what are we even doing here?" I stumble over a piece of thick tree root sticking out of the ground.

Dorian takes my hand and pulls me to the cabin. He walks very fast, which doesn't make it easier for me not to injure myself.

"Do you happen to be a psychopath who brought me here to kill me?" I step on a loose branch next, which cracks loudly and breaks in two. "Is that what your secret is?"

"No, but what I am isn't any better." He uses a shoulder to push open the creaky front door and lets me go inside first. "The cabin is empty. It's just you and me."

The first thing that hits me when we're inside is the scent of damp wood and rot. When Dorian flips on the light, I scan the interior. The place looks completely abandoned. All the furniture is covered with sheets, and the paint on the walls is shabby. A thick layer of dust covers every surface. All around are sepia photographs of people unknown to me.

Every corner of this place is mired in cold and gloominess.

We move to a medium-sized living room. My gaze is immediately drawn to a fireplace made from field stones. I drop onto a rickety, cream-colored couch, which is the only piece of the furniture without a foil cover. I don't mind the dust. The aura of this place matches my current mood.

I release a long exhale. My muscles quiver with tension. I'm so miserable that it takes away my willingness to utter even a single word, but I need to clear up the mess that's been fermenting in my head for several weeks.

Dorian falls to a bench in front of me. We remain at a distance from one another. I wonder why he doesn't feel like sitting beside me. My heart has been smashed, and he's the one who could help me bring all of the pieces back together. His warm arms could soothe the pain and comfort me.

"Why won't you sit next to me?"

"It's better this way. I need you to focus."

My heart sinks in disappointment, but I won't waste more time, and get straight to the point. "Can you finally tell me why you brought me here? I'd like to get it over with and go to the hospital as soon as possible because—"

"We came all the way here because it's the only place where you're safe. No one will know that you're here."

"No one? What do you mean by no one? I thought only one man was hunting me."

"Unfortunately, there are many more."

Silence hovers over us. I shift on the couch. At first the meaning of his words doesn't sink in, but when my brain finally registers what he's just said, my chest tingles.

"More? How many more?"

"As of now, there are at least four. It doesn't seems like a lot, but it's up to them whether or not that number increases to a few thousand more," Dorian says, stone-faced. I have no clue whether he's concerned, stressed, or completely uncaring. He seems indifferent.

"What?!" My jaw drops open. "You're lying to me! That's impossible!" I run my fingers though my hair.

"It's better if you listen and believe me instead of denying it."

"But *why?* What might anyone want from me? I'm a nobody!"

"You have something precious that they desire."

"Something precious?" I force a laugh. "I swear that I don't know what you're talking about." I shake my head in disbelief. How insane it all sounds.

"I find that unbelievable. Someone must have been keeping the truth from you."

His words reach my ears, but I don't want to process them. I can't even fathom the idea that he might be right.

"You're wrong! You're taking me for someone that I'm not—I've told you that multiple times." Frustration grows in me.

"How can you be so sure?" He furrows his eyebrows. "Didn't you tell me that you haven't heard from your family for years?"

A small part of me shivers. He's not mistaken. I don't

even know my real family. I've never heard from them, nor have I seen a single member over the years. Is it possible that Cynthia hid something from me? If so, was it at my mother's request? My stomach hardens at the thought.

"I'm sorry, but it's hard for me to even imagine that I might have been living in a lie my entire life. It doesn't make any sense." I bury my face in my hands for a moment, and sigh heavily. "Regardless of whether I believe you or not, what is this precious thing? Is it the reason why Rafael's been after me and broke into my house? To find it and steal it?" I raise my gaze back to Dorian. "Is he a thief?"

"Rafael isn't a thief." Dorian stares intently into my eyes and takes a deep breath. I can see the vein at his temple pulsing. He's about to tell me something thorny. He speaks up with the same calm voice that I know so well, unshaken: "*I* am a thief."

Time stops. The only noise around us at the moment is the wind beating against the windows.

"Say *what?*" I finally find my tongue. "You rob people? You burgle their properties and take their belongings?! That's what you do after dark?" I blink faster, my pulse quickening.

"Not really. Material things aren't of interest to me. My taste is a bit more… sophisticated. I take away the most precious thing that a human being possesses." His gaze is so intent, as if he's trying to burn a hole in me.

"Okay, now I'm very confused. I don't get how to interpret that statement." I frown, then say, "To me the most precious thing that a human being can have is a soul."

"You've understood, then."

Dorian's eyes are still on mine. Neither of us looks away.

"Right," I chuckle nervously, with no idea how to react. "Are you trying to tell me that you're interested in stealing… *souls?*"

He nods, his face still serious, without a shadow of amusement.

"That's ridiculous, Dorian." I rise from the couch as if propelled by an invisible force. *Now he's definitely lying. It's all bullshit. Maybe he'll tell me in a second that he uses a genie from a bottle to make his dreams come true. This is crazy.* Something holds me back from saying it out loud. "Stop fooling around. Do you think I'll believe you?" I wait for his response, but he remains silent. "Tell me the truth, because I don't feel like listening to some made-up paranormal stories. Just say something. Anything."

"I *told* you the truth," he eventually replies. "It's up to you whether or not you believe it."

For a moment it seems to me I'm dreaming. In fact, I hope it's just a nightmare, and I'll wake up soon. I've been waiting for the truth, but now he's revealed it, I'm not satisfied. I expected anything but what he said. Every cell of my body rejects his words.

"Wait, wait, wait," I say and raise my index finger, "are you trying to tell me that… that you're…"

"A soul thief."

A soul thief.

Those three words echo in my mind for a long while after they have been said. My brain strives to assimilate this information somehow, but such news is so exceedingly improbable that it's hard to grasp.

I look away from Dorian and begin snickering. "And you think that I'll believe that? That you're a *soul thief?*"

"As I just said, you don't have to believe me—but in that case, I think we're done here," he says, and gets up off the bench. "Let's go. We're leaving."

"No!" I rush to him and grab his hand to stop him. We can't just leave like that. "Okay, let's say I believe you. No matter how implausible it sounds. But does it mean that you…" I don't even know how to formulate my question not to sound dumb. "Steal souls?"

"Yes."

His assurance petrifies me for a fraction of a second. I still can't believe that it's not either a stupid joke or some kind of a test to see whether I'm mentally stable.

"How come?" The corners of my eyes crinkle. "How is that even possible? A soul isn't a thing that you can just take from someone and put in your pocket."

He drops his gaze to my nails, still biting into his hand. I didn't realize that I was using so much force.

"I'm sorry." I let go of him.

"We'd better sit down." He motions to the couch.

"I'd rather stand."

"Okay, but it will be a long conversation."

CHAPTER TWENTY-FIVE

W E STAND IN SILENCE for a lingering while. Tension grows between us. The tree branches scrape against the cabin, and a few pinecones, from the sound of it, bounce off the roof. I've been waiting for this conversation for a very long time, but now that it has come, I'm not certain if I really do want to know the truth.

"So how do you steal a soul?"

"There's a whole process. Sometimes time-consuming, sometimes quick. It depends on many factors."

Did he just say PROCESS?

I've heard that word at least twice. First when Dorian explained to me that all his women had undergone a process, and secondly, a few hours ago when that strange guy in the parking lot by the market looked me in the eye and said that the process had already begun.

"Hold on." I narrow my eyes. "You told me that all those women… All of them… Oh my God." I bury my face in my hands. Everything's falling into place and starting to make sense, even though I'm still too much of a rational person to fully accept it. "I'm one of them."

My discovery renders Dorian frozen. After about ten seconds of surveying me, he only nods without speaking.

I grow cold. I let out a forceful breath and toss him a reproachful look. "But why? Why did you choose *me?!*"

"Are you serious?" His face is grave. "Why did I choose you?" He approaches me, but I take a step back to avoid letting his warmth influence me and take away my ability to focus and stay persistent. Getting mushy is the last thing I want now, even though my heart longs for him. "So many times I kept telling you that it couldn't be you, that it would be better for you if you gave it a rest, but you were so *stubborn*. All the time you tenaciously came back to our house to sniff around, you were searching for any form of contact with me, regardless of my warnings. You didn't want to listen, and now you're trying to blame me, but *you* were the one who opened the can of worms yourself. I continuously pushed you away, discouraged you. I was even snippy and curt to you, but it wasn't enough."

His tirade leaves me speechless for a few seconds. Nothing of what he's said is untrue. I did it to myself, and I'm well aware of that. How could I have known, though? Nobody of sound mind would've suspected what his secret was.

"You should've told me the truth in the first place!" I pinch my lips together.

"First of all, would you have believed me?" He pauses to let me answer, but I don't agree, shake my head, or give him any other form of response, so he continues, "Secondly, even if you had known, would you have stayed away from me?"

Good question. I'm positive I wouldn't have, even if I'd been aware of what the truth was. Most likely, I'd have made multiple attempts to be closer to him regardless of the consequences.

I'm conscious of these things, but reluctant to admit them to Dorian. He's right. The more he pushed me away, the more I tried to get close to him. I was jealous of all those women that he was with. I couldn't restrain myself from peeking out of my bedroom window every night, hoping that I'd see him for just a moment, walking out of his part of the house. I wasn't able to focus my thoughts on anything else than Dorian Hatch. I was so vulnerable to his influence.

"Is that why you told me that I should be afraid of you? Because your plan is to… Uh… Is stealing a soul equal to killing?" My heart plummets. His response will change everything. It's not about being a thief anymore. The issue now is whether he's a murderer.

"Yes and no."

"That doesn't explain anything."

"Well, you're asking me whether the act of separating a soul from a body equates to killing." Dorian crosses his arms in front of his chest. "Obviously, a body can't live without a soul, so, theoretically, stealing a soul is killing. At least in earthly life terms. But remember, a body can't live without a soul, yet a soul can live without a body." That doesn't put me at ease. In fact, I'm genuinely confident that Dorian is being confusing on purpose. He wants to tell me the truth, but in a way that won't seem as cruel and dramatic as it actually is.

"What happens with the stolen souls after they're, I guess, pulled out from their bodies?" It's hard for me to find appropriate terms to describe this act, which is so far beyond the scope of my cognition.

"The only thing I can tell you at this point is that stolen souls are kept in a special place, from which they can't break free."

"But why do you hold them there?"

"Me?" He chuckles and shakes his head like my question amuses him. "There are tens of thousands like me out there. I'm not the only thief. They steal the souls of unwary men and women every day. They suck what's best out of you. They take away your vitality, your positive energy, the will to live, thrive and breathe. Soul thieves beguile, leading their victims to madness."

My heart feels like it's shrinking when the reality hits me. Dorian is a predator—the same one I saw last night. I remember the wild rage in his black eyes, and a sudden chill shudders through my body.

"Are you a human being? Do you have your own soul? What are you?"

"On the one hand I am, and, on the other, I'm not. I don't want to discuss that with you, though."

I knew it. I could've anticipated from the very beginning

that he'd explain to me only the things that he considers relevant. Nothing more than that.

I feel like rolling my eyes and throwing the objection that he promised to tell me everything at him, but I don't. For one thing, I detect a somehow tortured expression on his face, which discourages me from pursuing the subject. Secondly, after all, there are only the two of us in this cabin, and as much as I don't want to believe he'd hurt me, I prefer not to irritate him. Especially after I witnessed his dark side last night.

I move on to my next question: "Who are those strange people who showed up at your house? Are you one of them?"

Dorian nods. "Yeah. Those people are responsible for supervising certain… things."

"What things?"

"Simply put, they make sure that everyone fulfills the designated tasks."

"So you aren't just a random bunch of individuals? You have to report to somebody?"

"We have our hierarchy."

I start pacing around the room. I need a moment to digest what I've learned. Based on Dorian's explanation, I gather that the world of so-called soul thieves has its own structure—they have a whole society, where everyone has a certain role to play. It blows my mind to realize that such beings live alongside regular people. *Have I ever come across a different thief in my life?*

"Where are you in the hierarchy?"

A shadow swings across his face. He averts his eyes from me, looking somewhere into space before him. He wants to spare me from this knowledge.

"I'm just a tool. That's it."

I don't have to be a mind reader to know that it's not true. I remember Blair praising Dorian for being one of the best. He can't just be an ordinary one. There must be something special about him in their world, something that other thieves can't do. However, for some reason Dorian isn't eager to share his position in his community. I suspect that the truth might be too hard for me to handle, and that's why he'd rather keep it to himself.

"Enough straying from the point." He fixes his eyes back on me. "There's one thing that you need to know about, and that's why I've dragged you here. I need to make sure that no one will either hear or disturb us, and also that you're not in danger."

"You need to be sure I'm not in danger?" I frown. "Why would you even care whether or not I'm safe?"

He comes closer. "You have to know what the process of losing the soul looks like." He turns a deaf ear to what I said and gets to the essence of the matter. "Only then will you grasp what's been going on with you lately."

I'm perfectly aware what this means: I've been subjected to the process against my will. I'm one of them—a victim. He, on the other hand, is the monster who's chosen me, or rather to whom I have given myself voluntarily.

He takes one more step towards me. I can sense some

sort of electricity between us. It's like an invisible pull that draws us to each other. "Let me use simple terms. Thieves have a couple of reasons for collecting souls."

"What's yours?" I immediately chime in. That's the only reason that interests me.

A bitter expression cloaks his face. His jaw flexes.

"To survive. Thieves like myself need to steal souls primarily to maintain their existence. The ones above us benefit from that and that's why they created, or rather programmed, us like that."

I suddenly recall the conversation with Dorian when he said that he didn't want to hurt me, but he had to, as it was his nature. At that time, I didn't understand his words—I even found them ridiculous—but now I begin to comprehend.

"So it's true." A lump forms in my throat, and I swallow hard. "You're not human."

My heart splinters into hundreds of pieces when it dawns on me that the man who's caught me, body and soul, in an obsessive trap of passion for him has almost nothing resembling humanity in him. The feelings I have for Dorian are more profound than anything I've ever felt in my life. He's the embodiment of everything I've ever desired. He's the fulfillment of my greatest dreams. Yet I'm only his quarry. He needs me solely to survive.

My eyes fill with tears. I hold my breath for a moment. The pain in my heart is excruciating.

"So, go ahead—enlighten me." My voice trembles. "How do you do it? How do you steal someone's soul?"

"In various ways, for instance through murder." I flinch at that word. "But the problem with that is that a soul is resistant and fights back, and as a result often weakens the one who's taken it away."

"Have you ever murdered anyone?" I ask, in a weak, almost inaudible voice.

"Does it matter to you?"

It's like icy cold is slowly covering my heart. Dorian's silence is more than an answer to me. He just doesn't want to admit it.

He's a murderer. He's taken someone's life in cold blood. My heart thumps an erratic rhythm in my chest. I instinctively take a few steps back to increase the distance between us. I still can't believe all this is happening.

"There's another, more effective way," he continues. "A soul can be also possessed; then it gives up by itself."

"Possessed?" My feet hit the wall behind me. "Do you mean…"

"By physical contact."

"Are you trying to tell me… that… that when we were…" Despondency creeps into my heart.

"You gave yourself away of your own free will," he says quietly.

It now makes sense why he was so reluctant to be intimate with me. I finally realize why all his inner fights were coming from. He lusted for me, but he also recognized what severe consequences surrendering to his desire carried. It's such a paradox that it was *me* who kept insisting and pushing him to give in, deaf to his resistance. It doesn't make me feel better in any way to realize that. I might have been too persistent, sure, but he should have never come into my life in the first place. If he hadn't moved in next door, then I'd have never fallen for his charm.

But do I really regret it?

"That explains why you asked me how much willpower I had. To check whether I'd resist." I have the impression that if I blink, tears will run down my cheeks.

"Actually, you're wrong there. I asked about your willpower not to establish whether or not you'd resist, but rather how long you'd be able to fight it off."

"What do you mean?"

Dorian clears his throat. "When a thief finds an object of his interest, he checks out its aura, which informs him how vulnerable the victim is to his allure… influence… call it whatever you want. If the aura is very palpable and radiates thoroughly from the person the thief's going to attack, it means that he's dealing with a strong soul, which won't be easy to possess and will be unconsciously fending off the attack. Even though at the end it will give itself away to the thief anyway, the whole process is longer than it would have been with a soul that has a barely perceptible glow around them. That's the rough explanation."

"Why did you ask me how much willpower I had if you could see my…?"

The answer dawns on me. How many times did Dorian claim that he couldn't see me? It was my *aura* that was invisible to him in the basement when I asked him to help me fix the lights in the house. He couldn't determine how vulnerable to his influence I was.

"I couldn't see your aura. It's been a mystery to me ever since. Like you're some sort of an anomaly. Or perhaps you're special." He takes one small step toward me.

My fingers and toes tingle. The closer he gets, the more confused I feel. Somehow, Dorian is eerie and menacing, but at the same time unbelievably appealing. I'm scared, but also excited. I fidget, holding his intense gaze.

"So that had never happened to you before?"

"Never." He takes one more step. My knees go weak and a light chill of fear travels along my spine, but simultaneously every fiber of my body tingles for his touch.

"Every human being has an aura. Even if it's extremely dim, it still exists." One more step. "It reflects your life energy, personality, thoughts, and emotions. It depicts the state of your mind and soul. Thieves use it to decipher their victims; they are like an open book that we can browse as much as we want. You, however, are totally opaque to me." Another step. "Rita can't see you either, which clearly proves that it's not just my affliction. I couldn't predict what to expect from you. Every physical contact with you could've been the last one, ending up in you being unable to wake up again."

I wet my lips. "Isn't that the point, though?"

"I'm not stupid. We would've been forced to move out right away not to arouse any suspicion."

That sounds like Dorian cared more about maintaining his façade than my life. But why am I surprised? He even admitted himself at one point that he wasn't able to feel anything for anyone. I didn't take those words seriously either. Now I know that the only thing that matters to him is collecting souls.

"Yeah, that's obvious. I don't know why I didn't figure it out myself," I say, striving to sound as indifferent as possible, even though it feels like my heart has just been shattered. "It also explains why you pushed me against the wall that night in the basement. Was it because you couldn't see my aura and were wondering who I was?"

"I suspected that you were… someone other than the person you claimed to be."

"Who?" I blink faster.

"I'll get to that point."

There's another mystery that has been burdening my mind since the basement incident. "When you were holding my hands, I felt freezing cold running through my arms. Why?"

"I don't know why that happened."

That's hard to believe, but I move on to the next question. "Why did you pull away so suddenly?"

"Because you literally burnt me," he says, and closes the distance between us to merely two steps. He's been stalking up to me like a panther in a jungle. "That's why I let go. I wasn't able to stand the touch of your skin. I can't explain that either. But I know one thing for a fact; at that moment, some kind of electromagnetic field was generated between us, and was robust enough to bring back the electricity in the house."

"Electromagnetic field?!" I open my mouth as if I want to say something further, but nothing comes to my mind, so I close it again.

"Yes. What's more, I'm sure that the same sort of energy made the fuse blow in the first place. I wasn't around, so it must've come directly from you."

If I told him the truth, I'd die from humiliation. There is no proper way to concede that I was thinking about Dorian, imagining him touching me while whispering dirty words in my ears. My cheeks burn when I recall the steamy images that ran through my mind that night.

"I don't really remember what I was doing."

"You're lying."

Dorian has shortened the distance between us to two or maybe three feet. He's way too close. My hands tremble. A hurricane of conflicting emotions rages through my soul. Longing and fear. Lust and loathing. A desire to be close to him and at the same time as far away as possible. I'm dizzy, unable to tame the growing yearning to be with him, yet the realization of what he really is fills me with dread. I don't know what to do.

"Don't come any closer to me," slips from my lips.

"Are you afraid of me?"

"I don't know…" A cold wall behind me reminds me that there is no escape. "You're my worst nightmare and most desired dream. I have no idea what to think about you. You can't be afraid of someone and simultaneously feel lust for them."

Time suddenly stops.

You're my worst nightmare and my most desired dream echoes in my mind.

"A nightmare…" I repeat more to myself than to him. I force my brain to a superhuman effort and scour every recess of my mind. This has happened to me before, multiple times. A terrifying fear combined with overwhelming desire for the same person. I eventually solve the riddle that's been haunting me for weeks.

"It was you in my dreams." My facial muscles go slack. "You're the man who's been haunting me in those nightmares."

"What nightmares?"

"About the creepy forest. Every time I run through it, I come across this ominous man. I've never seen his face because he has a hood on, but I can sense that he very badly wants to hurt me. I'm horrified by him, but I'm kind of… infatuated with him too." I narrow my eyes. "It is you, isn't it?"

"I don't know what you're talking about."

Is that possible that he really doesn't know? But it all makes sense. He's the only person who triggers the same reaction in my body and soul as the man from my dreams. I have no guarantee that he's telling me the truth, but I also can't help but trust him.

There is a secret to those dreams that I have to unravel.

Dorian ignores my request not to come closer. The distance between us is now down to one foot. I'm swamped by his scent; my body tingles as I fill up my lungs with it.

"You feel fear, but you're trapped in your desires, too." He's so close to me that I can feel the warmth of his body, which has a disarming power over me. "I affect you like a drug; you're addicted more and more every day. You can't stop thinking about my touch," he runs his index finger down my cheek, "my scent, my taste. I'm the first thing on your mind right after you wake up, and the last before you fall asleep." He keeps going down from my cheek to my neck, then my chest, which is immediately covered with goosebumps. "You aren't able to focus on anything else but the memories of those moments when we were together, united as one. You're hungry for more and won't rest until you get what you crave. You're ready to do anything to have me again." I close my eyes and lean my head back against the wall; I'm not strong enough to resist him. "You're fascinated by me, and don't even realize how slowly but surely I weaken you, how I suck out your life energy, how it slowly gets disconnected and isolated from your etheric body every time you give yourself away. I break all the ties that bind them together. You begin to have difficulties in telling what's real from what's not. You don't know who you are anymore."

Keeping my eyes closed, I instantly remember how I felt after the first night I spent with Dorian. So he *was* to blame for the hallucinations I suffered. I instantly open my eyes. "That was when you began stealing my soul. The process had started…" Tears flow down my face.

"Forgive me, Zara…" Dorian presses his forehead into mine.

"That's what you apologized for that day when you and Rita saved me from Rafael, when I almost passed out in your arms."

"I honestly didn't want you to be one of them, but you didn't even think about leaving me alone." As he says this, he grabs me by my shoulders and squeezes them gently as if he's trying to express how much he regrets what he's done.

"Why didn't you want me to be one of them?" I sob.

"I just didn't want you to go through all that, condemn you to such a fate."

My eyes are locked on his. I try to blink my tears away, but unsuccessfully; there are too many of them.

"But why?" My voice is shaking. "Why did you want to spare me?"

"You're different. You were from the very beginning." He wipes my cheek; the spot that he touches prickles. "The way you influence me. The way your presence makes me feel… Those are unknown to me. I can't even put into words what you do to me. I just… didn't want that for you, but I couldn't keep fighting it." He lifts his eyes to mine again. For the first time I can see something in them. Is that a trace of anguish? Regret? Remorse? It bothers him, what he's done to me. His expression gives me a pang. I'm genuinely sorry for him, even though I shouldn't be. I'm the victim here.

As though he can tell I sense his pain, he pulls away. We remain silent. Some acute, unspecified tension hovers over us. He's a predator and I'm his prey. Nothing will ever change that. Sooner or later, I'll end up like the rest of his victims — an empty body, lacking a soul, which will be trapped in some remote place. Maybe even in the depths of hell itself. Perhaps underground, or in some different reality. And he's the one who will sentence me to that.

Yet we both know that, even though Dorian has to hurt me—that's the way the process works—he's reluctant to do so. He doesn't want me to share the fate of his other victims. My life is in his hands, but can he *save* me?

CHAPTER TWENTY-SIX

DORIAN PACES THE ROOM with his hands behind him. Not a single word escapes his lips. His features are straight, as if someone has erased any emotions from his face. I can't read anything from him again. He's deep in thought, contemplating something. I don't move, glued to the wall behind me. I still don't know how to react to everything that I've learned. I feel disappointment, anger, fear, and longing blended together.

"If I left, would I be safe? Far away from you?" I gulp air, a knotted feeling forming in my chest.

"No; you'd be an easy target for others. Plus, you'd go insane without me."

The latter I can imagine. Even the mere thought of never seeing him again makes my stomach turn.

"Will I die, then?"

Dorian stalls. "Under normal circumstances I'd say yes, but there's something different about you that I've never dealt with before. Perhaps I'm wrong, but maybe... maybe you're capable of fighting it off."

That must be the matter he's been pondering over the past several minutes—whether there might be something to be done that would keep me alive. He's never thought about it before because he didn't care about anyone until now. *Am I deluded to think so? Is he deceiving me on purpose? Didn't he mention to me once that he wasn't able to feel anything— no love, no empathy?*

"What makes you think so?"

"For starters, not being able to see your aura. That's never happened to any thief. But mostly, the evening when you fell from the bicycle."

"What about it?"

"You ended up without a single scratch, whereas a different person would've wound up in a hospital with a concussion. You have some power in you, which you're not even conscious you possess."

"That accident wasn't as severe as it seemed."

"You know that's bullshit. You had a lot of bruises and were bleeding, and no longer than an hour later there was no trace of them. Do you think that's *normal*?" He slides me a dark glare.

"No, I don't think it's normal, but…" I really don't have any arguments to support my theory. Even though I didn't witness what the accident looked like from a bystander's perspective, the remnants of my bicycle suggested that it wasn't just a gentle fall to the ground. He's right that it's not typical for wounds to heal at such a dizzying pace. However, I just can't entertain the thought that I might have some sort of superhero power.

"There's no 'but,' Zara," Dorian says, grabbing my shoulders again. "That miraculous recovery wasn't accidental. You have a hidden power that not only heals you, but also makes your aura invisible." I can hear excitement in his voice, maybe even hope.

"Don't be ridiculous."

"Have you ever had a similar accident?"

"Not that I would know of."

"You never cut yourself with a knife?"

"Many times."

"Do you have any scars?

"No."

"Exactly."

The tears stopped flowing a while ago; now it's pure astonishment painted on my face.

"That doesn't prove anything," I insist.

"Have you ever broken anything?" Dorian's relentless.

"No..."

"Twisted or sprained?"

"No."

"Do you still think that doesn't prove anything?"

"I've always been very cautious."

"Right. I don't think you really believe that." He lets my shoulders go and shakes his head, clearly irritated.

I know he must be right, yet I don't want to believe that what he's saying is actually true. I've never analyzed my life like this before. Does the fact that I've never suffered from any form of bodily injury and have no scars or marks really prove that I possess some power that is unknown to me? If so, does it mean that, like Dorian, I'm some weird, inhuman creature and that's why I affect him in such an odd way?

"That evening you gave me some sedative."

He raises his eyebrows. "Where do you get *that* idea from?"

"I conveniently dropped off out of the blue when we started touching on an uncomfortable subject."

"That wasn't a sedative. It was Rita." He turns around, his back to me, and walks over to the window by the fireplace. "She has the power of hypnosis. She made you fall asleep."

"She can hypnotize people?" My jaw drops open again. As if the fact that they aren't human beings isn't enough, now I find out that they also have supernatural powers. "Can she rummage through people's minds, then?"

"Sort of."

My eyes narrow in consternation. *What else am I going to find out tonight?*

"Does every thief have powers?"

"Each and every one of them." Dorian peeks through the window as if he's making sure that no one is hovering around the cabin.

"What are yours?" I swallow, praying that it's not mind-reading.

Dorian doesn't respond immediately. Instead, he moves to the window on the other side of the room, pulls away a dirty, dusty curtain, and scans the area outside with watchful eyes. He must've heard or spotted something. Is someone out there? Is that his skill? Sensing people from afar?

"I," he wheels around to look at me again, "can absorb people's energy, manipulate their auras, and take control of someone's power and use it as my own."

My first reaction is a nervous laugh. He cannot be serious. Everything he's just said sounds ridiculous. I've never believed in things that were beyond the scope of normal scientific understanding—but then why am I surprised? Isn't the sole act of stealing a soul supernatural enough?

"Did you learn all that by yourself?" My tone is incredulous.

"It's in me." He goes back to staring at the window. "It's like with human beings—they're born with certain skills."

"Dorian, is there someone outside?"

"No, why?" He abruptly draws the curtain with one smooth motion.

"I thought you noticed something outside."

"No, it's nothing," he says, but I don't buy it. He ambles around the room again, rubbing his neck. He's analyzing something, but, as usual, he isn't willing to share his thoughts.

A plethora of questions frantically rattles in my head. I'm aware that we must have a limited time to clarify things, but all the things Dorian has been keeping secret from me are like a poison slowly spreading through my system. If I don't dispel my doubts and reach the truth, my brain will explode under the rising pressure. Among dozens of questions, there is one that can't go unanswered. It's been bothering me ever since I eavesdropped on him and Rita for the first time. If this evening is my only opportunity to ask Dorian for explanations, I need to bring it up.

"I never told you this," I begin, pulling him from his trance, "but that evening when I passed out on your couch, I actually woke up not too much later and tried to find you and Rita to ask what had happened." I decide to leave unsaid the fact that I deliberately sneaked upstairs with the purpose of eavesdropping in the first place. "By accident, I overheard your conversation with Rita. I didn't want to be rude and interrupt, so I waited—"

"Who are you trying to fool?" he cuts me off.

I sigh. I've already confessed to eavesdropping on them once before; there's no point in trying to hide the truth. Besides, Dorian apparently has one more skill that he didn't mention to me—extraordinary lie detection.

"Okay, you're right," I admit. "I'm sorry for being overly nosy, but it doesn't matter now. What's significant is what I heard."

I watch his reaction for even the slightest sign of annoyance, but he doesn't seem to be bothered. He only sprawls on the couch where I was sitting a while ago and says: "I'm all ears."

My heart urges me to sit beside him, yet my gut does the opposite. Still cornered, I decide to stay where I am.

"Rita was terrified that someone would find something

out. Which, now that I think about it, makes me assume she had your recent guests in mind." He nods. "When you made an attempt to calm her down, she pointed to something, I didn't see what, as proof that her fear wasn't groundless. What was it?"

Dorian hesitates for a moment, as though wondering how I'll take what he's about to say. He grasps the pendant that he never parts with and that nobody is allowed to touch and says: "She pointed out the number on this."

"The number?" I repeat, to make sure I've got it right. "But didn't you say that it had no meaning whatsoever?"

"It has significant importance."

"I knew it. Even though you tried to deny it."

"You noticed that the number changes," he says, twiddling it in his fingers, "but you couldn't know what it reflects."

"Will you tell me now?"

He shifts his eyes from the pendant to me. I observe something in the way his face changes, but I can't read his thoughts.

"Are you sure you want to know the truth? It will be irrevocable."

"I'm positive."

"If I tell you, there will be no going back," Dorian insists, as if he hopes for me to change my mind.

"Tell me." I hold his gaze, unblinking.

In spite of my brave words, my stomach quivers and my breathing quickens. Panic wells within me. He's going to tell me something devastating—maybe even something that will change the way I perceive him forever. Perhaps I *need* him to do so. I can't live in constant doubt; the worst truth is better than endless delusions.

Dorian lingers over the revelation, but he can't hold it off forever. He pulls in a breath. "The number on the pendant shows the number of the stolen souls."

"Wait, wait, wait… But your number is…" I turn my memory back to the last time I had a chance to take a closer look at Dorian's pendant. "2002…" I mumble. "Does it mean that you… You…" I don't let that thought come out of my mouth, as though it will come true the second I utter it.

"Yes. It means exactly what you think."

The world stops. My breath gets trapped in my lungs. I raise my hand to my temple and shake my head. My lips move, but words refuse to form. I can't even imagine such a huge number of people whose lives have been taken. I wasn't prepared for this revelation. When Dorian told me what thieves do, somewhere in the back of my head it dawned on me that he must've taken more than one life. Nevertheless, the number *2002* far exceeds my tolerance.

"Oh my God…" My knees are too weak. I can't take it anymore and drop to the floor, where I lean my back against the wall again, pull my legs to my chin, embrace them, and start to tremble. I'm not certain what emotion is dominant. Fear? Disgust? Distress? Something that I have no doubt about is that Dorian is a cold-blooded *monster,* and that thought makes me nauseous.

"You're a murderer!" I rasp.

He stares at me with a frightening stillness. "I've been telling you that you didn't want to know what I was. I tried to assure you that it was better for you to stay away from me." He stands up from the couch.

"Don't you dare come any closer!" I scream. Dorian pauses, but keeps his eyes locked on me.

Dread builds in my veins. I remain dazed, unable to move even my toes. It takes a good while for me to regain my senses. I have to cool down and collect my thoughts. After all, Dorian is still the same man (or creature, or thing, or whatever he is) that I've known for over a month. But how can I treat him the same way as I have been after this confession? I'd have to be ruthless to get over what he's done and pretend that everything's back to normal. That I'm not aware of the crimes he's committed.

The avalanche of emotions that slides through my soul annihilates all my feelings, one by one, leaving me empty. I feel like someone has ripped my heart out of my chest.

The silence between us stretches forever, but Dorian doesn't insist on continuing our dialogue; he waits until I'm ready to talk again.

"Why was Rita so concerned about the number on the pendant?" I ask, my voice flat.

"You don't want to know the truth."

"I do."

"If you find out, I guarantee, you won't be able to cope with it."

"What difference does it make to you?" I stare blankly at him, my tone sharp. "You're not the one who's locked in the same room with a murderer whose intention is to kill you!"

"I don't want to kill you!" he says indignantly.

"Hard to believe, considering that you've just told me the process of taking away my soul started a good while ago!"

"Then maybe you should try listening to my advice for once."

"Why is that? Because it's you who decides when it's over?!"

"Yes! It's me who decides when it's over!" Dorian's patience wears thin, and he loses his cool. His eyes turn as black as coal. My breath catches in my throat as I'm reminded of what he really is once again. He zips toward me, ignoring my previous objections. "So shut up and hear me out!"

If there was anything human in his expression before, now it's all gone. I hope he can still control his impulses. He stretches out his arm to help me get to my feet, but I don't want to touch him. The thought of how many innocent lives he's taken fills me with revulsion.

I slowly hoist myself up. When we're at eye level, I'm still pierced by his black, eerie gaze. I shiver, wanting to get away from the dark and disturbing stare. I can't tell what's more horrifying: the truth about him or that there's still a hint of something attracting me to Dorian that doesn't let me truly hate him. *But how can that be? Why am I still so hungry for his presence after learning all these cruel facts about him?*

His rapid breathing slows down. I notice blue dots appearing in his irises, replacing the black. "The thieves you saw in our house carry out monthly inspections, checking how many souls we managed to steal within a certain timeframe." His voice is calm again. "The more souls stolen the better. The low number indicates that something's wrong and has to be fixed."

"Fixed?"

"If a thief doesn't provide a decent amount of souls each month, then he or she will be *encouraged* to be more active in the hunt."

I swallow hard. "It doesn't sound too good."

"Because it isn't. Those thieves are subjected to excruciating pain and suffering to drive even the smallest shadow of an idea of rebellion out of their heads."

I remember one of the thieves mentioning ripping someone apart. *Is that one of the ways they give "encouragement"? Is that what the man meant?*

"Has it ever happened? A rebellion, I mean?" I walk away from him and start circling the room to make the distance between us as long as possible, but he follows me no matter where I edge.

"Of course. There's not much left of those who dared to stand up. They served as a lesson to the others. No one likes insurgencies and uprisings."

"So thieves can be killed, then?" I try not to look at him. It gives me physical pain.

"You can't kill something that isn't alive. But we can be destroyed."

I could swear that for a split second I heard a noise coming from outside. Did I imagine it? However, judging by Dorian's reaction—he pads to the window—the noise must have reached his ears as well. He regards the area outside, but I'm certain he can't see much; the world is already shrouded in darkness.

"Is there someone outside?"

"It's just an animal," he replies, but I don't really believe him. He said it to spare me from being even more afraid. Or, also possible, to prevent me from screaming for help.

There's something inside me that won't settle down. Perhaps Rafael being on the loose makes me uneasy. *Could that be him lurking outside? Did he follow us all the way here?*

"You haven't told me yet who Rafael really is and what he wants from me."

"I promised I'd come back to that." He's still by the window, keeping an eye on what's happening on the other side. "He used to be a *hunter*."

"That means nothing to me."

"Hunters have one objective: destroy all thieves."

"I sincerely hope they'll succeed." The statement tumbles out of my mouth before I know it, but I don't regret those words. My fists clench when I try to imagine how many innocent lives they've possessed. They are all killers, who *should* be exterminated.

But do I really wish that for Dorian?

"Can you tell me more about them?"

"They don't stand out too much." He glances back at me. "They look like ordinary people who blend into the crowd. You would never spot one unless they wanted you to. Anyhow, even though they camouflage themselves very well, there are two things that help us—thieves—single them out." Dorian clears his throat. "First, they have a tattoo in the shape of a wide-open eye. Each of them has it tattooed, no exceptions. Second, they always carry a dagger, a so-called Black Heart. You've already seen one. It's the dagger Rafael has on him."

It's hard not to remember the magnificent thing he pulled out of the sheath which sparkled with dozens of inlaid gems. It was mesmerizing yet dreadful, with those two shining blades that popped out of both ends. I tremble at the thought that he might have used it on Cynthia.

"Why did he attack my aunt? She's not one of you."

Dorian still hasn't moved. His relentless stationing at the window gives me a jittery feeling. I study his profile—so beautiful, not cold or scary.

"Rafael had a moment when he decided to rebel. It even crossed his mind to join the thieves. Everything went according to his plan until his conspiracies were discovered, and he got deprived of his hunter rights by the Hunters' Tribune. He was accused of betrayal and was awaiting execution."

"They were going to kill him?!"

"Yes. But he managed to miraculously escape and steal the dagger that had been taken away from him. Now, to worm his way into the hunter's society again, his goal is to prove he's worthy and wreak havoc among as many soul thieves as possible. Especially the ones who are the Creators' favorites."

"How do you know all that about Rafael?"

"I have my sources."

"I still don't get why he's after me."

"He's so insanely determined that he blindly believes you're one of us. I'm still trying to figure out what made him think that. Maybe it has something to do with your aura, or maybe some other abilities you have and of which I'm not yet aware." He runs his fingers through his thick hair. "One thing is sure—he's convinced that you're a thief. That's why he's been chasing you."

"That's ridiculous!" I shake my head. "I didn't do anything to make him believe that I'm a murderer! Why the hell would he come up with such nonsense?"

"He's blinded by fear, anger, and hatred. The fact that he saw you dealing with me and Rita might've been enough evidence in his eyes that you are one of us. I'm not sure about that, though. This whole situation is very complicated. He's been trying to get me and Rita for quite a while, but he knows that by himself he can't harm us too much."

"Why didn't he break into *your* house? Why did he choose mine instead? Oh my God!" I close my eyes. The nagging sense of blame shudders through my body. I'm reminded again that whatever happened to my family was all my fault.

"You're asking me about things that I'm unable to tell you," Dorian says. He continues, unfazed by my little outburst. "I never spoke to Rafael, and my suspicions are only guesses. I'm not sure about anything. I've never dealt before with a rebellious hunter who's trying to claw his way back into the ranks of the rest of his society at any cost. No hunter has ever mistaken a human for a thief, let alone attacked them. It's contrary to their code of conduct. One of the crown principles is destroying thieves and defending people. He did something totally contradictory. Plus, hunters tend to keep the world of thieves secret from people. That's why I was confident Rafael wouldn't hurt you during the day when you were in the company of others. As it turns out, he's completely unpredictable."

"So it *was* him who kidnapped all those girls who've been the number one topic in the news recently!"

"No. It wasn't him." Dorian slides his gaze to the window.

I'm a bit confused by his assurance. How does he know it wasn't Rafael? I've been blaming him for everything that's been going on in Keizer. Rafael's the only villain who's shown up in our town. At least, that's what I thought up until now.

He's not the only one anymore. There are also… thieves.

I gulp and then, with a quivering voice, ask Dorian a question to which I'm afraid I already know the answer.

"Was it you?" The dead silence stretches between us.

"Did you abduct Leslie Dean?"

Still silence. Dorian neither nods nor shakes his head, but I know it was him. It's hard for me to breathe.

"You're evil!" I yell, hoping that it will soothe me. Why am I even surprised? After all, Dorian has just confessed to killing thousands of people. Is kidnapping those girls any better? They were all the same. Innocent women whose only fault was falling in love with the wrong man. A serial killer. "What did you do with Leslie Dean? Did you murder her? She was so young and innocent! She wanted to live a happy life like the rest of the women you killed." I feel so hopeless "You're a monster! I don't even want to be in the same room with you! Let me out of here!" I dash over to the front door, but Dorian is faster and cuts me off.

"I never claimed I wasn't evil."

He's right, but so what? It doesn't change the fact that I can't come to terms with it and accept it. So far, simply knowing that Dorian is a murderer has been enough to make my blood run cold; however, at least those women were anonymous to me—I wasn't aware what they looked like or who they were... Unlike Leslie. She wasn't just a name I heard. I remember perfectly well the way she dressed in all those family videos, even the way she smiled and moved. It's insane.

Dorian blocks my way out. I'm not strong enough to move him or push him aside.

"Let me out! Right now! You can't keep me here against my will! You have no right to stand in my way!" It's the adrenaline ripping through me that gives me the courage to punch my fists against his chest, but it's still not enough. There's no escape. Finally, Dorian restrains me by grabbing my wrists and holding them behind my back. I'm pushed against the wall, which I bump into with my chest. Even though he did it as gently as he possibly could, it still hurts me.

"Calm down! You don't get anything!" Dorian presses me against the wall.

"Do you think you can call the shots for me?! I don't give a fuck what you want!" I cry aloud. I'm incandescent with rage, like a furious animal that just got caught in a trap. "Those are your intense relationships, huh?! You lure women, fuck up their minds and then kill them?" I'm trying to yank away. "You only care about the number! You don't give a shit who they are." He tightens his grip; I must've hit a nerve. "But what am I even talking about? It completely slipped my mind that you don't have any feelings. Each night you hung out with a different woman. Did you drag each of them to bed? Did you cross every one of them off your list after the job was well done, huh?!" I'm so nasty that I don't even recognize myself. I feel like a different Zara is talking through me. "Is that why you moved to Keizer? To find a new territory to hunt?"

I'm scared to death, but I have nothing to lose. If he ends up killing me in a fury, at least he'll know what I think of him. I don't even care anymore. All these recent revelations have taken away my will to live. I fell in love with a creature that has been slowly killing me. He can put an end to it now, for all I care. It would actually spare me all the sorrow and misery that will probably kill me before Dorian even makes it to stealing my soul.

However, although my mind is drowned in anger, in some deep corner of it I still can hear a weak voice telling me that he kept rejecting me like he didn't want to hurt me. Does that sound like something an emotionless serial killer who lacks empathy would have done? What is that odd thing about me that didn't let him touch me at first? What is the thing that he needs from me so badly? Isn't it my soul after all?

Dorian doesn't respond to my stream of words. He simply keeps holding me tight, probably waiting for me to cool down. But it's not that easy after everything I've found out. *How can he even expect me to relax?*

Becoming aware that I don't have the slightest chance of freeing myself from his grip, I sigh heavily and lean my head against the wall. My pulse still pounds in my ears.

Dorian leans forward and says directly into my ear, "Zara, you aren't thinking reasonably. You can't associate the facts and just let your tongue run riot."

The closeness of Dorian's body and his scent, along with his voice so near to my ear, affect me instantly. The tension in me gradually goes away, as though Dorian has just injected a sedative into me. My furious heartbeat slows down. I regain my composure as if by magic. My shoulders loosen up and I become drowsy.

Apparently not only Rita can put me to sleep.

"What are you doing to me?"

"Have you ever wondered why, when I met you, the first thing I told you was that you weren't a good fit for an intense relationship? Why I didn't just jump on the opportunity as it came about?" I twist my head. Words seem like too much of an effort right now. "I was confident you were a hunter who camouflaged yourself very well, but when I checked your neck, there was no tattoo. You couldn't be one of them. On the other hand, the lack of a visible aura didn't let me believe that you were a human being either. I was far from taking any risk and bringing any danger into our life. But as time passed, your presence started affecting me in a very peculiar fashion. I didn't know what to think about you. I felt an urge to defend you rather than attack you."

My brain starts to get foggy. I hear his words, but it takes me time to register their meaning. I have the impression that Dorian's voice comes from behind a thick wall. My limbs become heavy; I need to sit down.

"Whatever you're doing to me, can you stop it?" I try to move my hands. "I'm uncomfortable."

"I'll stop if you promise you won't behave like a wild animal again."

"Promise."

"Good. For your information, if you are planning to escape, you'll end up in this position again, but next time I won't set you free," he warns me.

"I understand."

As soon as he liberates me, I turn around to face him. I feel much more confident having Dorian in front of me rather than behind my back. My mind is still blurry, but I steadily regain clarity. His eyes examine my face as though he's trying to determine which emotion dominates in me: disgust, fear, or perhaps hatred. I'd like to know myself. I can't sort my own feelings out. I'm empty inside.

"How old are you?" I ask in a weak voice, barely able to stand on my own.

"Older than you think."

"Have you ever loved anyone? With a real, pure, and innocent love?"

"It doesn't matter."

"So you have… But how come, if thieves can't love?"

"I've never had, and I never will have, any feelings for any woman." He says it loud and clear, as if he's talking not to me, but someone standing far behind me.

His raised voice doesn't affect me; I'm still emotionally chewed up. Indifferent. Besides, even though he's told me time and time again that he isn't capable of having any feelings, I know that it can't be true. A man who can't love wouldn't look at me like Dorian has many times, nor would he protect me by putting his own life at risk. It almost feels like he tries to disguise his real self for some reason. Maybe behind the mask of a tough and heartless creature there is actually a broken and tormented being. I hate that he'd rather pretend than face who he really is.

I look into his ocean-blue eyes, trying to see into his soul, which he may not even possess, and say, "You're a coward, Dorian. You're nothing more than a coward who can't even face his real feelings. You would rather live a constant lie and take away innocent lives to make up for your own misery."

I'm not even certain why I said that. Maybe I just want to put an end to everything. Maybe I'm done with all these secrets and mysteries with which Dorian cloaks himself. Or maybe I don't want to live anymore, knowing that there is no happy ending for us. All I know is that my words will have consequences.

I've touched a sore spot. Dorian's face takes on the same ghastly expression that I saw a while ago. His eyes are instantly swathed in black; his facial features sharpen. As he transforms into this ferocious version of himself, I'm unable to avert my eyes from him becoming what he really is. A monster that is ominous and simultaneously magnificent. A strange piece of art. At this moment, he certainly isn't the same man I know. He's enraged to the limit, unable to control himself. He's a beast of prey incited to attack.

Fear blended with lust bursts out inside me and pours out of my every particle. I'm accustomed to this mixture; it's come over me dozens of times before in my dreams. Only Dorian can trigger such a profound combination of two opposite sensations. As I look at his face, cold, inhuman and deprived of any emotions, I'm convinced for once and for all that I'm standing face to face with the man from my nightmares. I can finally see him. Every piece of me knows that it's him.

Dorian pushes me into the wall across from us. This time he's less gentle than before. He pins me to it, not allowing me to move. His eyes find mine. There's an unspoken message that he tries to convey, yet I can't decipher his thoughts. His cold fingers wrap around my throat. I don't try to shout or yank away; I'm ready for what's coming. In this very moment Dorian is entirely the creature he's been hiding from the rest of the world—a soul thief.

Seconds drag as I wait for my execution, yet surprisingly, he loosens his grip. A strangely familiar drowsiness comes over me. It makes my limbs feel incredibly heavy, and my eyelids are impossible to keep open. I'm completely immobilized. *What's happening?*

My heartbeat slows down. So does my breathing. I suddenly realize that this is Dorian's last mercy to me. Instead of killing me in cold blood, he's putting me to sleep first. I suppose that's a kindness from him.

With difficulty, I manage to mumble a final few words. "I knew… it was you… all along." I look deep into the eyes of my executioner; the eyes of the man who's been haunting my dreams.

"I'm sorry," he whispers, right into my ear.

When I close my eyes, somewhere far away I hear a bang, followed by other loud sounds. Maybe it's just my brain deceiving me right before I die.

"Leave her alone, Hatch!"

It's someone's voice. It belongs to a man. I can't see his

face, but I'm too weak to stay conscious.

Darkness falls.

EPILOGUE

A COLD BREEZE BRUSHES MY face. Still immobilized, I strive to open my eyes, but my eyelids feel as though they've been glued together.

Someone is carrying me, striding very fast, maybe even running. I have no idea where I am. The only sound that reaches my ears is the echo of quick, heavy steps on a hard surface. I don't even care where I'm being taken. All I want is to fall back to sleep.

"You're safe now. Nothing bad is going to happen to you," a male voice says. It's rough and uneven. I don't recognize it.

I'm balancing on the edge of dozing off. Am I dreaming?

ZARA

It's another voice, but this one I know very well. It's him. He's calling my name. I wish I could respond, but my lips refuse to move.

I'LL FIND YOU.

Everything is shrouded in darkness. Is that a promise or a threat? I don't know if I should be relieved or terrified, but as an intense, familiar scent surrounds me, I know that he's with me. It's my last thought before I fall asleep.

CAN'T WAIT TO FIND OUT WHAT
HAPPENS NEXT?

READ ON FOR A SNEAK PEEK OF BOOK
TWO OF THE ENTHRALLMENT SERIES

I TAKE A FEW MORE STEPS, and right by the round coffee table, I walk onto something hard that stabs my foot. The thin sole of my shoe doesn't protect me from its sharp point. I flinch in pain and drop onto the couch behind me, holding my left foot. Taking a closer look at the sole, it becomes clear to me that there's something stuck to it. I detach the tiny thing immediately to examine it. It resembles a black stone.

Wait. Isn't it the same exact one that Blair gave to Dorian right before she and her creepy friends left the house? What did he call them—gems? He must've dropped it…

I turn the stone over in my hand a couple of times and realize something strange. It feels warm to the touch, as though it's absorbed sunlight for several hours.

How bizarre.

Suddenly, another memory comes flooding back. Dorian mentioned the gems get warm in the presence of other gems. *Does that mean that there are others hidden throughout this house?*

"What the hell are you doing here?" a deep man's voice demands from behind me.

I almost jump out of my skin, my heart thumping an erratic rhythm in my chest. There's no time to think; driven by instinct, I stuff the gem deep into my sweatshirt pocket and jerk to my feet. I whirl around to face the intruder, but there's no one there. Adrenalin whips through my body as I scope the room. I feel vulnerable, unable to tell where the danger is lurking.

"Do I need to ask you again?" The voice comes from the hallway, out of my field of vision. I've never heard this man before; he has a British accent.

Is he a soul thief who's going to kill me now? Did he notice that I picked up the black gem? Maybe that's why he's here.

"Why did you come here unattended?"

He knows I'm alone. I'm screwed. Panic starts to take over. I need to come up with a good reason for being here, and quickly.

"I came here to see Dorian, but apparently he's not home," I say, with a slight tremor in my voice.

"Liar." Judging by his heavy tread, the man is approaching the living room. I take a few steps back; my legs are shaking so hard that I'm afraid I'll collapse.

"Why do you say that?" I ask, pretending that fear hasn't gripped my entire body.

"Neither Dorian nor Rita have been here since Rafael attacked your aunt three days ago."

His dark shape unfolds from the hallway.

I see a tall man clad in a black leather cloak. Beneath it,

I detect small tactical pockets around his waist and chest. Strapped to his shoulders are several weighted pouches that appear to be full – of what, I cannot tell. Then my eyes fixate on the sheath and a hilt with familiarly engraved gems in it, just visible under his cloak. It must be the Black Heart: a weapon that can kill soul thieves. The sight of the dagger gives me a glimpse of hope.

"You're not a soul thief," I toss out, staring hard at him without blinking.

"No," he says, pacing toward me. "My name is Vincent. I'm not here to hurt you; I'm a hunter."

I deflate and let out a long sigh. Even though the tension slowly subsides, my limbs still jitter. When he stops a few feet from me, I take in a staggeringly handsome, strong and defined face with a rugged beard. Vincent's hair is a dirty blonde; his blue eyes, full of intensity, are steeped in a serious expression but not unkind. There's something about him that feels familiar. Have I seen him somewhere before? I frown.

"Have we ever met?"

"Nope."

"But you know who I am."

"Of course I do," he says, as if it's obvious. "You're Zara Logan, the target of the most dangerous soul thief out there—Dorian Hatch. News spreads fast, especially the part where Hatch's victim has survived. That's something unheard of. Everyone in the hunters' world is aware of your identity."

Apparently I'm famous. But not exactly in a way that I'd like to be.

"You know me, but I know nothing about you. That's unfair, don't you think?" I examine his unusual outfit, trying to figure out what is hidden in all of those pockets.

"That's perfectly fine," Vincent says, walking away a few steps. "The less you know about me, the better."

Frustration rises in me. That's the line that Dorian used to give me whenever I asked him questions. I don't give up that easily anymore. "How did you find me? Did you follow me all the way here?"

"No, I didn't expect to find you here." He fixes his stern eyes on me. "Are you aware that you shouldn't be here?"

"Why?"

"You've come to the house of the creature that wants to kill you. Do you think that's a clever thing to do?" he says condescendingly.

"Maybe I *want* to be dead…" I drop my gaze to the floor. My heart has definitely felt dead since the incident in the cabin.

"Right. Enough chitchat. I'm taking you with me."

"What?! No way!" I shake my head. "I'm not going anywhere with a stranger."

"Yeah, whatever you say." Vincent obviously doesn't care about my objection. Instead, he reaches into one of the satchels adorning his outfit and fishes something out of it. A second later, he throws the thing at me with a quick "Heads-up!" warning.

I catch it with one swift motion inches from my face, preventing it from hitting me between my eyebrows. It's a small, cold, metal ball, no bigger than a thumb. No sooner does it end up in my hand than I feel it releasing something flexible and elongated, like tentacles, that wrap around my wrist. At first they're soft and sticky, but after they finish lapping my wrist tight, their texture completely changes and now they feel hard like metal. The ball is gone, absorbed into this strange device that now resembles a handcuff.

"What the hell is this?" I lift my hand up to examine it.

"It's an essential measure to ensure you're not going to escape." He raises his hand, which is cuffed by the same thing. "Ready?" he asks, taking the first step toward the door.

Before I can react, a strong force attracts me to Vincent like an invisible lasso. The handcuffs act like magnets, pulling each other. I can't resist it; it's too powerful.

"Let's go."

"But—"

"Have I mentioned no questions yet?"

He puts his hood on, so that now I can only see the silhouette of his lips. My blood pressure rises. I'm trapped and helpless. I came here to sniff around, not to be caught and imprisoned by some stranger. I *have* to go back to the hospital and find out if my aunt's condition has worsened. And what about poor Maddie? She needs me there – she's so sensitive. I try to struggle against the pull of the handcuffs as Vincent heads out the door, but the force is far too strong, dragging me behind him. The realization sinks in: wherever this stranger is taking me, I'm completely at his mercy now.

ACKNOWLEDGEMENTS

Writing this book was an amazing experience. However, I shouldn't steal all the credit. Enthrallment would have never come to life without the help of many amazing people.

The first person I'd like to thank is my mom. You've been my most devoted reader since I can remember. I appreciate you being an honest critic. Dad, I have to mention you right after mom, thank you for the hundreds of books that you read to me in my childhood. That time we spent together exploring different worlds, immersing in various realities, and accompanying multiple protagonists in their journeys has had an immense impact on me as an author.

Jesse, thank you for supporting me regardless of my bad days. You've been there for me when I needed it the most. Plus, I always appreciate your wonderful ideas that inspire me.

Thank you, Emma O'Connell aka my hero, for making Enthrallment shine. You've gone above and beyond to perfect my book. Enthrallment would never be as great as it is without your careful eyes. You're not just my editor, you're one of my dearest friends.

Thank you to all the wonderful beta readers who provided me with their valuable feedback during the editing process: Grace Tudor, Kate Crane, Stephanie Berumen, Bethany Votaw, Zoe E., and Tanja G.

Publishing can be a very overwhelming process, but I was fortunate and could count on advice of a few great authors. I'd like to thank E.G. Radcliff, Mary Ann Tippett, and Robin Lyons for your valuable tips.

Thank you, Mila Milic, for creating a masterpiece cover that has a powerful symbolism hidden within. You're a talented artist, who's also very patient. I appreciate your commitment and attention to detail.

I can't skip all of my friends and family members who've been rooting for me since the very beginning. Thank you for never giving up on me.

Finally, I'd like to thank you, my reader, for giving this book a chance. The literary world wouldn't be the same without you!

ABOUT THE AUTHOR

Meg Evans is a certified health coach passionate about wellness. Although she's a hardcore gym rat, she likes slowing down and getting absorbed in a riveting page-turner. Meg is the author of Enthrallment, her debut paranormal romance, and the first book in the Enthrallment series. When not writing, Meg enjoys a good conversation over a soy latte, and laughing until her face hurts with her friends.

She currently lives in New York.

KEEP IN TOUCH WITH MEG EVANS

www.megevansauthor.com
info@megevansauthor.com

@megevansauthor